**Allis released a fluttering breath. "Is he dead?" she asked, dread in her eyes.**

Leon dropped to his knees, saw the pulse beating in Sir Philippe's neck and the gentle rise and fall of his chest.

"He's alive."

*More's the pity.*

Allis let out a sob, dropped the prayer book and ran toward him.

Leon wasn't aware of rising, but he must have, for he found himself on his feet with his arms about her. She was trembling from head to foot. Her veil was gone, and her blue eyes were swimming with tears.

"Thank you, Leon, thank you!"

Wholly absorbed by the feel of her fast in his arms—temptation beyond temptation—it took him a moment to realize that her arms had crept up around his neck. Her fingers slid into his hair. He groaned and she tugged his head down.

"Kiss me. For pity's sake, Leon, kiss me."

## Author Note

Warning: be careful what you wish to write about!

My imagination is usually sparked by visits to intriguing places. In 2019, after some research, I booked a longed-for trip to Avignon. TGV through France. Car rental. Hotel. Then COVID-19 struck.

There are two stories in the Convent Brides miniseries, and with the first one begun, I had blithely shut away my feisty heroine, Lady Allisende, and her shy sister Lady Bernadette behind the walls of a convent. Now we were as cloistered as my characters.

So fourteenth-century Avignon just had to be imagined...

# CAROL TOWNEND

—

## A Knight for the Defiant Lady

**HARLEQUIN**
HISTORICAL

# HARLEQUIN®
## HISTORICAL™

Recycling programs for this product may not exist in your area.

ISBN-13: 978-1-335-72387-1

A Knight for the Defiant Lady

Harlequin Enterprises ULC
22 Adelaide St. West, 41st Floor
Toronto, Ontario M5H 4E3, Canada
www.Harlequin.com

**Printed in U.S.A.**

**Carol Townend** was born in England and went to a convent school in the wilds of Yorkshire. Captivated by the medieval period, Carol read history at London University. She loves to travel, drawing inspiration for her novels from places as diverse as Winchester in England, Istanbul in Turkey and Troyes in France. A writer of both fiction and nonfiction, Carol lives in London with her husband and daughter. Visit her website at caroltownend.co.uk.

### Books by Carol Townend

#### Harlequin Historical

##### Convent Brides

*A Knight for the Defiant Lady*

##### Princesses of the Alhambra

*The Knight's Forbidden Princess*
*The Princess's Secret Longing*
*The Warrior's Princess Prize*

##### Knights of Champagne

*Lady Isobel's Champion*
*Unveiling Lady Clare*
*Lord Gawain's Forbidden Mistress*
*Lady Rowena's Ruin*
*Mistaken for a Lady*

##### Palace Brides

*Bound to the Barbarian*
*Chained to the Barbarian*
*Betrothed to the Barbarian*

Visit the Author Profile page
at Harlequin.com for more titles.

To the Harlequin editors for their patience in waiting for the first draft of this novel, which was lost in the ether for six months! Particular thanks are due to Linda, who has now retired, Bryony, Carly, Julia and my new editor, Soraya.

# Chapter One

*Castle Galard, Provence, France—1341*

Lady Allisende lifted the latch and went into the solar. Her mouth was dry with nerves. A shiver ran through her as she braced herself for what was likely to be the most challenging conversation of her life.

Supper had ended and her father and stepmother had retired from the great hall. As was their habit, they were sitting on a cushioned settle. Since it was high summer, the hearth in front of them was empty.

Her father, Lord Michel Galard, Count of Arles, was a formidable-looking man in a lightweight green surcoat embroidered with gold thread. His hair and beard were streaked with grey. Next to him, Allis's diminutive stepmother, Lady Sybille, looked tiny.

Lady Sybille's forehead was creased with worry lines. Briefly, Allis closed her eyes. It was horrible knowing that she was responsible for her stepmother's anxiety. Indeed, she felt so guilty about it that she was amazed when her father gave her a welcoming smile.

'We were just talking about you.' Her father's signet

ring flashed as he waved her in. 'Sybille tells me you have taken her in dislike. Tell her it is not so.'

Allis was certainly unhappy, but Lady Sybille was a dear, she couldn't be blamed for Allis's woes. Allis crossed to Sybille and took her hand. 'My lady, I could not wish for a better stepmother. All our hearts are in your keeping.'

Sybille searched Allis's face and the lines on her brow eased.

'There, Sybille,' Lord Michel said, stroking his beard. 'I said you were mistaken.'

Releasing her stepmother, Allis went to the settle opposite and tried to find the right words. Her father was the most stubborn of men and even though she had reassured Sybille, Allis was expecting anger. This was her last chance to get him to understand. She could not marry Claude. Swallowing, she opened her mouth only for Sybille to beat her to it.

'Allis, dear, I was under the impression that we had agreed to discuss which gown you'll be wearing on your wedding day. I'd like you to have a posy and I need to know which flowers will match it. Yet when I came to join you in your bedchamber, you were not to be found. And then there's the wedding feast. The hall is at its best with flowers on the tables and we only have a few days to make the final arrangements.'

Allis grimaced. 'Sybille, I am sorry if you don't understand, but I've been speaking very plainly. I will not marry Claude. It's not my fault that no one is listening.'

Sybille closed her eyes and let out a faint moan.

'By the Rood, Allis, not this again.' Her father scowled. 'You are the most stubborn young woman. Always harping on the same note.'

'If I must, Papa, I will repeat myself until the message gets through.' Allis stiffened her spine. 'The wedding cannot take place.'

Sir Claude Vaucluse of Carpentras was her father's godson. Carpentras was roughly forty miles away and despite the distance between Carpentras and Castle Galard, her father regularly invited Claude to stay at Galard. Allis held in a sigh. Papa was the least subtle man on earth. Long ago, she had realised that her father issued these invitations in the hope that Claude and Allis would grow fond of each other. Well, Allis liked Claude well enough, but she could never marry him. Never. The fact that he was the son of Lord Robert Vaucluse, Count of Carpentras and her father's close friend, was irrelevant. Claude was not for Allis.

'Be reasonable, Allis.' Her father's nostrils flared. 'It is too late to back out. The match was agreed years ago.'

'I never agreed to it.'

Lord Michel clenched his fist. 'You are impertinent, Daughter.'

'Papa, I am truly sorry to cross you. I would love to marry according to your wishes, but I can't.' Allis took a sustaining breath. 'I will not marry Claude. I've been telling you for months.'

That was no lie. Allis had told her father as much many, many times. The last time had been the previous evening.

Lord Michel regarded her through eyes turned to slits. 'That is your final word?'

Throat tight, for Allis loved her father and hated disappointing him, she nodded. 'I refuse to marry him.'

Lord Michel rose from the settle and came to stand over her. Or rather, he towered. He was a tall man. Allis had inherited her height from him. And, she thought ruefully, her stubborn temperament. Her fair hair and blue

eyes she had from her mother. When his gaze shifted
to a glass lamp on the side table, he looked as though
he was miles away. She ached to reach him. What was
he thinking?

'Please, Papa, tell me you understand.'

'I understand.'

That distant look had not gone, and Allis felt a pang
of doubt. Sometimes, her father looked so sad. Was he
thinking of her mother? She knew he loved Sybille, but
Sybille was his second wife, and everyone knew that the
Count of Arles had been devastated when his first wife
had died after Bernadette's birth. That had been seventeen years ago. Since then, Allis had been told many
times that she bore a strong resemblance to her mother.

'Papa?'

A large hand came out to touch her cheek. 'Allis,'
he said quietly. 'Dear Allis. Be assured that I hear you.
I shall take your views into account.'

'You'll write to Lord Robert?'

'Certainly.'

Delighted by this unexpected capitulation, Allis
sprang to her feet. 'Thank you, Papa! Thank you.'

Her father gave her a tired, abstracted smile. 'Goodnight, my dear. May the angels guard your sleep.'

*May the angels guard your sleep.* From as far back
as Allis could remember, that had been her father's
night-time blessing.

'Goodnight, Papa. May the angels guard you too.'

Giving him a last searching glance, for he really
did look weary, Allis gave Sybille a quick curtsy and
left the solar.

Several days later, Allis stood on the castle steps
with her maid and stared in disbelief at the grand cav-

alcade—it looked more like an army—snaking over the drawbridge and into the castle bailey. Knights' pennons fluttered. Hoofs clattered. Harness clinked.

Her gaze went straight to the banner in the centre and her heart dropped like a stone. It was the banner of Lord Robert Vaucluse, Count of Carpentras.

How could this be? Thoroughly bewildered, Allis put her hand to her forehead. She was beginning to doubt her own memory. Father had agreed to write to Lord Robert. He'd promised to explain that she could not marry Claude. Had the letter not arrived?

It was well known that Lord Robert had long wished to unite their two families. Had he decided to ignore Papa's letter? Was he trying to shame her into marrying his son? If so, Lord Robert would soon discover that Allis would not be shamed into anything.

The procession was winding in past the gatehouse. It looked exactly like a wedding procession, and that was because it *was* a wedding procession.

'Unbelievable,' she muttered. 'Unbelievable!'

As her mind worked, her anger built. Her first reaction had to be wrong. This might not be Lord Robert's doing. She had known him for years and she doubted very much he would insist the wedding took place if her father had made it plain that he had changed his mind about the marriage alliance. Her father on the other hand...

She turned to her maid and spoke through gritted teeth. 'Estelle, did you know this was going to happen today?'

Estelle looked away, which told its own story. 'Lord Michel is set on this match, my lady.'

Allis clenched her fists and swore under her breath.

'I'll kill him,' she muttered. 'This time I will actually kill him.'

She stormed back into the keep, so angry that she was through the great hall and up the winding stairs in no time. When she reached the landing outside the solar, she paused, reaching for calm. Behind her, Estelle was muttering and moaning as she rounded the last turn of the stairs.

'My lady, please be sensible. You cannot fight your father. Remember he loves you. He's doing this for your own good.'

*No, he's not,* Allis thought. Outrage burned in every vein. Her father was doing this because he and Lord Robert had made an absurd agreement when Claude was born. And her wishes were completely irrelevant. Her father had pretended to listen to her—and now this. It felt like betrayal. It *was* betrayal.

She snatched at the latch and shoved back the door. Her father and his Countess were peering through the window overlooking the bailey, watching the procession. As the door thumped against the wall, her father turned. With a smile, he beckoned Allis forward.

'Come and look. This is in your honour.'

Allis seethed. Typical. Papa was acting as though he had never made that promise to take her views into account. That conversation, and the dozens that had preceded it, might never have happened. Truly, he was the most pig-headed man in creation.

Sybille was biting her lip—she knew that Allis was beyond angry. Sybille was waiting for Allis to explode.

Sybille gave an almost imperceptible headshake and something extraordinary happened. Allis's anger didn't leave her, but she understood, very clearly, that the best way to get her message across was to speak calmly. Sybille often employed this tactic with her father, and it often met with success. It wasn't infallible, but it was worth a try.

*Calm, Allis. Calm.*

She moved to the window and began counting to ten. By the time she'd got to four, she'd spotted her so-called betrothed in the chaos below. Claude was mounted on a vividly caparisoned horse that he seemed to be having difficulty controlling. Claude had a tendency to favour horses he couldn't control. If Allis hadn't felt so desperate, she might have smiled.

*Calm, Allis.*

She gestured at the cavalcade milling about in the bailey. 'This is in my honour? Papa, I don't understand. When we spoke the other night, you said that you would take my wishes into account.'

Her father took her hand and enfolded it in his.

'So I did. I still do. Allis, be realistic. Tomorrow is your wedding day. It's been planned for months. I could hardly put a stop to it at this late stage.'

Swallowing, Allis took a sustaining breath. 'You said you'd write to Lord Robert.'

'I wrote to confirm the date.'

'You deceived me! You allowed me to think you respected my wishes. I thought you were writing to put an end to the betrothal.'

'I am sorry if you put that interpretation on my words. As you are aware, it is a daughter's duty to obey her father.'

Allis felt as though the walls of the solar were closing in on her. 'Papa, you do know that Claude doesn't want to marry me any more than I want to marry him?'

Her father drew himself to his full height and his face seemed to freeze. Allis had seen that look many times before. She was looking at Lord Michel Galard, Count of Arles, an illustrious descendent of Merovingian kings. Her father had vanished.

'Papa, please—'

'Enough! Allisende, you and my godson will marry. Tomorrow.'

Allis's heart started jumping about in her breast. 'Papa, I can't.' She backed away, shaking her head. 'I will not. Papa, I am sorry if this causes the family embarrassment, but I have made it plain. This marriage cannot take place.'

Her father's face reddened. Veins bulged at his temple. He stalked to a side table and reached for the hand bell.

'Daughter, you are overwrought.'

'I am not overwrought. All things considered, I am extremely calm.'

The Count—Allis could see little of her father in him now—rang the bell. 'I am giving you one last chance,' he said coldly. 'Will you greet the wedding guests tonight?'

'No, my lord, I will not.'

Footsteps in the stairwell announced the arrival of Sir Hugo Albret, one of the household knights. Allis released a quiet sigh of relief. Hugo had been fostered at Galard, and he and Allis had played together as children. Hugo was an ally, the brother she had never had. As was Claude. Of the two of them Allis felt closer to Hugo, their friendship was strong as steel.

'You rang, my lord?'

'Sir, Lady Allisende is feeling unwell. She will not be greeting her guests tonight.'

'I am sorry to hear it, my lord.'

'No need to look stricken, Hugo, it's merely wedding nerves. Be so good as to escort my daughter to her bedchamber and ensure she stays there. She must look her best tomorrow.'

'Very good, sir.'

'And Hugo?'

'My lord?'

'Make certain the kitchen understands my daughter is feeling queasy. She is to have bread and water tonight, nothing more.'

Allis hung on to her temper as she, Estelle and Hugo traipsed up to her bedchamber. She remained calm even when Hugo looked apologetically at her and produced a key.

'My lady, do you recognise this?' he asked.

Her jaw tightened. 'It's the key to my bedchamber.'

The key hadn't been used since Allis had been a young girl. After her mother, Lady Genevieve, had died, Lord Michel had often confined his eldest daughter to her bedchamber as a means of disciplining her. Happily for Allis, these periods of confinement never lasted— she was invariably released the next day.

The bread and water penance was another of her father's favourites, and that didn't worry her either. Allis had learned her way around that one years ago. Judging by the sympathy in Hugo's eyes, it wasn't going to present a problem today either. Hugo was her most loyal friend. They hadn't just been playmates. Allis had kissed him once behind the stables. It had been a first kiss for both of them and it had been short and sweet and rather clumsy. Afterwards they had agreed that it had felt all wrong.

'My lady, will you give me your word not to set foot outside this chamber until I get back?'

'I will.'

Formalities dispensed with, Hugo shoved the key into his purse. 'Very well. Allis, I ought to convey your father's instructions to the kitchens. Is there anything you require?'

Allis hesitated. Thoughts were flying through her head at dizzying speed, chief among them the understanding that her father wasn't going to change his mind. Unless she took drastic action, tomorrow would be her wedding day. And her wedding night. And since that wasn't going to happen things were about to get ugly. Extremely ugly.

'Bless you, Hugo. Before you go to the kitchens, I'd like you to find my sister and ask her to come to my bedchamber straight away. I suspect you'll find her in the chapel.'

Hugo nodded, his small smile telling her that he had anticipated her asking for Bernadette. 'Anything else?'

Allis glanced at Estelle. 'We'll need bread for four.'

Hugo's eyebrows lifted. His smile wavered. 'Four? What are you planning?'

'I am hoping that you two will agree to help. In truth, I am pleading for support.' When Hugo and Estelle murmured a somewhat reluctant agreement, Allis continued. 'We'll have some of that lamb we had last eve and a flask of ale. Wine, if you like. Cheese and fruit too. We won't want to ride if we're hungry.'

'Ride?' Hugo frowned and took a step closer. 'Wherever you go, Lord Michel will find you.'

'No, he won't. I've thought of the perfect place.'

'Allis, your father has allies everywhere. Nowhere is beyond his reach. Besides, I cannot permit you to put yourself at risk.'

Impatience had Allis gritting her teeth. Hugo was

a dear man, but sometimes he irritated her beyond belief. 'Hugo, it isn't up to you. If I stay, I will be forced to marry Claude.'

'Aye, but Claude would never hurt you.' Hugo jerked his head towards the window slit. 'Out there, beyond your father's protection, you could come to real harm.'

Allis smiled. 'Not where I'm going.'

'And where might that be?'

'Avignon. Saint Claire's Convent.'

Hugo stared.

'No, my lady, that won't do,' Estelle said, shaking her head. 'You'll hate being in a convent, particularly Saint Claire's. It's fearfully strict. The nuns are like prisoners, they are hardly ever allowed out. Personal possessions are forbidden, and their vows mean they must embrace poverty, remain chaste and be obedient.'

'Obedient?' Hugo let out a huff of laughter and gave Allis a look. 'You'll have trouble with that one.'

'No, I won't. As a guest I shall be exempt from their Rule.'

Estelle's eyes were huge with anxiety. 'My lady, the nuns in Saint Claire's don't encourage guests.'

'They will if that guest is accompanying a young lady who has her heart set on becoming a nun. Bernadette is just such a lady and, if she decides to stay, her dowry would soon follow. We will be welcomed with open arms.'

A silence fell. When it was broken by the tolling of the chapel bell, Allis could scarcely believe her luck. What perfect timing. 'That will be Bernadette,' she said coolly. 'Ringing the bell for Vespers, as she does every night.'

Hugo and Estelle exchanged glances and Allis's spirits lifted. Everyone in the castle knew that all her sister had ever wanted to do was to become a nun. Hugo and Estelle would probably agree to help her, because of Bernadette.

Hugo cleared his throat. 'Allis, if you insist on going to Saint Claire's, I can ensure you arrive there safely. But you mustn't delude yourself, you'll loathe it. You? In a convent?'

'That is irrelevant, Bernadette's been asking Papa if she can test out her calling for years. She will love it there.' Allis faltered, gripped by a moment of uncertainty. 'At least I think she will. With luck, she'll soon find the life of a nun is not for her. We can return home when Papa accepts that I won't marry Claude.' She looked pleadingly at Hugo. 'I'll crawl to Saint Claire's on my hand and knees if I have to, though for Bernadette's sake I would prefer to have your escort. You will escort us, won't you? If you don't, we shall go without you.'

Hugo's eyes begged for understanding. 'Allis, this isn't an easy decision. It's one thing to arrange for food and drink to be brought to your bedchamber, and quite another to deliberately go against your father's wishes. I have sworn fealty to Lord Michel. It's an oath I do not take lightly.'

Allis lowered her gaze. 'Hugo, I do understand. I feel terrible placing you in this position. If Papa discovers you are involved, he is likely to have you in the stocks. But I don't know what else to do. I am desperate. If you can't help, please don't fret. I'm aware I'm testing our friendship to the limit. Maybe one of the stable boys can accompany us.'

'A stable boy would be useless as an escort.'

'Then we shall take two, perhaps three. Hugo, I know you're fond of Bernadette. This is your chance to help her as well as me. She needs to test her vocation and Papa is very much against it.'

Hugo held up his hand, a resigned expression in his eyes. 'Very well, I'll take you to Avignon, but don't think you're deluding me about your reasons for storming off. This is as much about your dispute with your father as it is about Bernadette.'

Allis bit her lip. She wasn't being completely honest, and it wasn't a pleasant feeling. Hugo was the closest thing she had to a confidant and the urge to tell him all was strong. It must be resisted. No one must know about her fall from grace. 'Hugo, I beg you to say nothing of our whereabouts to my father. If he gets wind of where we are, he'll have us out in a trice.'

Hugo studied her for what felt like an eternity. 'Your secret is safe with me,' he said. 'We could leave in an hour, just after sunset. In the meantime, I'll ask Lady Bernadette to join you and I'll arrange for the food to be sent up.'

'Thank you, Hugo, you are a true friend.'

Her true friend left the bedchamber scowling.

'Estelle? Will you come with us? Do say you will.'

'My lady, you are forgetting, I cannot ride.'

'How stupid of me, of course you can't. Never mind, you are probably right about the convent. It sounds ghastly. You'll be better off here.'

'Yes, my lady.' Estelle brightened. 'I can help you pack. You don't have long.'

'Pack?' Allis snorted. 'I shan't need much, just a couple of drab gowns, so I don't shock the nuns. First, find a dark gown and then help me with my laces. I need to blend in with the night.'

Estelle rushed into action and her fingers were soon

moving swiftly down the laces. 'Will you take your grey cloak, my lady? It's rather threadbare.'

'The grey cloak will be fine, it's a warm night.'

When Estelle's fingers stopped moving, Allis turned. 'Estelle?'

Her maid's cheeks had gone white. 'My lady, it's occurred to me, Lord Michel is bound to ask me where you've gone. What shall I say?'

'You will tell him nothing. You know nothing. Tell Papa that you went to sleep as usual at the foot of my bed and in the morning when you woke, I was gone.'

'Will Sir Hugo stand by me?'

'Estelle, it's not far to Avignon, Hugo should easily be back before sunrise. All you have to do is to wait until morning. You will find Hugo outside that door, exactly as my father instructed. I shall ask him to rouse you late. Papa knows perfectly well that the kitchen feeds me, even when I am put on bread and water. The two of you can say you suspect I put a sleeping draught in your ale.'

'A sleeping draught?' Estelle looked doubtfully at her. 'Will Lord Michel believe it?'

'Papa knows how angry I am, I'm sure he will. Estelle, whatever happens, it's vital you say nothing of our whereabouts. Vital.'

'Very good, my lady.'

Estelle resumed unlacing Allis's gown and Allis closed her ears to the uncertainty in her handmaid's voice.

# Chapter Two

*A month later*

The sun was blinding, and the horses' hooves rang hollow on the baked ground. Sir Leonidàs of Tarascon and his troop had almost reached their destination—Castle Galard, the main residence of Lord Michel Galard, Count of Arles. Leon had yet to meet the Count of Arles. All he knew was that one commission had ended and his men had been delighted to learn that a summons had come from Lord Michel.

The image of Othon writhing about in agony in the dust sprang into Leon's mind. Othon was Leon's captain and most longstanding friend and, fool that he was, he had dislocated his shoulder while demonstrating a showy circus trick on his horse. If Leon could choose his family, Othon would head the list. Crucially, Othon needed time to heal.

Leon was hoping that Lord Michel's proposal need not involve the entire troop. Othon would be out of action for a while.

The times were certainly lawless. As commander of an elite troop of mercenaries known locally as The

Lions of Languedoc, Leon had rendered aid in many disputes: border disputes between France and England, disputes between warring Italian counts, disputes with the Holy Roman Empire… The list went on. There were always calls for help when one led a strong, reliable fighting force. Sir Leonidàs of Tarascon and his thirty or so seasoned men were rarely idle.

Lord Michel had not employed Leon's troop before, and his message had been unusually cryptic. Leon had no idea of the task in hand. Whatever the challenge, Leon was confident that he and his men would be equal to it. Leon hated having time on his hands. More precisely, he hated it when his men had time on their hands. It happened rarely these days, and when it did, he braced himself for trouble. The last thing he needed was for the troop to start quarrelling among themselves or righting old wrongs. That this had never happened to date was largely due to Leon's success at finding them one lucrative commission after another.

Today, Leon felt a twinge of foreboding. Why had the Count's summons been so short on detail? Whatever he wanted, it must be political. A matter of some sensitivity. Equally, experience had taught him that Lord Michel's delicate approach might indicate that the troop was required for something less than honourable. If so, he would be put straight. Swiftly. Missions of the cloak and dagger variety were *never* undertaken by The Lions of Languedoc.

Leon's squire, Peire, was riding alongside. Peire cleared his throat and waved away a cloud of midges. 'I wonder what the Count wants. Do you know anything about it, sir?'

Leon smiled. Peire was a bright lad—he liked to know what was going on. 'As yet, I have no idea. However, I

give you due warning, if he expects us to involve ourselves in anything underhand, we shan't be accepting
the commission.'

Peire sagged a little. He was alarmingly bloodthirsty
for one so young.

'Not even if the pay is good, sir?'

'Not even then,' Leon said firmly. A flash of black
and white—a magpie—flew past his horse's nose.
Titan, Leon's rangy grey, walked steadily on. The last
of the trees fell back and there it was. Castle Galard.

Peire gave a low whistle. '*Jésu*, it's almost as big as
that town we passed. Look at those walls.'

Leon ran an appraising gaze over the defences. There
was a moat. The water was dark, glossy in the sunlight,
save for the green landward margin with a border of
weed. A handful of ducks were paddling through it. The
gatehouse was solidly built, with loopholes at conve-
nient angles, and enough soldiers and sentries to man a
garrison. Helmets gleamed. Spears pointed skywards.

A square tower reared up from behind a cliff of a
curtain wall. It had a turret at the corners, and each one
was flying the Count's green standard. More loopholes
were cut into the stonework on the upper floors and the
turrets. In the side of the tower facing them, a handful
of windows flashed the sun back at them. They were
larger than Leon expected, and they told him that, whatever Lord Michel wanted, the man was confident that
no one would be attacking his castle any time soon.

So why call for Leon?

After announcing themselves at the gatehouse, Leon's azure shield with its silver sword and two daggers
gained them immediate admittance. He spoke briefly
to his sergeant.

'Vézian, let the men dismount for food but post sentries.' He raised his voice so that some at least could hear. 'Try and get them to look organised—unlike the disreputable rabble they undoubtedly are.'

There was laughter in the ranks.

Leon and Peire dismounted. They entrusted their horses to the care of the castle grooms and were shown into the great hall. A serving girl brought a jug of water and a basin and cloths for them to wash off the dust of the road. She bobbed a curtsy.

'Would you care for refreshment, Sir Leonidàs? We have ale or wine if you prefer.'

'Ale is fine, thank you.'

Having refreshed himself, Leon left his squire flirting outrageously with the serving girl and was ushered up a winding stair.

The door opened into a bright, airy chamber with windows on two sides and a wide hooded fireplace. The Count's coat of arms—a shield covered with honeybees—was carved into the stone above it.

Owing to the heat, there was no fire. A man and woman sat side by side on a cushioned settle by the hearth. Leon had the impression they had been there for some time. The man rose. Lord Michel, for this must be he, was wearing a full-length surcoat generously embroidered with gold thread. He had grey hair and a neat beard.

'Welcome, Sir Leonidàs.'

Leon bowed. 'My lord. Most people call me Leon.'

'As you wish.'

Leon inclined his head briefly at the woman on the settle and turned back to Lord Michel. His brown eyes were sharp, and his gaze penetrating. Leon couldn't read him.

'Sir Leon, you come well recommended.' The Count's

voice was dry. 'Indeed, you are so well recommended that I can scarcely credit what I have heard. Do you care to comment?'

'Since I am unaware what you've been told, my lord, all I can say is that when I accept a contract, I strive to fulfil it.'

Lord Michel waved dismissively. 'Your early years are shrouded in mist. No one seems to know anything about you until you appeared at Tarascon.'

Fully aware that mention of his childhood had stiffened his spine, Leon stood very still. 'My lord?'

Those sharp eyes narrowed. 'I think—I trust—that your childhood has no bearing on today. You were knighted at Tarascon, I believe.'

'Yes, my lord.'

'It is rare for a mercenary to be knighted. So rare.' Lord Michel glanced briefly at the woman on the settle and though neither of them moved a subtle communication seemed to pass from one to the other. 'Very well. Sir Leon, this is entirely confidential. If you choose not to undertake this commission, I assume you will keep what I am about to say to yourself.'

'You have my word.'

'Excellent. Sir Leon, I need your help with my daughter.'

Leon blinked. 'Your daughter?'

Lord Michel's mouth tightened. 'Aye, my daughter, Lady Allisende.' He cleared his throat with what Leon was astounded to recognise as embarrassment. 'She and I had a misunderstanding, and she has left the castle. I should like you to bring her home so we may reconcile.'

'My lord, you cannot be serious.'

'I assure you, Sir Leon, I am.'

'How old is Lady Allisende?'

'Twenty-three.'

Lost for words, Leon racked his brain for a polite response—one that wouldn't alienate the Count of Arles for ever. He had his livelihood to think of. If he turned down this commission, he might jeopardise the possibility of something more suitable in the future. Also, there was Othon to think of. His captain did need to recuperate.

One thing was certain: such a commission would certainly amuse the troop. They had never undertaken a task like this. The girl was twenty-three and Lord Michel expected Leon to act as a nursemaid? The best that could be said for this encounter was that it was a novelty. Usually noblemen, upon discovering that Leon made his living as a mercenary, threatened him with gelding if he went anywhere near their daughters. And this one was asking him to fetch his daughter home?

Leon bowed. 'My lord, I am truly sorry that you and your daughter have disagreed, but I confess to being puzzled.' He gestured in the direction of the gatehouse. 'There are plenty of men under your command. Why not ask them to fetch her home?'

Faint colour washed into the Count's cheeks. 'My daughter knows the name of every man here. She would know that I have sent them, and it's entirely possible she would refuse to speak to them.'

'Your daughter is in fear of you?' After an unpleasant episode when Leon had first come to Tarascon, he had learned to avoid noblewomen, but he didn't like the idea of a woman, any woman, being forced home against her will.

Lord Michel clenched his fists so hard his knuckles gleamed white. 'You are insolent, sir.'

Leon held that dark gaze. 'Am I?'

'Devil take you, my daughter is not at risk. If you must know, she can wind my men around her little finger. Half of them are in love with her, and the other half worship the ground she walks on. She's a wilful baggage and she needs to come home. Her place is here. If my men went to fetch her, she would wheedle them until they did her bidding, not mine. I need someone she will obey. I hope that man is you.'

Leon held back a grimace. Lord Michel's daughter sounded very like Lady Madeleine, the wife of the steward at Tarascon. Leon had met her when he and the boys had first arrived. Older than Leon and an atrocious flirt, Lady Madeleine had amused herself by toying with him. She blew him kisses when no one was looking. She teased him from dawn to dusk and, although she took care never to come too close, she was so brazen that Leon feared that he and the boys would be thrown out.

Determined not to lose the chance of winning his knighthood, Leon had confronted her and asked her to stop. Lady Madeleine had spat in his face, 'You lowborn cur,' she said. 'If you approach me again, I shall tell my husband you accosted me. He will have you whipped.'

For Lord Michel to call his daughter a wilful baggage, she sounded as though she was cast in the same mould as Lady Madeleine. Lord Michel's commission held little appeal, but for Othon's sake, Leon would have to accept it.

A rustling behind Leon told him that the woman was rising from the cushioned settle. A hand touched his sleeve. White and smooth, it was the hand of a woman who had never toiled in the fields or chopped wood. The most strenuous activity this woman was likely to have done was to lift her tapestry needle and embroider a few bed hangings.

'Sir, a moment, if you please.'

The lady was in her mid-forties. She was wearing a short veil and her fair hair was plaited and held in place at the side of her face by a golden net. Her over-gown was crimson with open sides and her under-gown was pale grey. Both were undoubtedly silk. She must be the Count's wife.

'My lady, you are Lady Allisende's mother?' Leon asked.

'Her stepmother. My name is Sybille.'

'Lady Sybille, I am honoured to meet you.'

Lady Sybille smiled, and her eyes crinkled at the corners. Instinctively, Leon liked her. She was not another Lady Madeleine. 'And I you. Sir Leon, I sense doubt in you. You need not fear for my stepdaughter's welfare, nor my husband's temper. He dotes on Allisende. It's true however that they both have a fiery disposition and that, in a nutshell, is the problem.' She shrugged. 'You know how it is with families.'

Since Leon could barely remember his actual family, he knew nothing of the sort. It occurred to him that the men under his command had become his family. He opened his mouth to comment and shut it again. His men were mercenaries. Peasants for the most part, there could be no comparison between them and Lord Michel's noble relatives.

Lady Sybille gave him a comfortable smile. 'I knew you would understand. Please consider our offer. You will be well rewarded.' She clasped her hands at her breast and looked at him with disarming confidence. 'It won't take long. Avignon is not far away.'

'Avignon?' The hairs lifted at the back of Leon's neck. 'You say Lady Allisende is in Avignon?'

Lady Sybille gave him another comfortable smile. 'Yes, sir.'

Avignon. *Mon Dieu.* Leon kept his expression under control as his mind worked. Despite past tragedies and some of the men's murmurings about vengeance, Leon had managed to steer them clear of Avignon. For years, a handful of the troop still lived with one aim in mind.

Revenge.

He gritted his teeth. Those men's desire for vengeance was a burden Leon had been carrying for too long. Naturally, he needn't tell them that Lord Michel's orders would take them to Avignon. Thus far, Peire had heard no mention of the place, so the men had no need to know. Except…

Leon would have to dissemble, which wasn't his way. He prided himself on being direct.

He looked speculatively at the Count. 'My lord, as you will have gathered, your proposition isn't one I would normally consider. However, my captain is injured, and I'm loath to take on anything too strenuous before he has fully healed. If I accept your offer, would you and your good lady grant him house room?'

Lord Michel's expression lightened. He was almost smiling. 'Why, of course. Sir Leon, we have much to discuss. You will need a reasonable escort to protect my daughter, but I doubt your whole troop will be needed. Provided they know to behave, the rest can make themselves at home.'

'My men are not animals, my lord.' Leon made his voice dry. 'Well, not quite.'

Lord Michel laughed. 'I am aware of that. It is why I sent for you. Rest assured, your men will be well fed. They can always help with sword play and spear training. They will want for nothing and be kept busy until this is over.'

'Thank you, my lord.'

'Please, sir, come with me.' Lord Michel gestured at the door. 'My steward is in the estate office. He can set down the finer points of our agreement, including your fee, in writing.'

Lady Sybille coughed to draw her husband's gaze. 'My lord, pray remember Allis is so strong-willed we may need Sir Leon to keep watch over her for some weeks.'

The Count tugged at his beard. 'She wouldn't dare try this again.'

A plucked eyebrow lifted. 'Wouldn't she?'

The Count made a sound of exasperation. 'I'll bear it in mind,' he said. 'Sir Leonidàs, this way, if you please.'

As Leon went back down the winding stair and was directed towards the estate office, he felt a distinct stirring of curiosity. What was he letting himself in for? For Lady Allisende's own father to name her a wilful baggage, she must be completely ungovernable. A termagant.

Well, if Leon couldn't stand the sight of her, he would simply leave when Othon was well again.

He caught the Count's eye. 'My lord, my men and I may not be available for long. I'm afraid I cannot commit to remaining in your employ for longer than a month.'

'As you wish,' Lord Michel said tersely. 'As you wish.'

*Saint Claire's Convent, Avignon*

Allis's old grey gown flapped around her ankles as she strode the length of the cloister. She was looking for Bernadette. The cloister was deserted, so she went round the entire walkway, checking every nook and cranny before finally pausing for breath. Where had her sister got to? Allis had already searched the herb garden. She had poked her head around the door of the chapel. Nothing. Was Bernadette finally beginning to loathe Saint Claire's as much as Allis?

A week ago that hadn't been the case. Bernadette had assured her that her calling to become a nun was as strong as ever. She had admitted that the convent life wasn't quite as she had imagined—none the less, she was happy to stay and enter the novitiate.

Had that changed? Allis hoped so. She prayed so. When she left, Bernadette must come with her. If her sister stayed behind, the Mother Superior—a harpy in human form—would peck away at her from dawn to dusk.

'Dear Bernadette,' Mother Margerie would say in that sickly voice that was anything but sweet. 'There is grit on the cloister paths. Did you forget to sweep them?'

'Bernadette, the kitchen flagstones are greasy. Did you forget to wash them?'

'Bernadette, my dear child. Discipline is all, particularly in a house devoted to poverty. I know you understand our Rule. Did I imagine it, or did I see you take not one but two bread cakes at the noon day meal?'

Mother Margerie was a monster and Allis couldn't stand the thought of someone as sensitive as Bernadette being left here alone.

Was Bernadette baking? Allis went to the kitchens. No Bernadette. She peered into the washhouse. Still no Bernadette. It was beginning to look as if Bernadette had grown wings and flown away. Allis gritted her teeth and marched towards the portress's lodge. Bernadette was only seventeen and she was such an innocent. If that harpy had driven Bernadette into the edgy streets of Avignon on her own...

The convent being in the heart of the town, it was surrounded by a high wall. The only entrance—an oak door—led directly from a lane into the narrow convent courtyard. The portress's lodge overlooked the courtyard so the nun on duty would have clear sight of both door and courtyard. The door in the wall was usually locked. When Allis and Bernadette had arrived, there had been much key turning and bolt drawing before they were admitted.

Sister Teresa was acting as gatekeeper today, which was a relief because Sister Teresa liked to talk. Generally, Mother Margerie expected the sisters to remain silent, unless it was an emergency. Some nuns adhered to the rule of silence, many did not. Allis heard them whispering to one another when Mother Margerie's back was turned. It was a great irony that Mother Margerie herself was rarely silent.

As Allis swept into the courtyard, the nun's gnarled fingers were moving slowly over her rosary beads. She looked up.

'May I help you, Lady Allisende?'

'I hope so.' Allis hid her impatience and smiled politely. 'I am looking for my sister.'

Sister Teresa's fingers went still. 'Lady Bernadette is not in the convent. She has gone to tend the vegetable garden.'

'The vegetable garden?' Allis felt a flash of fury. There was no doubt, the harpy had been at work again. She kept her voice calm. 'Whose idea was that?'

Sister Teresa gave a quiet smile. 'Actually, it was

mine. Lady Bernadette looked miserable. I thought a change of air might help her.'

'She'd been talking to Mother Margerie?'

Sister Teresa nodded.

'Very well,' Allis said. 'I need to speak to her. Sister, will you be so good as to tell me how to find the vegetable plots and let me out?'

Sister Teresa rose. 'If you wish. However, you would be ill advised to go alone, my lady, there are some rough characters in town these days. If you wouldn't mind waiting, I'll fetch a novice to bear you company. She can show you the way.'

'Thank you, Sister, you are truly kind.'

'It is my pleasure. As long as you are all back in time for Compline, no harm will be done.'

That made sense—the harpy wouldn't care if Bernadette missed supper, but she would raise hell if she wasn't in the chapel at Compline.

'Sister, you are an angel.'

Allis was so focused on finding the convent garden that the streets passed in a blur. She and the novice walked past unsavoury alleys and she hardly saw them. She was vaguely conscious of much dilapidation. The wooden houses were so decrepit they sagged against each other as if they needed something to lean on. Rubbish lay where it had been flung in gloomy backstreets, reeking in the summer heat. The wider streets were paved, most were not. Allis ignored it all, hurrying past hovels and stone-built palaces with the same unwavering focus.

Was Bernadette all right?

At length they reached the vegetable garden, a sloping parcel of land overlooking the River Rhône. Beyond the city walls, the river curled south towards the sea. Allis glanced at a tower on the opposite bank—it belonged to the King of France. Her family had originally come from France and she had heard the tower faced the town, though she'd no idea it was visible from here.

Shading her eyes against the lowering sun, Allis caught sight of her sister. *Dieu merci.* Thank God. Bernadette was unharmed. She was hoeing, of all things— moving between rows of cabbages with her grey skirts tucked up into her belt to keep them out of the way. Bernadette looked thin, scarcely more than a bundle of sticks. She worked too hard. Mother Margerie should allow her to eat as much bread as she wanted.

If Papa should see her…

Apart from another novice in a grey habit, Bernadette was quite alone in the field. Allis picked her way between the furrows until she was close enough to see tear tracks on her sister's cheeks. 'Bernadette, please stop. If you don't pace yourself, you'll become exhausted.'

Bernadette looked up and gave a shaky smile. 'I don't like to be still. You can help if you like.'

'Certainly not. I have no idea how to hoe and absolutely no desire to learn.'

'You don't need to stay. You hate it here. Go home. Papa will forgive you.'

Allis's stomach twisted. If only she had had Bernadette's certainty. 'I haven't come to talk about me.'

'Perhaps you should.'

'No.'

'Tell me again why you wouldn't marry Claude,' Bernadette said. 'Please, Allis, I'm trying to understand.'

'I don't wish to discuss it. I've already told you that Claude was Papa's choice, not mine.'

'That's no answer. It's no secret that the two families wish to unite. Everyone's been expecting you to marry Claude for years. Why not marry him? I know you like him.'

'Of course I like him.'

'Then why are you here?'

'Bernadette, please stop.'

'No,' Bernadette said, in her most stubborn voice. 'I need to know. Is it because he is younger than you?'

'It isn't that.'

'I thought not. Allis, I'm grateful you brought me to the convent, but I know that you did so partly because it suited you to leave Galard. You say the reason you helped me was because you didn't wish to marry Claude, but I'm not entirely convinced. I suspect there's more to it than that.'

Allis felt herself flush and found herself wondering how her naive sister could sometimes be so knowing.

Bernadette pursed her lips. 'It's time you trusted me.'

'I do trust you!'

'Then tell me. Tell me everything. Why not marry Claude? If you married him, you would be lady of not one, but two holdings. That would suit you far better than life in Saint Claire's. Yet you left the poor man at the altar to bring me here. What are you hiding?'

Allis bit the inside of her cheek. Her sister was not going to let this go, Allis would have to tell her the truth. Or rather, part of it. She couldn't possibly tell her everything. 'I'm refusing to marry Claude because he's in love with someone else.'

Bernadette's eyebrows lifted. 'Oh? Who?'

'Eglantine.'

Bernadette stared. 'The daughter of our village reeve?'

'Aye. You must have noticed that Sir Claude is always staying at Galard.'

'I thought he came to see you. Papa is determined to throw the two of you together.'

'That last is certainly true, but as far as Claude is concerned, I was the pretext. He comes to see Eglantine.'

A gust of wind tugged a strand of Bernadette's hair free of her headscarf. Frowning, she used her forearm to push it out of her eyes, smearing a streak of soil across her cheek.

'Allis, as the daughter of the village headman Eglantine isn't noble. I doubt Lord Robert would allow Claude to marry a simple villager.'

'No, I'm afraid he won't.'

'Claude has to marry you. Goodness, Allis, I don't understand your reluctance. He won't be the first knight who marries to please his family. It's distressing, I'm sure, but Claude is young. He will recover.'

Allis smiled sadly. 'You sound just like Papa.'

'Do I? It's true though, Claude will get over his disappointment.' Bernadette looked thoughtfully at her. 'Have you tried speaking to Sybille? She cares about you and she's extraordinarily good at making Papa change his mind.'

'I spoke to Sybille before we came here. It was a waste of breath. Papa has dug in his heels.' Allis lifted her shoulders. 'Sybille's no match for him when it come to a clash of wills.'

'So, Claude loves Eglantine.' Bernadette frowned in the direction of the river and shook her head. 'Allis, Claude must be realistic. So must Eglantine.'

Truly, Allis thought, Bernadette was such an innocent. She was untouched in so many ways. 'Those remarks,' she said slowly, 'prove how little you know about men and women. About love.'

Bernadette gave her a strange look. 'And you are the expert?'

Allis's cheeks burned. Guilt. 'Heavens, no. All I know is that Claude loves Eglantine. And that love is a rare and precious gift.' Even as she spoke, Allis realised she was going to have to tell her sister a little more. The last thing she wanted to do was to destroy her innocence. Yet Bernadette had asked for the truth. She prayed she was doing the right thing. 'Bernadette, you need to know that Eglantine is great with Claude's child.'

Bernadette's mouth fell open. Dark colour ran up her throat and into her cheeks. 'She's having his baby. Oh, no! Allis, I am so sorry.'

'Don't be.' Allis laughed. 'It was a relief when I discovered it. I knew all along that Claude wasn't for me.' Bernadette did not reply and Allis was left searching her sister's face for the tear tracks beneath the smearing of soil. Her heart clenched. 'My turn to listen?' At her sister's nod, she continued. 'I can see you're upset. What did Mother Margerie say this time?'

Fiercely, Bernadette shook her head. She bent over her hoe and rooted out a stray poppy, quite viciously for Bernadette. 'Nothing.'

'Now who's lying?' Allis asked, mildly. 'Very un-nun-like. Please, tell me.'

'Mind that cabbage, you nearly trod on it.'

Allis sighed, reached out and caught hold of the hoe. 'Put this thing down, will you? You look like a peasant—what would Papa say?'

'That we both disappoint him. of course.' Bernadette tugged at the hoe. 'Allis, do let go.'

'On one condition. Dearest, I know that harpy upset you. What did she do?'

'She says I must hand over the whole of my dowry before I join the novitiate. She insists on having it immediately.'

'Saints, she has nerve. Isn't poverty one of their foundation stones? It shouldn't matter when your dowry arrives.'

'I'm afraid it does. For now, all I can do is work hard to try and impress her.'

'Bernadette, Mother Margerie knows that your dowry will eventually arrive. We've just got to sort it out with Papa.'

'It's no use, she wants it now. She is most insistent.' Bernadette lowered her gaze and kicked a piece of chalk with the toe of a dusty boot. 'She also said that you were an expense the convent can ill afford.'

Allis felt like snapping the hoe in two. Instead, she released it. 'She's a difficult woman. She enjoys making other people's lives a misery.' A sob rose in her throat. 'Bernadette, you can't really wish to stay. Galard needs you.'

'Does it?' Solemnly, Bernadette touched her arm. 'Allis, please understand. I'm not like you. God has called me to His service. I cannot ignore His bidding.'

Allis felt her throat close. 'You won't change your mind.' Her voice was hollow, and her eyes stung. Tears weren't far away. She had come to the convent to avoid an unacceptable marriage and she'd brought her sister with her in the hope of bringing her to her senses. She'd been certain that being cut off from the hurly burly that was life would do the trick. It seemed she couldn't have been more wrong. 'You and I are indeed so very different.'

Bernadette squeezed her hand affectionately. 'So we

are. You can barely drag yourself to chapel, whereas I find it inspiring.'

Allis managed a rueful smile. 'Contrary to your expectations, I have been praying. Several times a day.'

'Oh?'

'Morning noon and night, I pray you will change your mind about taking the veil. Do you enjoy being treated as a drudge?'

Bernadette waved that aside. 'That is nothing. I belong here, Allis.'

Allis stared at her sister's broken, dirt-encrusted nails, lost for words.

'It is my calling, Allis.' Bernadette's voice firmed. 'My vocation. I'm staying.'

## Chapter Three

The cloisters were quiet. Honeybees were buzzing around the lavender. Allis was perched, a somewhat mangled scrap of embroidery in hand, on a low, sunlit wall overlooking the cloister garth. She wasn't the most enthusiastic of embroiderers, but embroidery was preferable to working in the laundry, which was the other task Sister Mary had offered her that morning. Instead, Allis had found cloth and embroidery silk and had set about embellishing a bookmark for Bernadette's Book of Hours.

Guilt was eating away at her and it had nothing to do with her failings as an embroiderer. Allis wasn't ready to go home and face her father, but considering her sister's insistence on entering the novitiate, she was beginning to see that she must. She could not hide here for ever.

Would Papa have her beaten? Allis was aware that many fathers beat their daughters, but hers had never done so. She found his forbearance baffling. Her will was as strong as his and she'd roused his anger on many an occasion. This time though…

By refusing to marry Claude so publicly, Allis had

provoked him as never before. Yet her worries were
nothing compared to Bernadette's. Her sister was seventeen and young for her years, and her nature, shy and
contemplative, meant she found it hard to stand up for
herself. Papa didn't want his youngest daughter to become a nun. He was bound to try and prevent that happening, which meant that Bernadette would need help
getting him to relinquish her dowry. Money wasn't the
problem. Their father's intransigence was.

In normal times, Allis would simply have used her
wiles on him to ensure that Bernadette got her dowry.
Unfortunately, these were not normal times. Allis had
angered him beyond bearing. Would he forgive her?

It was time she faced the enormity of what she had
done. As Bernadette had indicated, Allis had used her
sister's desire to take the veil to escape marriage. Poor
Claude. Claude no more wanted to marry Allis than she
wanted to marry him, but in leaving him to face their
fathers alone, she'd probably lost his friendship too.

Allis stared blindly at her needlework. If only Papa
could see how wrong Claude was for her. She didn't
want *any* husband. She wanted a man she could love
and respect because she understood him. A man who
loved her despite her less than perfect past. A man who
stirred her blood. Her mouth twisted. She wanted the
impossible. No such man existed.

When Allis had kissed Hugo behind the stable, she
had felt little more than curiosity. The rest of her experience was limited to one other man, a squalid episode
which had become her most shameful secret. Admit-
tedly, Allis only had herself to blame. She had been
both foolish and impulsive to encourage him. She had
been attracted by the man's looks, and her insatiable
curiosity had made her an easy target. She, fool that

she'd been, had thought a flirtation would be divert-
ing. No such thing. The man had taken her innocence
without a qualm.

Her needlework blurred and she shook herself. She
should leave the entire episode in the past, but she
wasn't sure how to. She was no longer a virgin and for
a noblewoman, that mattered.

For the first time in her life, Allis had no idea what
to do next. Should she send word to Papa, asking him
to send an escort to bring her home? With a sigh, she
leaned her spine against the cool column behind her
and looked up at a perfect blue sky. The house martins were shooting joyfully hither and yon. Usually,
she loved hearing the martins chattering cheerfully to
one another. She'd always imagined they were telling
her that everything was as it should be. Today it was
hard to believe them.

She tried to relax. She wanted to marry. More than
that, she wanted her marriage to be a meeting of heart
and soul. Never mind that the man she yearned for was
naught but a dream. She was ruined.

'Lady Allisende!'

The hated voice jolted Allis out of her thoughts so
violently, she jabbed herself with a needle. She managed
not to grimace. 'Good afternoon, Mother Margerie.'

'My lady.' Mother Margerie's tone was accusatory,
as usual. 'Shouldn't you be in the laundry?'

'I don't think so. I understood I might embroider a
bookmark for my sister.' Allis rose, holding up the tangled needlework. She was careful not to mention Sister
Mary by name, she didn't want to get anyone in trouble,
not on her account.

Mother Margerie's mouth pursed. 'Never mind. It is
fortunate I found you. You are needed in the courtyard.'

'The courtyard? Which courtyard?'

'The one by the portress's lodge, of course. Run along.'

Allis blinked. What on earth was she meant to do in the courtyard. Sweep it?

'Don't stand there gawping. A man who claims to be a knight is waiting to speak to you.'

'A knight?'

'So he says.' Mother Margerie's tone was disdainful. 'He has a message for you.'

Allis's stomach dropped. Merciful heaven, Papa had found them. 'What is the knight's name?'

'Sir Leonidàs of Tarascon. Does he answer to Lord Michel?'

'I've never heard of Sir Leonidàs of Tarascon,' Allis said. Even so, her father had sent the man, she was sure.

Her mind raced. How had Papa found them? Had they been betrayed? When Allis and Bernadette had left Galard only Hugo and Estelle had known of their destination and both had been sworn to secrecy. Hugo was strong enough to withstand their father. But Estelle? Allis muffled a groan of pure frustration. She could just see what must have happened. Her father had suspected that Estelle knew where his daughters had gone, and he had harangued the poor woman until she told him all. She should never have left her maid behind.

Mother Margerie sniffed disdainfully. 'Lady Allisende, duty compels me to offer a word of warning. This man does not look like a knight. I would take everything he says with a pinch of salt. Should he threaten you in any way, call for aid immediately. Sister Teresa will sound the alarm.'

Allis's eyes widened. If she didn't know better, that sounded like concern. Except she did know better.

Mother Margerie was afraid that if harm came to her, their father would never part with Bernadette's dowry. Allis dropped into a brief curtsy, shoved her needlework into her purse, and left the cloister.

Leon strode up and down in the narrow passageway the Mother Superior had pretentiously referred to as a courtyard. He knew precious little about convents and if he were honest, he would rather be at the nearby tavern where his men were waiting. All Leon knew about nunneries was that the women inside them had taken vows promising to follow strict rules such as poverty, chastity, and obedience. How many obeyed their Rule? He scowled at the convent walls. The stonework was as old as time. Patches of mortar had crumbled away, and if Leon weren't mistaken, the worn course of bricks near the base looked as though it had been put there by the Romans. He snorted. Anyone who voluntarily immured themselves behind walls such as these must be touched in the head.

A few feet from him, safe in her cell, an elderly nun sat by a window, rosary in hand. She chose that moment to look across at him. When their glances met, she looked swiftly away. That woman recognised him as an interloper. She knew he didn't belong anywhere near a convent.

Religion hadn't been kind to Leon. Little did the nun know that he had spent most of his life avoiding anything to do with the Church. If it weren't for this commission, he wouldn't be here now. Leon was here for Othon. He was here for his men, several of whom were at this moment happily ensconced in The Crossed Keys, an inn recommended by Lord Michel.

Leon had already worked out Lady Allisende's char-

acter. By her doting father's admission, she was a termagant. A disobedient, surly girl who took pleasure
in crossing Lord Michel. Idly, he wondered what she
could possibly have done to have upset him so. For all
his bluster, there was no doubt that Lord Michel had
been knocked back by his daughter's disappearance.
She must have done something truly appalling to war-
rant fleeing to this place.

While Leon waited for her to grace him with her
presence, he amused himself by imagining what she
looked like. Despite her father telling him that half the
castle was in love with her, she must be as ugly as sin.
Yes, that was it. Her nature was sour and her face repel-
lent. She was an ill-tempered witch. Her eyebrows were
thick and hairy and met in a permanent scowl. She…

Light footsteps sounded in the passageway leading
from deep within the convent and Leon turned.

A vision of loveliness stood before him. Lady Allisende was breathtaking. Tall and graceful, she had a
wide brow and deep blue eyes. Leon's stomach lurched.
Her mouth was prettily shaped and her lips— Lord, she
had the most kissable lips he had seen in his life.

Her clothes, however, were appalling. Grey convent
rags. Her veil and wimple were an insult. They served
merely as a sombre contrast to her arresting beauty.
Leon couldn't say how it was, but life seemed to shine
from within her. Her blue eyes sparkled. Her cheeks
were faintly flushed. Lady Allisende was a rose coming into bloom.

As to her figure—Leon felt an instant and disturbing
tug of awareness and fought to keep his face blank—it
was all gentle curves. Her body was as intriguing as sin.

God save him, Lady Allisende was a beauty such as
Leon had never seen. If ever there was a woman less

suited to convent life it was the woman before him. She
was formed for love. Made to be cherished.

It went without saying, Leon would never touch her.
She was a high-born lady, while he—knight or no—
was simply a jumped-up mercenary, chosen by her father to escort her home.

He waited for her to break the spell. It would happen
the instant she opened her mouth. Any moment now the
termagant would show her face....

Goodness, Sir Leonidàs of Tarascon was tall. And
large. Allis frowned as she looked him over to see if
her assessment matched Mother Margerie's.

On the face of it, her father's envoy wasn't dressed as
a knight. He wasn't wearing a helm, allowing her to see
that his hair was dark as night. She ran her gaze down
past a pair of wide shoulders, past the belt circling a
trim waist. She noted a fine scabbard and the gleam of a
subtly chased sword hilt. So, he was wearing his sword.

She allowed herself a small smile. Mother Margerie
had misjudged this man. He had been knighted. There
was no way the town watch would allow anyone bearing a sword this far into the city unless he was a knight.
She continued her inventory as far as his boots, her gaze
lingering on his gilded spurs. Truly, Mother Margerie
didn't have a clue.

She looked up, surprising a cool gleam in eyes which
were an arresting shade of green. Her pulse thudded.
The arrogance of the man! He thought she was admiring
him. Which of course she had been. After being cooped
up here so long she would admire any man. Particularly
one as powerfully built as this one.

Saints, he was handsome enough to make her wish
he were a hero. Her hero. Which was utter nonsense.

She had been away from her father's hall too long. Life had shown her that men were far from perfect, every one of them had flaws. Every woman too, of course.

Physically however, Sir Leonidàs was magnificent. His flaws must be hidden in his soul.

A dark eyebrow lifted. 'I take it I pass muster?'

His voice was low, and Allis was alarmed to feel a responsive flutter, deep inside. It felt like nerves, but it couldn't be. This man must have been sent by her father—what did she have to be nervous about?

She lifted her chin. 'I understand you are Sir Leonidàs of Tarascon.'

'And you must be Lady Allisende.'

He bowed, giving Allis leisure to study more than his physical appearance. He was wearing a blue linen jacket and black hose, and although they were of obvious quality, they were plain rather than showy. Most of the knights Allis knew paraded about in heavily embroidered silks and damasks. Not this one. She could see why Mother Margerie had been wary. Sir Leonidàs looked more like a blacksmith than a knight. That was it, a well-to-do blacksmith. The way those shoulders and biceps strained against the blue cloth of his jacket…

Heavens, she'd spent so long here her wits had gone.

'I don't recall meeting you, sir. To what do I owe the honour of this visit?'

Sir Leonidàs slid his hand into his jacket and handed her a small scroll. 'My credentials, my lady. I bring greetings from Lord Michel.'

Allis stared at the blob of wax bearing the imprint of her father's seal. 'Thank you.' She broke the seal and began to read.

Given that her father must had been in a towering rage when he had dictated the letter, it was more mea-

sured than she expected. It was curt certainly, saying
simply that he wished her to come home, that there
were matters of great import that needed to be discussed, and that she was to put her trust in Sir Leonidàs
of Tarascon, who had come highly recommended. Sir
Leonidàs would bring her home. Her father closed by
saying that he looked forward to seeing her around sunset that evening.

She was expected that very evening? Allis frowned
and looked up. 'Sir, you have only just arrived. In his
letter my father says he expects us to be home by dusk.'

'That will cause difficulties, my lady?'

Allis hesitated. Ought she to mention Bernadette?
Her father hadn't asked about her in his letter, and this
knight had given no hint that he even knew of her ex-
istence. For the sake of Bernadette and her vocation it
might be best if Allis left Saint Claire's as swiftly as
she could. Without Bernadette. Mentioning her sister
might lead Sir Leon to drag her home too. And if Bernadette was taken home, Allis wasn't confident her father would allow her to return to the convent. No, she
couldn't mention Bernadette.

'Sir, I need to ask you a question.'

'My lady?'

'Did my father tell you how he discovered my whereabouts? Was it Estelle?'

'Estelle?'

'Estelle is my maidservant.'

'Lord Michel told me very little, my lady. I am simply employed to serve as your escort.'

Allis narrowed her eyes on him. 'You are a knight,
sir. No doubt you observe the laws of chivalry. My father trusted you to come for me, he must have said
more.'

'On my honour, he did not.' A weary expression crossed his face. 'Lady Allisende, you need to know that I am a mercenary. I have been knighted, though as the nun who greeted me clearly saw, I am not of noble stock.'

Allis didn't quite see why that was relevant. 'Why are you telling me this?'

'My lady, your father is mindful of the gulf between us, yet he has entrusted me with escorting you to Castle Galard. He knows I will not harm you. He is also aware that some of the niceties you are used to mean nothing to me.' Sir Leonidàs spoke calmly and with great deliberation. 'In brief, he knows I will bring you back to him, come what may. All I need to know at this point is whether you are happy to obey your father's summons.'

Allis stiffened. 'Are you threatening me, sir?'

Briefly, the faintest of smiles lifted the edge of his mouth, an attractive glint of humour that was gone so swiftly she found herself wondering if she had imagined it.

He shrugged. 'That is entirely up to you, my lady. And, please, most people call me Leon.'

If only he were not so tall. Allis was generally held to be tall, yet this man dwarfed her. She glowered up at him. This was his way of warning her that he would be taking her back—with or without her agreement.

'And if I am not happy to obey my father, sir? What then?'

There it was again, that brief smile. Was he mocking her? If only he was not so inscrutable.

'Lord Michel told me he misses you, my lady. He regrets your quarrel.'

Allis doubted that Papa had said anything of the kind. Further, a certain wariness in Sir Leon's eyes, as though he were braced for trouble and was prepared to use ruthless methods to overcome it, warned her. This man wouldn't think twice about binding her hand and foot and flinging her in a cart if that was what it took to get her home.

No matter. Allis wasn't going to admit it, not to him, but her list of reasons for going home was growing. She needed to patch things up with her father so arrangements could be made for Bernadette's dowry to reach the convent. She must apologise to Claude and, if possible, repair their friendship. She was longing to know if Eglantine was well. When her baby arrived, Allis would insist that her father spoke to Lord Robert. It might be possible for Claude to make a slightly unconventional marriage. It must be. Lord Robert's estate was vast, so vast that there was no real need for Claude to be forced into a dynastic alliance. Failing an unconventional marriage, Lord Robert must allow Claude to support Eglantine. If the baby was to bear the stain of illegitimacy, it was only right that Eglantine and the child be given the means to survive. Her father Isembert was getting old. He would not be village reeve for ever.

'My lady, are you happy to ride back with me?'

'I am.'

Sir Leon looked her up and down in a slow, slightly puzzled perusal that had Allis wondering if he was mocking her earlier study of him. Unfortunately, it also had her wishing she were wearing something better than the drab gown she'd thought suitable for the convent.

'You will wish for time to pack, I am sure,' he said.

'Thank you, sir. I need to make my farewells to the sisters.' Above all, Allis must bring Bernadette up to date with events.

'I understand. My lady, a small delay is of no matter, I have business here anyway. I shall return in two hours. One thing further—your father mentioned that when you left Galard, you took your mare with you. In case you no longer have her, he gave me coin to buy a new mare.'

'There's no need. My mare is stabled nearby.'

'If you give me the direction, I will collect her.'

'My thanks. She is at an inn called The Crossed Keys. She is black with white socks on her hind legs. Her name is Blackberry.'

'And she's at The Crossed Keys? How intriguing.' Green eyes bored into hers. 'The very inn that your father recommended.'

Allis felt her cheeks warm and looked away. Sir Leon was obviously intelligent as well as handsome. By naming the inn, she had virtually confessed that she had had the aid of one of her father's men. She glimpsed a fleeting smile and received a courteous bow.

'Very well. Until later, my lady.'

Sir Leon opened the door in the wall and strode into the street. In a trice, Sister Teresa scuttled out of the lodge. She had the door secured almost before it had shut, leaving Allis in no doubt that she had been eavesdropping on the entire conversation.

Unsettled, Allis returned to the cloisters, sat on the low wall, and stared blankly at the well head in the centre of the garth. Her insides twisted. She was leaving Bernadette behind. She had looked out for her little sister all her life and even though Bernadette wanted to stay and had suggested that Allis go home, it felt as though she was abandoning her. Throat aching, she pushed to her feet. She must go back. Alone. Bernadette's calling was unshakeable. In not mentioning her to Sir Leon, she was doing the right thing.

*If I have the right to dictate the course of my life, so does Bernadette.*

Heavens, Bernadette would be sorely missed. Without her, life at Galard Castle would never be quite the same.

Leon's squire was slouching against the wall in the alley outside.

'All is well, sir?' Peire asked, hastily straightening. 'Where's the lady?'

'The lady needs to pack and to make her adieus.'

'Oh, simpler than we thought.' Peire brightened. 'Back to the inn?'

'Later. I'd like to scout around first.'

Several people were squeezing by, so when Leon set off, Peire had to follow. It didn't stop him talking. Leon was expecting questions and he wasn't disappointed.

'Sir, why exactly are we here?' Peire asked.

Leon glanced back, hiding a smile. 'As you know, Lord Michel wishes me to bring his daughter home.'

Peire snorted. 'You can't fool me. Prising a wayward lady out of the convent isn't the sort of commission you would usually accept. Why are we really here?'

Leon stopped walking. 'Peire, you are both insolent and indiscreet. You must learn to guard your tongue. I never said Lady Allisende was wayward.' Even though, he thought ruefully, it was likely true. Now Leon had seen her for himself, he was beginning to sympathise with Lord Michel. A beauty like Lady Allisende must have spent her life winding everyone in the castle round her little finger.

'No, sir. My apologies, sir,' Peire said. 'I just—'

'Leaped to a conclusion, as usual,' Leon said drily. His squire's expression was priceless. If Peire was trying to look chastened, he was failing dismally. Biting the inside of his cheek to hold in a smile, Leon resumed walking and attempted to dismiss Lady Allisende from his mind. With looks like that, she must be utterly spoilt. Utterly wilful.

The lane opened out into a small square that was busy with workmen. One of the buildings facing them was lost behind a complex framework of wooden scaffolding.

Leon couldn't help it, his lip curled. He'd heard that since the Papacy had moved to Avignon much of the town was being rebuilt. The princes of the Church and their huge retinues had flocked here in their droves and this rundown trading town on the banks of the River Rhône had been found wanting.

Labourers were filling sling hoists with bricks or balancing on narrow wooden walkways with hods of cement. Barrows were weaving in and out of passing townsfolk.

Peire came abreast. He was watching Leon closely, a strange light in his eyes. 'Sir, I apologise for what I said about Lady Allisende. Why won't you admit why we're really here?' The lad lowered his voice, proving that at times he had sense. 'Are you sizing the place up ready for when we—?'

'Enough! Let it lie.'

A bright flash caught Leon's eye. There was a church at the corner of the square and to one side of the door sat a woman with a begging bowl. Leon stilled, his attention wholly on the beggar. A priest with a golden cross was processing towards her at the head of a procession of robed monks. Their hooded heads were bowed. The cross glittered with every step. The entire procession moved past and not one monk deigned to notice her.

'This place is bristling with churchmen,' Peire muttered. 'When do we strike?'

Exasperated, his gaze fixed on the beggar woman, Leon frowned. 'You've been talking to the men?'

'They want revenge.'

Leon shook his head. 'All that is in the past.'

'Sir, that isn't true. They've been biding their time for years, just as you have.'

'*Mon Dieu*, I don't know why I put up with you. You are the most bloodthirsty boy.'

'I'm a squire. You're training me to fight, I'm meant to be bloodthirsty.'

'Only when necessary, Peire. Every fight must be—'

'A just fight,' Peire said, finishing his sentence for him. 'Sir, I've learnt the rules.'

'It's a pity you haven't learnt what they mean. Or your place for that matter. Watch your tongue or I'll put you on half-rations.'

Peire subsided into a sulky silence. There was no real harm in him. The boy was too young to know what had really happened. At the time Leon's village had been cleared, Peire hadn't even been born. The lad had joined their troop years later. Leon had found him after yet another atrocity, a half-starved scrap of a child, wandering alone in a scorched corn field. Peire's village and its land had been burned by a passing army with no regard for the local people. Those left alive had been left to starve.

Leon never found the boy's parents. Grateful for being rescued, Peire listened to Leon. Unluckily, Peire also listened to the men, some of whom, rather foolishly, enjoyed boasting about battles where all wrongs would be righted. When Peire sided with them in these vengeful discussions, he was attempting to bond with them.

Leon didn't like it, but he understood it. They had all suffered, and loyalty was often born of shared hardship.

As a boy, Leon had been obsessed with the idea of avenging himself for the wrongs done to his family and his village. But exacting revenge was a chancy business, often resulting in the suffering of innocents. Leon had seen a man die after a jealous husband attacked him for sleeping with his wife. The dead man turned out to be innocent and the husband was arrested by the town watch and hanged for murder. The execution left two families grief-stricken.

The murderer's widow had three children to support, and her life became impossible. She found herself shunned, first by the family of the man whom her husband had killed, and later by her neighbours. Vengeance often rebounded on the innocent. The answer, Leon had decided, was for him to ensure that whenever he signed a contract on behalf of his men, that the commission was honourable and well motivated. Fighting to keep the peace was justifiable, vengeance was not.

Making a promise to himself to find the beggar woman later, Leon led the way out of the square and entered a side street. It was narrow and squalid. A ripe stench hung in the air. A streak of grey—a rat—shot out of a pile of mouldering rubbish and vanished into a hole in a wall.

Tired women with cynical, kohl-lined eyes watched them pass. Some leaned through rickety windows, tugging at their bodices as they vied with one another to capture Leon's attention. Leon smiled and shook his head and continued, examining each face in the faint hope of finding features that were familiar. As ever, his luck was out.

With Peire trailing behind like his shadow, Leon

found a broad avenue where the houses had been reduced to piles of rubble, presumably to build a grand
cardinal's palace.

In another spacious avenue, Leon was studying the
insignia carved above an imposing doorway, attempting to work out which cardinal's palace he was looking at, when a brightly attired clutch of young ladies
pushed past him in a swirl of scented silk. They went
into the palace, laughing.

The contrast between the finery of these lively young
women and the careworn women in the poorer quarter
was stark. These laughing girls could be the daughters
of the resident cardinal—it was common knowledge
that the rules of celibacy were widely ignored. Leon
hoped they weren't mistresses, they looked very young.

Leon didn't bother to find the papal palace. He'd seen
enough. Retracing his steps, he made for the square
where he'd seen the beggar woman sitting by the church.
She was still there. He tossed a coin into her alms bowl.
As her face creased into a smile, he studied it carefully.
Looking, even though he knew it was probably hope-
less, for something he might recognise after more than
twenty years.

'God bless you, sir.'

The woman's eyes were grey. The wrong colour. She
was too old. Leon's jaw worked. It was insane to keep
doing this to himself, but he couldn't stop. His sister
was dead. With a brusque nod, he strode on. After a few
yards he turned to his squire. 'Cheer up, Peire. You'll be
glad to hear we're headed for The Crossed Keys. When
you see the signboard, give me a nudge.'

Peire brightened. 'Yes, sir.'

Bernadette was in the storeroom, stretching up to
hang bunches of herbs on a row of hooks in a beam.

More herbs lay in bundles on the top of a nearby barrel. The air was rich with fragrance—bay, thyme, lemon balm…

'Bernadette,' Allis whispered. She was careful to keep her voice down because of Mother Margerie's strictures concerning unwarranted talking. When Allis had the temerity to ask what constituted unwarranted talking, she'd been told in no uncertain terms not to be insolent.

Bernadette turned with a smile and pointed. 'Pass me that rosemary, will you?'

'I am not sure how to tell you this,' Allis said, keeping her voice low as she passed the bundle across. 'I must be brief. Papa has sent someone to fetch me home. I shall be leaving today.'

Nodding calmly, Bernadette hung the rosemary next to a bunch of thyme. 'I'm glad. I cannot deny that I'll miss you, but you were not made for convent life.'

Allis let out a soft laugh. 'That is certainly true.' She sobered. 'I want you to know that I shall make it my mission to get you your dowry.'

Bernadette gave her a look. 'You'll have to make up with Papa first.'

'I will. I want you to be able to hold your head high in Saint Claire's.'

'Pride is a sin, Allis.'

Allis shook her head in exasperation. 'Don't be difficult, you know what I mean. You will no longer be treated as a slave.'

As far as Allis was concerned that would be the best of outcomes. After she had arranged for Bernadette to receive her dowry, she could concentrate on her own life. But it was vital Papa understood that she was not going to marry Claude.

Bernadette looked enquiringly at her. 'Who did Papa send to fetch you back? Hugo?'

'No, I've not met this man before. I believe he's a mercenary.'

Bernadette eyes went round. 'A mercenary? How strange.' A frown appeared. 'Allis, he might be anyone. Are you sure Papa sent him?'

'Be easy, he gave me a letter bearing Father's seal. He's been knighted. His name is Sir Leon of Tarascon.'

'What is he like, this mercenary?'

Sir Leon's green, dark-lashed eyes came into focus at the back of Allis's mind and she cleared her throat. It was dry in the storeroom. Dusty. 'He's tall. Dark hair. He doesn't dress like a knight. Do you still have those coins I gave you?'

'Aye, they're hidden in my cell. Do you want them?'

'Keep them, you may need them. If you don't hear from me or Papa within a week or so, use them to send word to the castle. Your horse will remain at the tavern, so at a pinch you could go to The Crossed Keys to collect her and ride home yourself. If you do that, remember to hire a groom to escort you.'

'Allis, I am no longer a child, I can manage,' Bernadette said, rolling her eyes. She opened her arms. 'Come, give me a farewell hug before you go.'

## Chapter Four

The lane outside the convent wasn't wide enough to accommodate Leon's men, so after he had prised them out of The Crossed Keys, he ordered them to assemble with the horses in a nearby square. The mare that Lady Allisende had described—black with white socks—was easily found. It was a fine animal with a good conformation, a strong musculature, and a glossy coat.

He got Peire to arm him. Body armour, leg armour, sword. He was, after all, returning a lady to her father. She needed to know she would be well protected.

He addressed the men. 'Wait here, I'll join you shortly,' he said, even as it occurred to him that most ladies seemed unable to travel without taking half their chattels with them. Innumerable trunks and coffers might well be returning with them to Galard Castle. 'Peire, you and Stefe had best come with me. You can convey the lady's belongings to the horses.'

'Very good, sir.'

Leon left his shield and helm attached to Titan's saddle and he, Peire and Stefe proceeded to Saint Claire's on foot. He pulled the bell rope and when the door opened, he went in alone. The sisters would not thank him for bringing soldiers into their sanctuary.

As before, it was quiet behind the convent wall. Convinced that Lady Allisende would leave him kicking his heels for some while in the narrow courtyard, Leon stood at ease by the wall, amusing himself by wondering how long she would be. In the event, the elderly nun had barely scuttled off to fetch her before he heard those light footsteps on the flagstones.

Lady Allisende had a smile for him. 'Sir Leon.'

He bowed, slightly disconcerted to see that her clothes were identical to the ones she had been wearing earlier. He'd expected—anticipated—a finer riding habit. Some decent boots, perhaps. A prettily coloured veil and maybe even a ring or two. Nothing. The only difference he could see was that she was wearing a slightly threadbare grey cloak. She had a small saddlebag in one hand and a riding crop and gloves in the other.

He stepped forward to relieve her of the saddlebag and looked enquiringly at her. 'Are your travelling chests in the convent?'

'I have no travelling chests, sir.' Her chin lifted. 'Sir Leon, the sisters of Saint Claire frown on worldly show. I am wearing what I brought with me.'

Astonishing. Leon was determined not to stare, but this was the first lady he'd encountered who was prepared to travel without one or two trinkets, a silk scarf, a pair of satin slippers. Her quarrel with her father must truly have enraged her.

'Very well. Your mare is waiting nearby. You have said your farewells?'

Her throat worked as she nodded, and Leon glimpsed the glitter of tears. It was enough to rouse his suspicions. Lord, she had better not change her mind about returning to her father's castle. He and his men needed the money Lord Michel had promised, Leon could not permit her to change her mind.

'You are coming with me, my lady. I hope you are not going to make a fuss.'

'Me? Make a fuss?'

She sent him a withering look which Leon ignored. He took her arm and, with a nod at the nun in the portress's lodge, marched her through the door and into the lane. She didn't look back, which was pleasing. Nor did she protest, which was even better. She simply stood outside the convent, calmly surveying Peire and Stefe as the locks and bolts of the convent grated shut behind them.

'These are your men, sir?'

'My lady, this is my squire Peire, and this is Stefe.' Leon passed her saddlebag to Stefe.

Lady Allisende nodded politely at Peire and Stefe before looking pointedly at the hand gripping her arm. 'I am not going to make a run for it, sir,' she said in a soft voice that startled him far more than if she spoken sharply.

Reluctantly, and not a little disturbed by the effect her voice had on him, Leon released her. 'I am very glad to hear it.'

In Leon's experience, her apparent acquiescence was unusual in a woman being forced to do something against her will. She must be keeping things from him. He smiled grimly to himself. She could keep her secrets, he wasn't interested. With luck, he wouldn't have to deal with her for long.

'The lady has no other baggage, sir?' Stefe asked.

'No other baggage,' Leon said shortly.

Sir Leon, once he had relinquished that tight grip on Allis's arm, proved quite civilised, which was a relief.

Being so large, he was a daunting figure in his body and leg armour. A war machine. Thankfully, he had left his head bare, which made him more human. His dark hair was ruffled as though he had recently dragged his hand through it. His green eyes were watchful.

The lane was thronging. When he offered Allis his arm perfectly politely, she accepted it. He guided her to a square where his troop of horse soldiers was gathered in the shade of a plane tree. She saw her mare immediately.

'Goodness, are these all your men?' she asked, as she headed to Blackberry and began petting her. Blackberry whickered a welcome and stamped a stockinged foot.

'Some of them,' Sir Leon said. 'The rest are at Galard Castle.'

Allis looked curiously at them. Mercenaries. There were over a dozen. Saints, Papa had honoured her by providing the strongest of escorts. A few moments' reflection however, and her heart sank. The size of the escort had nothing to do with her father's care for her safety. It was far more likely to reflect the scale of his anger. This was a show of force, and it wasn't directed towards the malcontents they might meet on the highway. No, it was directed solely at her. Papa was livid. This escort—fit for a queen and hired specifically for her—was his way of rousing her conscience. He wanted her to feel the enormity of what she had done. He wanted her cowed.

Blackberry nosed her skirts. Allis had an apple in her purse, the mare could smell it. She stroked Blackberry's neck and gave her the apple and tried to absorb the realisation that her father might be extremely difficult to handle.

Her reflections kept her fully occupied for the time

it took to mount up and ride on to the road that led out of the city. Vaguely, Allis was aware of Sir Leon arranging the cavalcade about her. There were horsemen ahead and horsemen behind. Unsurprisingly, people were staring. Conscious of her shabby attire, it occurred to her she must look more like a felon than a lady. She stifled a laugh.

Sir Leon turned to her. 'My lady?'

'It is nothing, sir.' Allis retreated into her thoughts. What if her hasty flight had alienated her hot-tempered father for good? She'd gone too far. Lord, let it not be so. For all their differences, she loved her father.

When Allis next glanced at Sir Leon, he was riding at her side. He had put on his helmet. The professional warrior was very much in evidence. It was disconcerting because when he glanced in her direction, she couldn't be sure where he was looking. Behind them, Peire and Stefe were whispering. The horses clattered over the flagstones towards the city gate.

All at once, Sir Leon gave a crisp order and held up his hand. The troop reined in sharply. Allis could hear chanting and the tinkle of bells. A religious procession was crossing their path. In Avignon, such processions were commonplace, but this one put the others in the shade. Incense swirled around not one but three golden crosses. A group of priests were followed by dozens of monks. Then came the cardinals and a richly decorated banner. The banner was followed by an enormous, tasselled sunshade. Walking beneath it, flanked by more cardinals...

'Look, sir!' Sir Leon's squire hissed from behind them. 'That's the Pope's insignia!'

Sir Leon's saddle creaked as he twisted to face his squire. 'Peire, be calm.'

'But, sir, something's going on.'

'Steady, Peire. Don't be rash.'

Peire subsided muttering and Allis turned to Sir Leon. 'Your squire need not be alarmed,' she said. 'Religious processions take place many times a day in Avignon. And when His Holiness himself is taking part, this is the result. The Pope is likely to be moving from one cardinal's palace to another.'

'Peire is not alarmed, my lady,' came the dry response.

'There he is, sir!' By now, Sir Leon's squire was practically jumping out of his saddle. It was all rather strange. Face filled with hostility, the boy pointed directly at His Holiness. 'Do you recognise him, sir? Do you?'

'Hold your tongue, Peire.'

'But, sir, just look at him. Parading about with golden crosses. That scented smoke. Costs a fortune that does.' The bitterness in the boy's voice was chilling. He was eyeing the Pope as though he were the devil incarnate, his face distorted by some powerful and ugly emotion. He seemed determined to work himself into a fury. 'It's outrageous, sir. Immoral. The men feel the same. All this pomp and fuss, and that monster sweeps past us as though we don't exist.'

'Peire!' Sir Leon growled. 'If you cannot control yourself, you will be dismissed. Permanently.'

Leon had himself been staring at the Pope with something akin to shock. He didn't recognise him. He'd been wondering what he would feel if this moment came. He felt nothing. The Pope was an old man who was stooped with age and leaning heavily on a glittering pastoral staff loaded with gems. He looked as though he could barely walk under the weight of his robes.

Hastily, Leon ran his gaze over his troop. Except for Peire, they remained silent. Obedient to his orders and years of training.

Without willing it, Leon's focus returned to the Pope. How could he not recognise him?

Every blessed day Leon thought about the village and the day his family had vanished. Every day. The emptied streets had been unnaturally quiet. In his mind's eye, smoke was forever rising from the burned cottages. He would never forget the acrid stench that scratched the back of his throat. He could feel the hunger cramps in his belly as though it were yesterday. A cold lump formed in his chest whenever he thought of his mother. His father. His sister. The choking misery had haunted him for years. Overnight, the village of Monteaux had become a desert. It had been scoured of people, of food, of hope. All that remained were ghosts.

Back then, Leon had been four years old. He'd felt guilty ever since. There must have been something he could have done. He had fled with a group of village children, many of whom were with him still, and not once had it occurred to him that when he saw the Inquisitor again, he wouldn't know him. It seemed impossible that he no longer felt the hot rage that was clearly sweeping through his squire.

You would think he would feel something. It was beyond strange. He held in a sigh. If it weren't for the opulence of the Pope's entourage, he would never have given him a second glance. An old man.

Well, it had been more than twenty years ago. Twenty-three years to be precise. A lifetime. More of a life than his sister had had at any rate. What had happened to her? Had she, as Leon hoped, escaped?

'Sir, is something amiss?' Lady Allisende asked.

'No, my lady. All is well.' And that was the truth. Peire was at last holding his tongue, and his men were obeying their orders.

Mercifully, the Pope's procession was snaking into one of the palaces. Thank God, they could get out of here. Leon raised his hand and signalled. 'Ride on!'

Despite his ruined childhood, Leon often felt uncomfortable about his lack of religion, but this place was making him think again. Avignon was filled with beggars and whores and thieves, and the great princes of the Church ignored it all. They acted as though people chose to live in squalor when many had no choice and nowhere else to go. No, the great princes turned a blind eye to all of that. They blithely tore down entire streets to build palaces. They sermonised about charity and justice while content to ignore the desperate plight of half of the townsfolk.

It was then that the anger hit him. A bitter surge roared up from Leon's belly to catch, pungent as smoke, in his throat. Inexplicably, he found himself looking at Lady Allisende. As though she could help. She, the spoiled and wilful daughter of a great lord, would never understand though she lived to be a thousand. None the less, those huge, intelligent blue eyes were watching him.

'Something is amiss,' she said softly.

And then Leon surprised himself. He allowed Lady Allisende to draw him into conversation. Most worrying of all, he gave her access to some of his thoughts. Nothing intimate, naturally. Nothing to reveal his miserable past. He wouldn't want to shock her out of those intensely practical riding boots. He gestured at the tail of the Pope's procession winding into the palace and, mindful of Peire, kept his voice low. 'That is religion? All that pomp. That is spiritual?'

Lady Allisende stared thoughtfully after the procession. 'I don't believe it is,' she said slowly. 'Sir, I am no expert, but in my opinion most of the nuns in Saint Claire's would agree with you. Their order is a simple one. As I believe I mentioned, the sisters frown on worldly trappings.'

Knowing his helmet meant she couldn't see his expression, Leon watched her face. Those blue eyes were incredibly expressive. 'My lady, the sisters cannot have expected you when you appeared on their doorstep.'

'No, sir, they did not.'

'Did they want payment for the hospitality you received?'

Lady Allisende flushed and bit her lip, which gave him his answer. The good sisters had wanted payment.

'My lady, the nuns in that convent are not angels.'

'No one is.'

'And they defer to His Holiness.'

Lady Allisende shrugged. 'The Pope is the head of the Church.'

The change in her voice was subtle, and Leon was surprised by how easily he read it. They were veering on to dangerous ground, and she was letting him know that she didn't care for it. He wondered whether that was because the topic bored her. It must be. Lady Allisende couldn't possibly suspect that he came from a village of heretics.

Leon took the hint and fell silent. It made a refreshing change to converse with a woman, and when this one used that soft voice, it simply undid him. It was passing strange. He *liked* talking to her. He would enjoy discovering how her mind worked, something which usually rang a few alarm bells. In this case, it didn't matter. Lord Michel had employed him to escort her home and if his daughter wished to talk as she rode, Leon couldn't see that her father would object. Particularly since Leon and the lady would be parting soon.

Still, it would be wise to speak only when she addressed him. It would not be courteous to ignore her. His men would accept that without comment. It would certainly raise eyebrows if he, after years of avoiding noble ladies, should be seen drawing her out.

He sent another glance her way and smiled quietly to himself. Lady Allisende's eyes sparkled, her cheeks were rosy, and a golden strand of hair had escaped her veil and was fluttering in the breeze like a glossy ribbon. His smile grew. He'd never seen a more fascinating bundle of contradictions.

She appeared to be the most practical of ladies. Take the way she was riding astride. Her gown had to have been made with riding in mind. The way the fabric fell ensured she wasn't displaying her legs to all and sundry, and the wide skirts easily accommodated the saddle provided by the inn. Leon had already noticed that it wasn't new—presumably, she had used it when riding away from her father's castle. Lady Allisende's back was straight, she had a good seat, and her grasp of the reins was easy and competent.

The lady had not come to Avignon burdened with belongings. Her clothing verged on shabby, her riding boots had seen better days—in short, there was an attractive no-nonsense side to her Leon could not but admire.

She turned towards him. 'We shall arrive by nightfall, I believe you said?'

'Yes, my lady.'

Lady Allisende was an intriguing woman. Not many noblewomen quarrelled so fiercely with their fathers. Many would call her foolhardy for doing so. Yet she was also intensely practical. They had only just met and already Leon knew that she was most uncommon. If he didn't watch his step, she would have him revealing too much. She would have him breaking his unwritten rule and he couldn't afford to forget the lesson taught to him by Lady Madeleine at Tarascon. Noblewomen were out of bounds.

Besides, Peire and Stefe were riding so close any conversation Leon had with her would hardly be private. Talking to Lady Allisende risked undermining his authority. He never unburdened himself to anyone. Least of all to a spoilt, wilful lady, however down to earth she might appear.

But that voice. Those eyes. If he weren't careful, Lady Allisende could be his undoing. With men to lead, Leon mustn't forget his responsibilities. She might appear approachable, but she was a noblewoman.

It took Allis about an hour to get used to being free. The streets seemed wider than when she had last ridden along them. The sky was bluer than blue, and the sun so bright it hurt her eyes. After the cloistered peace of the convent, there was so much going on. Carpenters and builders strode the avenues as though they owned them. Housewives forced their way to the best of the market stalls. Porters pulled handcarts through the throng. The noise was deafening.

'Watch your back!' came the constant cry. 'Make way!'

As they left the city behind them and the packed streets gave way to the open highway, Allis felt her mood shift. She was especially conscious that she had hardly set eyes on a man in weeks. It seemed odd to be riding alongside Sir Leon, amid his troop. Living in the convent had been…

'Ghastly,' she said, with a shudder. 'Utterly ghastly.'

That helmeted head turned her way so promptly, he must have seen her grimace.

'I hope, my lady,' Sir Leon responded, rather stiffly. 'You are not referring to me.'

She laughed. Was he always so distant? Or could it be he was making a joke? If only she could see his face. 'Of course not. That, sir, was exhilaration.'

'Exhilaration, my lady?'

'I confess I've found the past weeks something of a trial.' Allis gestured at a chestnut tree by the road. 'This—being out in the open—is all rather wonderful.' She felt as though a weight had lifted from her shoulders.

His head dipped. 'I am happy you think so,' came the careful reply.

His voice was a shade warmer than it had been. Was he smiling? Sir Leon certainly kept himself well shielded. That helmet ensured Allis had no way of knowing what was in his mind. Was he using it to hold her at arms' length? Was he like this with everyone?

He was so formal. Quite different to her father's men, most of whom had known her since childhood. He wasn't obsequious, though he was polite. Yet he made no attempt to be especially pleasant. He was simply doing the job he'd been paid for. His manner told her that he wouldn't dream of overstepping the bounds.

It should have been irritating but, oddly, it was far from irritating. It was rather reassuring. This man had discretion. Provided, of course, she had read him correctly. 'That wretched helmet,' she muttered.

'My lady?'

Allis sighed. 'Sir Leon, I doubt very much our party will be attacked. Is your helmet really necessary?'

'It's best to be prepared, my lady.'

'I find it hard to converse with someone when I cannot read their expression.'

'My apologies, but my helmet stays on. If you require conversation, I am at your disposal. What do you wish to converse about, my lady? Your time at the convent?'

This time she heard it, the faint edge of laughter. Very well, she would take him at his word.

'Frankly, it was a nightmare. For weeks I've been cooped up with a group of nuns who are content to have their lives ruled by bells. Apart from one excursion to the convent field strips to find my sis—a sister,' she hastily corrected herself, 'I have been penned inside those walls the entire time. Everything is so alive out here. The brightness of the sun. The jingle of your harness and the creak of your saddle as you turn towards me. Everything seems sharper. Louder.'

'Aye, you've been confined too long,' he said.

She heard sympathy in his voice and was warming towards him when he spoiled it.

'My lady, did you not consider how you might feel before you quarrelled with your father?'

She sat very straight. 'Quarrelled? Is that what he told you?'

'My apologies, my lady. I must have misunderstood. What Lord Michel actually said was that you and he had a misunderstanding. He gave me no details.' Sir Leon's voice changed, and she heard it again, that trace of warmth in his tone. 'I assumed there had been a quarrel.'

Allis twisted the reins about her fingers and glanced away. 'Had I remained at Galard Castle there would have been definitely have been a quarrel. I left to avoid one.'

'That sounds awkward,' Sir Leon said mildly.

Allis nodded and swallowed. They were riding past a wayside shrine. It was surrounded by a sea of flowers and candles—offerings for prayers that had yet to be answered.

She turned to look at Sir Leon, or rather to look at his wretched helmet. They were riding so close, she could have counted the rivets if she'd felt inclined. The eye slits were so narrow, it was a wonder he could see out. 'I had strong reasons for leaving home.' She heard a distinct huff of laughter.

'I don't doubt it. My lady, if you wish to talk, I am accounted a good listener and I keep my own counsel. When I met Lord Michel and his wife, I received a strong impression that they regretted your hasty departure.'

Allis hung her head. 'I am sure that they did.'

'What happened?'

Apart from the steady clop of hooves there was silence. Allis sent him a sidelong glance. On an instinctive level she trusted this man. He did indeed appear to be a sympathetic listener. So much so, she wanted to tell him what had happened.

She drew in a breath. 'Sir, without telling Papa, I borrowed one of his knights and rode to Saint Claire's.'

'That's hardly a hanging offence.'

'Not in itself. I should add that I left the fiancé my

father chose for me waiting at the altar. Worse, the wedding guests had assembled.'

'What, you missed your own wedding?'

'I did. So, despite the impression that Papa gave you when you spoke to him, I can tell you he is furious. I say this by way of warning. When we arrive, brace yourself for a barrage of fury.'

Sir Leon laughed, he actually laughed. It was deep and full throated, and Allis felt a tingle run right through her. He cleared his throat, saying gravely, 'Thank you for the warning, my lady.'

# *Chapter Five*

After Lady Allisende's warning, Leon had no idea what to expect. A barrage of fury? It didn't seem likely. Still, when they clattered into her father's bailey and drew rein before the stable, he saw at once that something was amiss. Galard Castle was in uproar.

Servants dashed across the yard like chickens startled by a fox. Lady Sybille was tearing down a path, a willow basket hooked over one arm. Leon had already learned that the path came from some outbuildings next to the castle herb garden. The instant she saw Lady Allisende, Lady Sybille altered course and flew towards her, veil aflutter. Her usually placid features were marred by a worried frown.

'Allis, thank the Lord you are back!' Lady Sybille gestured frantically towards the keep. 'You are sorely needed. Please, dear, come with me.' Her basket contained bandages, several sackcloth sachets such as were used by herbalists, and pots of what Leon knew must be salve. He had seen the like in many an infirmary.

The roses left Lady Allisende's cheeks. 'Someone's hurt?' She swung from the saddle and a groom took her mare's reins. 'Not Papa?'

'No, no, your father is fine. It's Claude.'

Lady Allisende caught her breath. 'What happened?'

'Hurry, Allis, I beg you. You're needed in the guest room.'

Puzzled, Leon watched the two of them speed toward the steps of the keep. Claude? Who the devil was Claude? The erstwhile fiancé?

Lady Allisende's reaction—it was obvious this news disturbed and distressed her—would seem to imply that she felt a genuine fondness for the man. Was she toying with him? Was she toying with her father? Leon frowned after the ladies as they swept up the steps. No, that didn't fit with what he'd seen of her. Not that he knew her. He might have misjudged her, she could be toying with Leon too. Still, he'd give a handful of silver to witness what must surely be the most awkward of reunions.

Halfway up the steps, Lady Sybille turned back. 'Sir Leon!'

'My lady?'

'My lord wishes to speak to you.'

Leon inclined his head. 'Very good, my lady. Where is he?'

'Try the armoury.' Lady Sybille threw Leon a harassed smile and followed her stepdaughter into the keep. Whoever this Claude was, Leon was left in no doubt but that he was dear to both ladies' hearts.

'Sergeant, dismiss the troop,' he said. 'More orders later.'

As Leon reached the armoury, his captain, Othon, appeared. His sword arm was strapped up in a sling.

'That looks uncomfortable,' Leon said.

Othon grimaced. 'It is, sir. It aches like the devil every time I move.'

'These things take time,' Leon said. 'In a few days you'll be free of the sling. For now, take it easy. You'll soon rebuild your strength.'

Othon gave him a doubtful look. 'I hope so. The Countess says it is more than a dislocated shoulder. My collarbone is broken.'

'Broken?' Leon swore softly. He had intended to ride on with the troop and find a more suitable commission once Lady Allisende was reunited with her father, but Othon ought not to ride until his bones had had a chance to knit.

'Aye, Lady Sybille warned me it might take a while to heal. I was a fool to try that circus trick, sir. It won't happen again.' Othon's eyes filled with anxiety. 'You weren't planning on leaving with the lads for a few days, were you?'

Leon shook his head. 'Othon, you're my captain. I won't go anywhere without you, and I am not about to cripple you by pushing you into the saddle early.'

Othon let out a great sigh. *'Dieu merci.'*

Giving his captain a parting nod, Leon went into the armoury. A vague memory surfaced. Earlier, Lady Sybille had mentioned that they might need his services for a while. The idea of keeping a watchful eye on the Count's wilful daughter for longer held as little appeal now as it had done then. Irritation brought a frown to his face. For Othon's sake, he must think again.

The Galard armoury was a huge cavern of a place. Dozens of helmets were stacked on shelves. Shields hung from hooks on a wall, and spears were grouped together at intervals like stooks of hay. Lord Michel and a man Leon assumed to be the castle armourer were standing before a trestle table laden with pikes. The Count nudged one towards the armourer.

'Erec, you couldn't cut butter with this. Check them all, will you?' As Leon's shadow fell over them, Lord Michel turned. 'There you are. Thought you'd never get here. Is my daughter well?'

'Lady Allisende is well, sir,' Leon replied. It was hard not to stare. It had been only a matter of hours since Leon had seen Lady Allisende's father and the man appeared to have aged ten years. Impossible though it seemed, new lines had appeared on his face. He looked haggard. Worn. Worried half to death. 'Lady Sybille told me you wished to speak to me, my lord.'

'Indeed. I must thank you for bringing Allis home.' The Count tipped his head towards the door. 'As you may have gathered, the situation has changed since you left. When we last spoke, you were uncertain as to your plans. Considering what's happened, I need to know whether you are prepared to give me your service for a few more weeks.'

Leon's heart lightened. Well, that would certainly give Othon time to regain his strength. But what exactly had happened? Leon recognised that he was unlikely to get the full story and hesitated before going ahead and asking anyway, 'My lord, what's going on?'

'My godson, Sir Claude—he is betrothed to Lady Allisende—was knifed this morning.'

'I am sorry to hear that, my lord,' Leon said as his mind worked. Lady Allisende had told him that she had left her fiancé waiting at the altar. And both she and her father had given him the distinct impression that she had left the castle days, if not weeks ago. If she had indeed jilted Sir Claude all that time ago, why hadn't he gone home? Why was her father insisting they were still betrothed? Someone wasn't facing reality.

'If we were to stay, what would our duties be?' Leon

asked. In truth, his mind was already made up. Othon needed to recuperate. The fact that Leon was himself intrigued to learn what was really going on in this castle had nothing to do with it. And he certainly had no interest in finding out whether the owner of a fine pair of sparkling blue eyes was as honest as she appeared to be.

'I need you to watch Allis. After what has just happened it is more important than ever.'

So, we were back to nursemaiding, were we? There had to be more to it than that. Leon had the distinct impression that the Count wasn't being entirely frank with him. 'Watch Lady Allisende, my lord?'

'Stick by her at all times. Don't leave her for a moment. If you must leave her, have one of your most trusted men stand in for you. And in case she tries to give you the slip, charge the others with watching her too.'

Leon felt a frown gather. Lord Michel wanted his men to spy on Lady Allisende? The Count's tone—earnest rather than angry—gave him pause. What was the Count's main concern? 'You think Lady Allisende is at risk, my lord?'

Lord Michel stared blindly at a shield on the opposite wall. 'I am not certain what to think. Well, man? Will you do it?' He gave a faint smile. 'My daughter is dear to me, as you will have gathered. You may name your price.'

'How long will you need us?'

'Initially, I am offering you and your troop a month's hire. If I require you for longer, we can review it then.'

'Very well, I agree,' Leon said coolly, although the instant he'd suspected that Lady Allisende might be in danger he'd known it would be impossible to leave.

And then there was Othon. 'My lord, you are probably aware that my captain broke his collarbone?'

'Aye, Lady Sybille mentioned something about a fellow called Othon.'

The Count remembered the name of Leon's captain? Now that was impressive. 'My lord, Othon won't be ready to ride out for a while. You will have to excuse him from this commission.'

'Agreed. We can discuss precise terms later. Please, see to my daughter.'

'Very good, my lord.' Leon bowed and left the armoury, fully conscious that he wasn't accepting this commission solely because his captain needed coddling. Lady Allisende's father thought she needed a protector. Now she had one. Leon would follow his instructions to the letter. As her father had asked, he would become her shadow.

Upon enquiry, he was directed up the curling stairs by a smiling maidservant.

'The best guest chamber? It's on the next floor, sir. The second door in the right-hand corridor.'

The door was ajar. As Leon approached, he heard voices—an argument was underway.

'Dammit, Allis,' a man said, testily. 'It's but a scratch. I won't be stitched.'

That had to be the prospective bridegroom, Sir Claude. Leon knocked and opened the door. His jaw dropped. Much of the bedchamber was taken up with a wide, canopied bed. On it, propped up by a bank of pillows, lay a young man. A very young man. His chest was bare, and he was pressing a bloody cloth—it looked like what remained of his shirt—to his left arm.

Leon bit back a laugh. Sir Claude was little more than a boy. If he'd seen twenty summers, Leon would be surprised. He looked almost as young as Peire. Far too young for Lady Allisende. She would make mince-meat of him.

*Mon Dieu*, what a mismatch.

Hand on her hip, Lady Allisende was glowering at him. 'Claude, you're quite ridiculous. Allow me look at it.'

'I refuse to be stitched,' came the petulant reply.

Lady Sybille, still holding the willow basket, ex-changed glances with her stepdaughter. 'Claude, be sen-sible, dear,' she murmured. 'There's quite a lot of blood. Let Allis look.'

*Allis,* Leon thought irrelevantly, *everyone calls her Allis.* He rather liked it. He must have moved for Lady Sybille glanced his way. She waved him in with an ex-pression of relief, proving to Leon what he'd already suspected. Lord Michel and his wife were close. They had discussed asking Leon to guard his daughter be-fore approaching him a second time.

Lady Allisende pushed up her sleeves. Leon leaned a shoulder against the door jamb and waited to see how she would handle the boy her father wished her to marry.

'Let me see, Claude.' Her voice softened. 'Please.'

With great reluctance, her so-called fiancé removed his hand from his arm and Lady Allisende bent over it. She barely touched him, but her examination was thorough.

'It looks quite deep,' she said. 'If you don't want it to fester, it's best to stitch it.'

Even from across the chamber Leon could see that the boy had taken quite a slash to his upper arm, blood was trickling sluggishly down. If left untended, smaller wounds than that could kill a man.

Lady Allisende turned to wash her hands in a basin on a side table before returning to her patient. She probed gently.

'Sybille, please send for hot water, the hotter the better. And wine.'

Sir Claude let his head fall back again the pillows and closed his eyes. *'Dieu merci,'* he muttered. 'I could do with a glass or two.'

When Lady Allisende carefully lifted the boy's arm, he made no protest. She pushed several cloths beneath it, and he didn't stir. She peered again at the wound.

'You're lucky, it looks clean. There don't appear to be any threads caught in it.'

Her unwanted fiancé grunted. 'Get on with it, will you?'

A wine flask appeared and was un-stoppered.

'Hold still.' Lady Allisende laid a firm hand on the boy's chest and nodded at Lady Sybille. 'You may give him a drink now.'

The lad took the glass with a shaking hand. While he drank, a maid appeared with a steaming basin and Lady Allisende busied herself with needle and thread, dipping both the thread and the needle into the water. The needle was curved like the beak of an avocet. Leon had seen many such needles in his time. Lady Allisende seemed to know exactly what she was doing.

'Sybille, please take charge of the wine glass,' Lady Allisende murmured. When Sir Claude protested, she smiled. 'You may have it back presently. Then, in a swift, ruthless movement, Lady Allisende tipped the flask and poured wine over the wound.

*'Jésu!'* the lad yelped and wrenched away.

Moments later she was stitching, talking all the

while. 'How did this happen? Were you on the practice field?'

'No.' A gasp. 'Get on with it, Allis, for pity's sake.'

'I'm going as quickly as I can,' she said, calmly cutting the thread of the stitch and beginning the next. 'You wouldn't thank me for crooked stitches.'

She stitched with a swift competence that told Leon she had done this many times before. When her patient moaned, she ignored it, she stitched calmly on.

'Well, Claude, what happened?'

'Was set upon outside the castle.'

'Oh. Where?'

'Between here and the village.'

Lady Allisende bit her lip, snipped the thread, and began another stitch. 'Was it one man or more?'

'One man.'

'Did you recognise him?' She looked up and studied the boy's face. 'Would you know him again?'

Sir Claude stared at the canopy above him, white about the mouth. 'No on both counts. Fellow dashed out of nowhere and struck before I even knew he was there.'

Lady Allisende frowned and said nothing. She set a few more stitches.

Her patient shifted. 'Are you done yet?'

'Almost there. You must have seen something.'

'I tell you, Allis, I saw nothing. He was just a thief. A brigand.'

With a small smile, Lady Allisende cut the last thread. 'There, it's done, you can relax.'

Lady Sybille set the basket on the bed and bent to examine her stepdaughter's handiwork. 'I was so relieved you arrived home when you did, my dear. When it comes to stitching people, you have a steadier hand than I. Do you need any herbs?'

'No, thank you. If God wills it, Claude won't need the herbs.' Lady Allisende took a small earthenware pot from the basket. 'Honey is good for wounds. I'll use a little of that. And the bandages of course.'

Still looking at the wound, Lady Sybille shook her head. 'Allis, if I live to be a thousand, I'll never understand you. Your sewing is barely passable, but this— you are a wonderful healer.'

'Aye, my thanks, Allis,' Sir Claude said. His eyelids were drooping. The wine—and shock—were beginning to have an effect.

Lady Sybille tiptoed out, leaving Leon to watch as his charge smoothed honey over the wound on her fiancé's arm and bandaged him up.

Allis kept a thoughtful watch over Claude until he drifted into a wine-hazed sleep. She had much on her mind. She had hoped to ask about Eglantine, but with Claude in so much pain, it hadn't been possible to do much more than get him comfortable. Her question remained. How was Eglantine? It was frustrating, but Claude wouldn't be talking sense for a while. Luckily, her stepmother took a strong interest in the village. Sybille would certainly have heard if anything was amiss.

As soon as Allis was confident that Claude was fast asleep, she tidied the willow basket and left the chamber. In the corridor, she ran straight into Sir Leon, who was leaning his shoulder against the wall. His arm went to steady her and fell quickly away, leaving Allis with a strange sensation in the pit of her stomach and a rush of unsettling thoughts. What would it be like to be held by this man in the throes of passion? What would it be like to kiss him?

Goodness, this wouldn't do. Kisses were disappointing, Allis had discovered that for herself. Not to mention that if she kissed this one, the scandal would never leave her. As to the rest, she already knew that ruination lay down that road. Ruination and bitter frustration. She jerked back.

'My apologies, my lady.'

Half afraid Sir Leon could read her thoughts, Allis responded more brusquely than she intended. 'Have you nothing better to do than lurk in corridors? You startled me, sir.'

Sir Leon's mouth twitched into that almost-smile. And, just as before, a pang went through her. He was always so controlled. Did he know how to smile with his whole heart? She'd love to see it.

A trestle table had been set up in the solar. Sybille and her handmaid, Patricia, sat side by side, hemming a linen tablecloth. Estelle, Allis's maid, was also sewing and as soon as Allis entered, she let out a squeak of distress and shot to her feet.

Allis swallowed a sigh. Without doubt, Estelle was responsible for revealing Allis's whereabouts to her father. 'Estelle, that reaction speaks volumes,' she said. 'It was you, wasn't it?'

'M…my lady?'

'Don't insult me by pretending innocence. I'm not stupid. Estelle, how could you? I swore you to secrecy.'

Estelle hung her head, and a large tear ran down her cheek. 'I am truly sorry, my lady.'

Sybille frowned. 'Allis, don't browbeat the poor girl. She couldn't help it and she is truly repentant.'

'She betrayed me. I trusted her and she betrayed me.'

'Think, Allis, dear. You of all people know how forceful your father can be when he has a purpose in mind. You cannot have expected Estelle to withstand him.'

Allis glowered at her stepmother before relenting. 'True enough.' She turned back to Estelle. 'However, I would like her to explain how I can be comfortable with her as my handmaid when I cannot trust her.'

Estelle dropped her gaze to the tablecloth. 'It won't happen again, my lady, I swear. It was just that the Count seemed to know that I knew. He kept on and on and—'

Allis found she had moved towards Estelle. She took her hand. 'I know. Papa is unbearably persistent—even I have trouble resisting him.'

A choking sound came from the vicinity of the stairwell. Sir Leon was out there listening, and the insolent rogue was laughing. Allis clenched her teeth. She would have to have words with him. What did he think he was doing, trailing after her the whole time? And how dare he laugh at her!

Estelle saw her fierce expression and gulped. 'I am sorry, my lady. I feel terrible because Sir Hugo had to confess his involvement and your father put him on guard duty as a punishment.'

'Guard duty? Hugo wouldn't like that.'

'I know. Forgive me, my lady. Please don't dismiss me.'

'Of course I forgive you, you goose.'

'You won't turn me away?'

'Certainly not. It was just the anger speaking.'

'Allis, dear, it strikes me that you and your father are alike in many ways,' her stepmother said, eyes twinkling. She reached for the scissors. 'There, Estelle, I told you it would be all right.'

'Yes, my lady. Thank you, my lady.' Estelle sat down again and picked up her sewing.

Sybille nudged a stool towards Allis. 'Do relax, dear. Did you wish to speak to me? Or do you wish to put on something more becoming first?'

Allis cast a glance towards the doorway, wondering whether Sir Leon was still on the landing. Not that it mattered. Like all men, once she began talking about babies, he was sure to become bored. 'Thank you, Sybille, I'm fine.' Allis sank on to the stool. 'I came to ask about the daughter of the village reeve.'

'Eglantine?' Sybille smiled. 'That girl is a wonder with her basketmaking. And not just baskets—did you know she makes hen coops and even chairs?'

'She does indeed. Sybille, did you know she is with child?'

'Aye, her father informed me of her condition some while ago. He wanted to ensure that she wouldn't be drummed out of the village.'

'Oh, poor Isembert. He must be worried. I hope you reassured him.'

'I did my best.'

With a glance at the maidservants, Allis lowered her voice. 'Did Isembert mention who sired Eglantine's child?'

Sybille gave a small cough and looked brightly at her maid. 'Patricia, I am parched, be so good as to fetch me a tisane. Peppermint, I think. Bring one for Allis too. And some of those apricot pastries she is so fond of.'

'At once, my lady.'

Sybille smiled at Estelle. 'Estelle, we have been neglecting poor Allis. She has barely come home, and we set her to work without giving her the chance to refresh herself. She will welcome a bath, I am sure. Have a tub brought up to her bedchamber, and a lay out a fresh set of clothes. Wait for her there, if you please. She will need you to wash and dress her hair.'

'Yes, my lady.'

Estelle followed Patricia out of the solar. Allis raised an eyebrow at her stepmother. 'I wasn't going to mention any names, Sybille.'

Sybille looked ruefully at her. 'I hope not.' She heaved a great sigh. 'Although I fear it is already common knowledge.'

'That may be true. Sybille, you do understand why I can't marry Claude?'

'I understand,' Sybille said carefully, 'why you think you can't marry him.'

Allis stared. 'Claude loves Eglantine, and she loves him.'

'Don't be obtuse, dear, you know there's more to it than that.'

Allis blinked. The way Sybille was looking at her was most unnerving. Almost accusatory. An icy pang shot through her. Guilt. Suddenly, Allis felt as though there was no other emotion. Guilt, guilt, guilt.

'What can you mean?'

Sybille stabbed her needle into a pincushion bristling with pins. 'You know perfectly well what I mean. You and Claude. Our families have been looking forward to your marriage for years.'

Allis stared at the pincushion. It looked, she thought irrelevantly, like a hedgehog. 'I don't love him, at least not in the right way.'

'Is there a right way to love a man?'

'Now you are being obtuse. Sybille, Claude and Eglantine are in love. Saints, there must be something we can do. What will happen to Eglantine when the child comes?'

'Nothing will happen to her. She will have her child. Isembert will support her.'

'Isembert is not young,' Allis said. 'Claude must be made to accept his responsibilities. Something must be done for her.'

Sybille tipped her head to one side. 'Allis, I did try. While you were away, I asked your father if he could help.'

'And?'

'He said, quite rightly in my opinion, that Eglantine's plight wasn't his responsibility. Your father feels that Claude must be held accountable. My dear, there are times when your father is malleable. Sadly, this is not one of them. When Claude has recovered, you had best speak to him.'

'I most certainly will.'

'Good. As you said, Eglantine's father is getting old. Like you, I hate to think of that girl on her own.' Thoughtfully, Sybille tapped her forefinger on the cloth. 'She has a brother, as I recall. Handsome rascal. I wonder if he could help. I haven't seen him in some while.'

Allis looked steadily at her. 'Eglantine's brother's no good. He's a pedlar and he's hardly ever in the village.'

'A pedlar? Well, that would explain why he's rarely about.' Sybille brightened. 'So, will you speak to your father?'

Allis rose. 'I'll go at once.'

Sybille looked her up and down and pulled a face. 'My dear, is that wise? You don't look your best.'

'Father knows I've just come from the convent, he won't mind.'

'Perhaps not, but when I have a case to plead, I find it gives me confidence to dress well.'

Allis twitched the skirts of her shabby dress. 'I agree that this has seen better days, but—'

Sybille's laugh rang round the solar. 'Allis, it's a rag. And it's filthy. There's a distinct whiff of the convent about you.'

'Are you saying that I smell?'

Sybille tipped her head to one side and said mildly, 'Estelle is ordering you a bath. You may as well take it. By the by, in all the excitement, you haven't mentioned Bernadette. How is she taking to convent life?'

'Bernadette is not coming home,' Allis said.

Sybille's face fell. 'Her heart's still set on taking the veil?'

'I'm afraid so.' Allis frowned at the white expanse of linen on the trestle. 'I hoped a few weeks of convent life would change her mind. I was wrong.'

'My dear, we mustn't allow ourselves to be downcast. It's Bernadette's decision.'

'I know. Nevertheless, the castle won't be the same without her. Sybille, did you know that the nuns are encouraged to distance themselves from their families?'

'I had heard that, yes.'

'It isn't natural.'

'Natural or no, only Bernadette can make the decision.' Sybille made a shooing gesture. 'Run along. Make yourself presentable for your father.'

'Very well. To be frank, I've been longing for a proper bath for weeks. I'll see Papa after that.'

'I'll have the tisane and pastries sent to your chamber.'

'Thank you, Sybille.'

Incredibly, Sir Leon was still hanging about outside

the solar. Allis felt her anger rise. 'You're still here?' She couldn't understand it, Sir Leon didn't strike her as an eavesdropper. His gaze held hers, steady and irritatingly calm. Her anger—and, yes, the man knew exactly how she felt—simply washed over him. 'Sir, you are completely without shame.'

'My lady, you cannot be forgetting, I am a mercenary.'

The penny dropped. Papa was paying Sir Leon to watch her! The indignity of it left Allis gasping. 'Father asked you to follow me? Why would he do such a thing? As for you, sir, you must have known I wouldn't like it. How could you agree?' She clenched her fists, uncertain what angered her most—Sir Leon agreeing to spy on her, or her wondering what it would be like to kiss him. Kiss him? She'd rather hit him. Not that it would make any impression on him, the great brute.

Sir Leon opened his mouth to respond, and she held up her hand. 'There's no need for platitudes, sir. I understand perfectly. You are mercenary to your core. You will be glad to hear I shall make it easy for you. I am going to my bedchamber. You may not enter. Is that clear?'

'Abundantly, my lady.'

Anger roiling in her, Allis gave him a final glare and stalked off.

# Chapter Six

**W**hile Allis—Lady Allisende—Leon amended, was in her bedchamber talking to her maid, Leon remained on duty in the narrow corridor outside. A line of unglazed arrow slits ran along the outside wall. He folded his arms. The next few days weren't likely to present much of a challenge. He ought to be bored, though that was yet to be an issue. Leon had overheard much of what had passed between Lady Allisende and Estelle in the solar and it was obvious the lady was aggrieved at what she saw as her maid's betrayal. Fortunately, the two of them seemed to have declared a truce. He could hear them now.

'Do you care for this gown, my lady?'

'Thank you, Estelle. Excellent choice. My father likes that one.' Lady Allisende raised her voice. 'Not that he deserves such consideration when he hires a mercenary to keep watch over me.'

Leon grinned. The little madam. She knew he could hear her.

'I couldn't say, my lady,' Estelle's voice was soothing. 'Will you wear your silver rings?'

It was obvious that she was doing her best to keep her mistress calm.

Leon stood aside as a parade of servants shouldered past with pails of steaming water. It was only after the last of them had poured the water into the lady's bath and had closed the door on the proceedings within that his difficulties began.

It went quiet in the bedchamber. From behind the door came soft rustlings. Clothing was being removed. He heard a splash. A sigh of pure pleasure. The scent of lavender drifted into the corridor. Unfortunately, it brought with it a vision of Lady Allisende in her bath. It was disturbingly clear. Leon hadn't seen the actual tub, but it had taken enough pails to fill it, so it must be large. She would be sitting there, leaning against a white linen cloth with the water lapping around her breasts.

Leon blinked. *Mon Dieu*, this must stop. Resolutely, he marched to the opposite end of the corridor. The voices faded.

He marched back in time to hear Estelle saying, 'Your hair first, my lady.'

A murmur of agreement was followed by the sound of pouring water. Which left him with a vivid image of the lady leaning forward, her hair trailing down her back. An unruly pulse throbbed. Leon swore under his breath and marched back down the corridor. He didn't stop. Up and down he went.

As Allis—Lady Allisende—bathed, he made himself examine the outer wall. It was unusual. Having both windows and loopholes spoke of supreme self-confidence on Lord Michel's part. The windows had shutters to keep out winter chills. Leon studied the splays in the wall, noted that each window had a small ledge beneath it, and attempted to distract himself by calculating the thickness of the walls. He went back to the bedchamber.

'Is that under-gown to your liking, my lady?'

Ignoring that ungovernable pulse, Leon gritted his teeth and marched back down the corridor. Torture. This was torture and why it should be, he couldn't imagine. Or rather he could. Only too well. He reminded himself of the rules. No ladies. Ever. And Lady Allisende was undoubtedly a lady. Even if she had refused the boy her father wanted her to marry.

A boy. A huff of exasperation escaped him. Lord Michel was deluding himself if he imagined his daughter would be content with that lad. What that woman needed was—

The bedchamber door opened and with a rustle of silk and satin, Lady Allisende Galard of Arles swept into the corridor. Leon, famed for his coolness in battle and his sang-froid with high-born ladies, felt his jaw drop.

Her head was uncovered, and her hair flowed, an unruly river of gold, down her back. Partly plaited, expertly styled, it hung in artful curlicues loosely secured with ribbons and pins. Silver rings gleamed on her fingers. Her gown was pink—it was probably the one that her handmaid had recommended. It had an underskirt of a deeper pink which somehow brought out the blue in her eyes. Leon couldn't decide whether she looked like a rose with ruffled petals or a fairy princess.

Lady Allisende swished her skirts away from him as she brushed past him. *She's a rose,* he thought, *an angry rose with many thorns.* He wondered how long it would be before a thorn pricked him. He didn't wait long.

She tossed a disdainful look his way. 'Oh, are you still here?'

He bowed. 'As you see, my lady. Where next?'

'I need to speak to my father.'

Leon was conscious of an absurd pang of regret. He'd rather liked the simple frankness of the humbly dressed girl he'd met at the convent. This woman—this lady—came from another world. She was untouchable. Out of reach for ever. Telling himself this should be easy, Leon crooked his elbow at her. 'Allow me to escort you.'

She turned her nose up at him. It was just as well, Leon wasn't entirely sure he had himself under control. It was astonishing. Lady Allisende had the knack of making him feel like a lad of sixteen.

'I can manage, thank you,' she said and started down the stairs.

Leon followed, frowning. He was gripped by an inconvenient urge to ruffle her petals. To ruffle them as they'd never been ruffled before.

Lady Allisende went directly to her father's estate office. A scribe was seated at the desk and Lord Michel was walking up and down in front of it, dictating. His face lit up. 'Allis, my dear. It is good to see you looking so well. You look so like your mother.'

'My lord.' Ignoring her father's outstretched hands, Lady Allisende swept into a formal curtsy. 'How kind of you to arrange to bring me home.'

Lord Michel regarded her heightened colour and shook his head. 'You're angry.'

Her chin lifted. 'If I am, you have yourself to blame.' She sent Leon a withering look. 'Did you have to set a watchdog on me? How could you?'

Lord Michel sighed and nodded at the scribe. 'Thank you, Gervase, that will be all. This isn't urgent, we can continue tomorrow.'

'Yes, my lord.' The scribe set down his quill, stoppered the ink pot and left.

A silence fell. The lady glared at her father, who was

regarding her with sad eyes. Watching them, Leon was conscious of an ache in his chest. If this was what being part of a family was like, constantly arguing and jostling for power, perhaps he hadn't missed that much. All this passion had to be exhausting.

'Do we have to come to blows?' Lord Michel asked.

'Papa, I don't enjoy coming to blows with you. I do it because otherwise you would trample all over me.' Roughly the lady shook out her skirts. 'You insist I marry Claude, when I tell you plainly that I do not want him. I have cause to be angry.'

'All I wish for is for you to be at peace,' her father said, sighing. 'What do you expect me to do?'

'You can start by dismissing your watchdog.'

'That is impossible. Sir Leon stays. If you object to him personally, I could find someone else to watch over you.'

Lady Allisende glared at Lord Michel. 'I don't object to him personally, how could I? The man is a war machine. But I'd like you to explain why you have hired him to keep an eye on me. If you think Sir Leon will stop me from acting as I see fit, you can think again. I will not be controlled.'

Lord Michel gave a bark of laughter. 'Control? You think this is about control? Allis, my dear, I am thinking of your safety.' He stepped towards her and this time his daughter permitted him to take her hands. He kissed each of them in turn and as he did so, her expression softened, and the furious flush faded. 'You are my beloved child. Sir Leon is here for your protection.'

'Papa, I am safely home, what can you mean?' Her gaze sharpened. 'Something else must have happened—apart from the attack on Claude. What is it? What are you not telling me?'

Lord Michel kissed his daughter's forehead and she leaned in to accept his kiss. The affection between them was palpable. The two of them were both unusually strong minded and Leon realised that while they might often be at odds with each other, they were bound together by shared experience. By love. That ache was back in his chest.

He was wrong about families. To have someone look at him the way Lady Allisende was looking at her father—if this was what it meant to have a family, the anger and the arguments might be a price worth paying.

Leon had never felt so lonely in his life. He reminded himself it didn't matter. He was, as Lady Allisende suggested, a war machine. He was proud of that. It had taken years for him to develop the skills necessary for survival. He was a mercenary, he accepted all honourable commissions, and emotions were never allowed to cloud his decisions or his behaviour. So there was no need for him to feel aggrieved that she referred to him as a war machine. None whatsoever.

The lady arched an eyebrow. 'What has happened that I need protection? Papa?'

'Allis, you may not need protection, indeed, I pray that I am wrong.'

'Please tell me.'

'Very well. I have no wish to alarm you, but the attack on Claude smells all wrong. Until we learn more, we must be cautious.'

'That is why Sir Leon is here?'

'Aye. You're in the habit of going into the village without an escort. That must stop.'

'Papa, I have friends in the village. No one would hurt me.'

'I pray you are in the right, but I am disturbed by

what happened to Claude. As I hear it, he too has friends in the village, eh?'

She flushed hotly and looked swiftly away.

'Come, Allis, until we learn more, you must be cautious. Humour me. Accept Sir Leon as your escort.'

Lady Allisende nodded. 'Very well.'

'Good girl, I knew you'd understand. Claude's assailant might still be around.' Lord Michel turned to Leon. 'Do you not agree, sir?'

'It's certainly possible,' Leon said, thinking it through. 'My lord, it occurs to me that the villagers might be hiding someone, reckless though it seems. One of their own could well have attacked Sir Claude.'

Lord Michel scratched his head. 'They have banded together to protect the fellow? If that's the case, they're likely to be as close as clams.'

'I agree. I doubt your men will learn anything, but the villagers may be less guarded with strangers. Would you like my men to make enquiries? I could ask a handful to visit the tavern. They will be properly briefed, and they will approach the village from opposite directions. No one will suspect they are staying at the castle.'

'My thanks, sir. That is by far the best idea I've heard all day.' Lord Michel turned back to his daughter, who had been listening to this exchange with a small pleat in her brow. 'Allis, you have other things to ask me about, as I recall. We have dealt with the first, Sir Leon stays. What else did you want to discuss?'

'Bernadette. Don't you want to know how she is?'

Leon's attention was caught by the passion in those fine blue eyes. Bernadette? He'd heard the name but couldn't make the connection. Whoever she was, it was plain she was important to Lady Allisende.

The Count was shaking his head. 'Allis, that remark

is not worthy of you. Of course I do. When we discovered both my beloved daughters had disappeared, it was obvious you had gone together. And as soon as Saint Claire's was mentioned, I realised what you were up to. You hoped Bernadette would change her mind about taking the veil. Well? Did it work?'

Lady Allisende gave a heavy sigh. 'No, she is as determined as ever.'

'I take it she is thriving?'

'She is as well as can be expected. However, she has been burdened with hard physical labour and she's far too thin.'

As Lady Allis talked, Leon's heart sank to his boots. God save him, Lord Michel had *two* daughters? How had he missed that? Had the Count expected him to bring them both back from the convent?

He cut in. 'Excuse me, my lord. Did you expect me to bring Lady Bernadette back to Galard? If so, I apologise for the misunderstanding. On the morrow, I will send her an escort.'

The Count shook his head. 'Be at ease, sir, that isn't necessary. You weren't to know about Bernadette because I did not mention her. She can stay where she is.' He turned back to Lady Allisende. 'A few more weeks of physical labour might bring your sister to her senses.'

'I doubt it.' Lady Allisende bit her lip. 'Papa, you wouldn't believe what life is like for her. Bernadette has been working in the vegetable garden and cleaning floors. Mother Margerie rations her food by the mouthful.'

'Allis,' the Count said, softly. 'It's the path your sister has chosen, and it is the way of things in a convent. Mother Margerie is testing Bernadette's vocation by giving her the most menial of tasks.'

'That is as may be, but her position there could be improved. Not an hour goes by without Mother Margerie mentioning Bernadette's dowry. Bernadette would be given privileges if she received it. More food. Clean linen. She would be far more comfortable.' She clasped her hands in an attitude of prayer. 'Please, Papa, if you think she will stay at the convent, send her dowry to Mother Margerie.'

'I will think about it.'

'Papa, *please*.'

'I will think about it,' the Count repeated. 'Now, was there anything else you needed to say?'

'There is something else,' she said, quietly. 'It concerns Eglantine.'

'Eglantine? That girl's nothing but a nuisance.'

'I was hoping you'd talk to her.'

'Why the devil should I do that?'

'Papa, I know you're aware of the nature of the relationship between Eglantine and Claude. Don't you care about the baby?'

'You've been talking to Sybille.'

'Papa, this can't be pushed to one side. Eglantine will need help when her time comes.'

'She is not my responsibility,' Lord Michel growled, face darkening. 'She has a father, as does her babe.'

He leaned threateningly towards Lady Allis and Leon found he had clenched his fists. The Count had hired Leon to protect his daughter—surely he wasn't about to hit her?

'Allis, that child is not my responsibility,' the Count said. 'That honour belongs to Claude and Claude alone.'

'I know.' Lady Allisende's shoulders sagged. 'Nevertheless, I was hoping that perhaps you—'

'No,' Lord Michel cut in tightly. 'No and no again.'

In the depths of the castle a gong sounded. The Count stepped away from his daughter and the atmosphere in his office lightened.

'Are you hungry, sir?' Lord Michel smiled at Leon. 'That was the call to supper. Would you care to join us at the high table?'

'I would be honoured, my lord.'

With a sigh, Allis followed her father to the great hall. They arrived at the same moment as her step-mother and her ladies. While her father and Sybille went to the ewer on a side table to wash their hands, Allis paused—she was seeing the hall with new eyes. After the frugal convent suppers, the great hall of Galard Castle looked very grand. White linen cloths were spread on the top table. Lights burned in hanging lamps. Glass goblets glittered. Large platters were heaped with fruit—grapes, peaches, oranges. Servants lined the walls of the hall, napkins over an arm as they waited for those at the high table to take their seats.

Supper was sure to drag. If she weren't so hungry, Allis would happily have missed it altogether, but her father had made it plain that he would enjoy Sir Leon's company. And since she wanted her father to loosen his hold on Bernadette's dowry, she would do her utmost not to irritate him. She had just come home. Tonight, she would be the exemplary daughter her father no doubt wished for. She hated crossing swords with him, especially since she was honoured by his trust in her. Allis had grown up knowing that her father's vision for the future of Galard involved her. Allis would marry its new lord. If only her father's mind was not set on Claude. The thought of coming between him and Eglantine was unbearable.

After Allis had taken her turn at the ewer, Sir Leon followed. When he had finished, he guided her to the bench next to the throne-like chairs her father and Sybille used.

'Is this your place, my lady?' he asked.

'Thank you, sir, it is.'

She rearranged her skirts and tried not to frown. Supper in the great hall usually took at least an hour and instead of wasting an hour, she would rather be walking into the village. She had hoped to talk to Eglantine tonight. That no longer looked possible.

On a practical level, Allis wanted to see Eglantine. Her pregnancy would by now be obvious. How had the villagers reacted? Allis wanted to make sure the girl wasn't being bullied. Some of the villagers were extremely conventional, and the birth of an illegitimate child often caused discord. Marriage, as sanctioned by the Church, protected children from the shame of illegitimacy. It also protected mothers from criticism. As an unmarried mother, Eglantine's position in the village would never be quite the same.

Furthermore, Eglantine's father Isembert was the most law-abiding and God-fearing of men. Since he was the village reeve that was only to be expected, but there was no saying what Isembert might do if he felt angry or humiliated that his unwed daughter was with child. Were the villagers turning against Eglantine? Allis didn't want her punished. She would not rest easy until she knew both Eglantine and her unborn baby were safe.

And last, but by no means least, Allis wouldn't mind knowing if Eglantine had heard from that elusive brother of hers.

The bench shifted as Sir Leon took his place next to

her. He was careful, she noted, to keep several inches between them. Not that it bothered her. It wasn't as though she was going to pay him any attention.

It didn't work out quite as Allis had planned. When she caught herself glancing his way for the dozenth time, she realised he was impossible to ignore. It mattered not that he was silent most of the time, you couldn't ignore a man like Sir Leon. He was so imposing. He sat next to her like a rock. No, that was wrong. He was no more a rock than he was a war machine. She shouldn't have called him a war machine.

Sir Leon was…

Quietly confident.

Strong and silent.

Impossibly attractive.

Briefly their eyes met, and Allis felt a worrying quickening inside her. She looked swiftly away and the next time she glanced at him his gaze was hooded. Impenetrable.

Sir Leon was concealing something. What could it be? She shifted her gaze to the trencher in front of them. Her father liked the traditions and clearly intended that she and Sir Leon would share the trencher. It was then that she realised what Sir Leon was hiding. He was hiding his reactions. Those green eyes were taking an inventory, he was watching the entire household and he missed nothing, she was sure.

The banners of her father's knights were displayed high in the corners of the ceiling at either side of the great fireplace, splayed out in colourful fan shapes. Sir Leon was studying them. Doubtless, he knew all the knights' devices. He studied every blessed thing. Why, she even caught him fingering the white tablecloth as though testing its quality. He had accepted the honour of a seat next to her on the dais without as much as a blink. What did he really think? Why was he so concerned to keep his thoughts hidden?

He must have moved closer for Allis was suddenly aware of the heat of his large body. It wasn't her fault that the man had such a wonderful build—the problem was that she was more conscious of him than she ought to be. It was most disconcerting. She was about to shift away when she caught the tail edge of a mocking smile. He had anticipated she would do exactly that. Which forced her to remain exactly where she was. It was then that Allis made the most alarming discovery of all.

She *liked* sitting next to him. She recalled the moment that her father suggested replacing Sir Leon with someone else.

No! If she had to be guarded, it would be by this man. She didn't understand why she felt this way, it must be the novelty. She'd never had anyone assigned to protect her before. And her father had chosen well—with Sir Leon at her side she felt perfectly safe.

'Do you care for wine, my lady?' a servant asked.

She glanced at Sir Leon. Since he had been partnered with her this evening, she was to share a goblet with him as well as the trencher. 'Sir, are you happy with wine?'

'If that is your choice, my lady,' came the quiet reply.

'You must let me know your preference, sir.'

'I confess I should like to sample the wine.' Briefly, his focus was entirely on her—dark, intense, and full of secrets. Allis stopped breathing. This man flustered her, and she couldn't understand it. She felt safe with him and yet…

His attention shifted back to the knights' colours at the other end of the hall, and she breathed again.

Sir Leon of Tarascon. Allis liked the way he kept

himself to himself. She liked his distance. His calm. It made him mysterious. Intriguing. And there was truly no question of her being in danger with him at her side. Did Papa really believe her to be at risk? From what? He must be mistaken. She was surely safe at the heart of his stronghold.

The wine—a rich blood-red—streamed into their goblet.

A platter of mutton appeared before her. 'Meat,' she heard herself say. Her stomach growled and she felt herself flush.

Without asking, Sir Leon reached out, speared a piece, and pushed it to her side of the trencher. 'I don't suppose you had meat in the convent,' he said, smiling.

'Sir, we didn't even have fish.' At which point Allis's stomach groaned again and they both laughed.

At first, all she could think about was eating. Throughout the meal Sir Leon remained as though glued to her side. Unsurprisingly, he had a healthy appetite, the appetite of a warrior. After she had taken the edge off her hunger, she wiped her fingers on her napkin and reached for a peach. She found herself looking longingly towards the double doors at the end of the hall. She must see Eglantine.

'Sir Leon, do you think we might walk into the village tonight?'

He glanced at the window slits and shook his head. 'The light is almost gone, my lady, it wouldn't be wise. Perhaps tomorrow.'

'In that case, I should like ensure that all is well with Claude before retiring.'

'As you wish.'

Allis smiled. 'You are thinking of accompanying

me?' she asked, in as nonchalant a tone as she could muster.

'Of course. As your father commanded.'

'There is truly no need.'

His gaze was suddenly intent. Inescapable. 'Oh?'

'I wish to speak privately with Claude, I am sure you understand.'

His mouth went up at one side. 'All I understand is that you do not wish me to be present. My lady, much as I regret inconveniencing you, I shall not leave your side.'

She stared at him, smile fixed grimly in place. This was exactly what she feared. She prayed he couldn't tell how her heart had sunk. How on earth was she to talk privately to Claude?

There were questions of great importance that must be answered, and Claude could, Allis was sure, give her the answers without realising the implications.

Unhappily, the same could not be said for Sir Leon. More intelligent than Claude, Sir Leon was likely to work out exactly what she was doing.

In her mind, she resorted to a curse often used by her father. Hell and damnation.

# Chapter Seven

Leon marched into the guest chamber behind Lady Allisende and stood at ease near the door. If he felt a shade uncomfortable following her again, he shrugged it off. Her father's orders were clear. Besides, this was too interesting to allow room for embarrassment. Lady Allisende had, reluctantly it was true, accepted her father's wishes that Leon should guard her.

Yet down in the hall she'd tried to prevent him coming with her. Why? What was she up to? When Leon had met her, he'd taken her for a straightforward no-nonsense woman. It was becoming clear that wasn't the whole truth. Lady Allisende had secrets.

The willow medicine basket had been left on a side table close to the bed and the lad was propped up on his pillows, staring at it. His lips were tightly compressed. Clearly, he was suffering. It didn't look as though he'd be sleeping any time soon. Lady Allisende glanced at the basket and then back at the boy.

'You know who made that, don't you?' she said.

Sir Claude started. 'Made what?'

She tutted and picked up the basket. 'This,' she said,

depositing it in his lap. 'You were staring at it when we came in.'

'I wasn't staring at it, my gaze happened to fall in that direction.'

'Claude, please. You cannot deny you were staring at it because Eglantine made it.' Her attention shifted to her patient's bandages, and she let out a gentle sigh. Perching on the edge of the bed, she added, 'I can't help feeling that this is all my fault.'

The boy's eyes went wide. 'You're surely not talking about the stabbing? How can the attack on me be your fault?'

Lady Allisende shrugged, and Leon's interest intensified. That shrug was far from casual. What was going on?

'I'm sorry I left you in the lurch, Claude.' She glanced at the basket. 'If you had accepted my refusal, none of this might have happened.'

'What are you saying?' the boy asked.

Baffled, Leon listened attentively as they began wrangling with each other about whether she should have accepted him or not. Half of what they said revealed the strength of their friendship. The other half was pure exasperation. There was nothing remotely loverlike in the way they related to each other. Thank God. Though why Leon should be thanking God about that, he had no idea.

By the time Leon realised his mind had wandered, they had come full circle. She was teasing the boy about the basket.

'Admit it, Claude, you were staring at it like a love-lorn swain.'

Sir Claude reached for her wrist. 'Forget the basket, you have an important decision to make.'

'Oh?'

'You have to marry me.' The boy glanced uneasily at Leon and lowered his voice. 'Please, Allis. Neither your father nor mine will rest until we are wed.'

'You've had my answer a hundred times,' Lady Allisende said crossly. 'It hasn't changed. The answer is no, it will always be no.'

'Allis, please—'

'No!' She sprang to her feet, eyes flashing. 'Stop humiliating yourself. I refuse to marry you. I refused to appear on our supposed wedding day. Don't you care about Eglantine?'

'Of course I do! Eglantine is my world, but I am sorry to say there will be no peace from our parents until you and I wed.' He flushed bright red and stared at the wall behind Allis before adding clumsily, 'And we must produce an heir as quickly as possible.'

An unwelcome image sprang into Leon's mind. By the time he'd dismissed it, they were back to bickering about Eglantine.

The boy wanted an heiress and he wanted to keep his lover. Leon felt a flicker of contempt. Like many noblemen, Sir Claude assumed that he could have the best of both worlds. If Leon were included in this conversation, he would ask him what he imagined married life would be like with an angry and unhappy Lady Allisende as his wife. The boy was weak-minded. He was under the thumb of his father and likely his godfather too. He resented it while being too weak to resist them. If Lady Allisende married Sir Claude, it would be the most unequal match of all time.

And then it struck him. Lady Allisende had fortitude for two. Which was precisely why the boy was so desperate to marry her. Sir Claude—deluded young fool—

imagined that marriage to her would magically imbue him with her strength, whereas in reality...

Lady Allisende would tie him in knots.

Leon almost laughed aloud. He leaned against the wall and waited for her response to the idea of giving Sir Claude an heir.

Rather than berate him, she looked pensively at the boy, bent over his bed, and smoothed the bedcover before giving him a dazzling smile. Clearly, she saw he was never going to accept her refusal. Rather than being relieved, Leon felt a prick of alarm. If he were not mistaken, she had changed tactics.

'Claude, has Eglantine's brother been seen?'

The lad was running his fingertips along the handle of the willow basket. He looked up, frowning. 'Simon? It's strange you should mention him, I've been wondering the same thing. As I told you, I didn't see who knifed me, but for some reason I can't stop thinking about him.'

Lady Allisende swallowed. 'You suspect Simon was your assailant.'

It wasn't a question. Leon resolved to find out about this Simon as quickly as possible.

'If it was Simon,' Sir Claude muttered, 'he must be upset about Eglantine.'

'Upset?' Lady Allis flashed him a look of intense irritation. 'He will be furious.'

'I don't see why,' Claude said in a sulky voice. 'We've all been friends for an age. Simon must know that I won't abandon her.'

Leon drew his head back. *We've all been friends for an age.* What was the boy saying? Lady Allis had told him she was in the habit of visiting the villagers, and Sir Claude had obviously got Eglantine with child, but this sounded as though others from the castle were friendly with the villagers. Thanks partly to his unfortunate childhood and partly to the malicious Lady Madeleine, Leon was in the habit of keeping a distance between himself and those of noble blood. He would think about this later. He turned his attention back to the conversation.

'You won't abandon Eglantine?' Lady Allis's face lit up. A bright strand of hair fell forward as she reached to squeeze the boy's hand. 'Claude, that is most heartening. If you agree to me visiting her, I can reassure her of that in the morning.'

Her supposed fiancé frowned. 'I'd like to see her myself.'

'Certainly not. You can't ride until your stitches have healed and walking would be most unwise for the next few days. Besides, Papa would never allow it. He's concerned for your welfare. If anything else happens to you while you are our guest, your father—great friend or no—would never forgive him.'

'If you say so.' The lad's voice was a thread of sound. He was clearly exhausted. He let go of the basket and cradled his injured arm. 'Tell her I miss her and that I hope to see her soon.'

'I shall. And I shall be sure she understands that you are not abandoning her.' Her face softened. 'Is it paining you very much?'

'It throbs a little. Is there more wine?'

'I shall order a tisane to be prepared. It will help with the pain and make it easier to sleep.'

'Thank you, Allis.'

Leaning over the bed, Lady Allisende picked up the basket and put it back on the side table. Her patient's eyelids were closed and his jaw clenched.

'Claude, I'm sorry I abandoned you. If only you had listened.'

Claude grunted.

Allis sent down to the kitchen for a tisane for Claude and sat with him while he drank it. She was fully conscious that Sir Leon's watchfulness never wavered. When she eventually left Claude to his sleep, Sir Leon fell into step beside her, a colossus of a man who was surprisingly light on his feet. And surprisingly companionable.

Except Sir Leon was a little too quiet. He'd not spoken since they'd finished supper. Companionable though Allis found him, she was beginning to find the silence irksome. He was trying to fit in, she knew. She had been certain he would interfere, but on the contrary, he gave her full rein, allowing her to go about her duties without let or hindrance.

It shouldn't bother her, and yet it did. Sir Leon's presence, while reassuring was deeply unsettling. By the time Allis had climbed the stairs to her bedchamber, she realised why she was so out of sorts. Sir Leon's silence gave her space, and his presence was so commanding she couldn't help but fill it by thinking about him. By wondering. What was going on in that handsome head? What did he think of her family? Of her? Had he noticed when she had mentioned Simon? She had no answer to any of her questions. Sir Leon's expression revealed nothing.

When they arrived at her bedchamber door, a rolled-up bundle that looked suspiciously like a bedroll caught her eye. Next to it was a leather saddle bag. She eyed them with misgiving. 'Sir, are those your things?'

'Yes, my lady.'

'Why are they there?'

The sun was sinking. Dusk was closing in. The servants were yet to light the candles, but Allis could see well enough to catch a brief—and far too intriguing—flash of amusement in his green eyes.

A dark eyebrow lifted. 'I would have thought that was obvious.'

His low, soft voice sent shivers rippling down her spine. 'You, sir, are an insolent rogue. Please tell me you are not planning to sleep in the corridor.'

He shook his head. 'I shan't be sleeping in the corridor.'

'That's a relief. It's not necessary. Papa won't expect you to watch me the entire night. Someone ought to have mentioned that there is another guest chamber next to the one Claude is using. You are welcome to it. A proper mattress will be far more comfortable than your bedroll.'

'Thank you, my lady, I am sure it would.' Sir Leon stepped closer, forcing Allis to tip her head back to look up at him. 'But I shall not be sleeping in the guest room.'

'Oh.' Allis swallowed. She wanted to say more but her mouth had dried. And, lo, there was that glint in his eyes, except once again it had changed. His gaze was heavy lidded and knowing. Sensuous. It was almost as if he were thinking about kissing. Kissing her? No, no. He wouldn't dare.

Oh, if only he would. Allis just knew that Sir Leon's kiss would be exciting. Thorough. Mere thought of it weakened her legs and all he was doing was look at her.

Hastily, she cleared her throat. 'Where will you sleep?'

He gave her a slow smile she felt in her toes. 'Right there.'

He was pointing at the threshold of her bedchamber. Allis shook her head. There were butterflies in her belly, which was a novelty for her. Usually when she was attracted to a man, she felt little more than curiosity. Saints, what was she thinking? 'Sir, there's no need for that. My maid is just along the corridor. If I need anything, all I have to do is ring for her.'

'Your father is paying me to watch you and watch you I will.'

Another smile set an unseemly wish skittering about in her head. *Kiss me, sir. Please, kiss me.* Heavens, she'd known the man's smile would be worth waiting for. It was so potent it was wreaking havoc with every sense. Filling her with impossible longings. *Touch me. Hold me.*

'My lady, you might take it into your head to go into the village without me,' he said, contriving somehow to make every word a caress. 'I might lose you, and you might get hurt.'

'I won't do that,' Allis said, in a breathless voice she didn't recognise. The corridor felt hot. Airless. The wind must have dropped. 'I give you my word, sir. I won't leave the castle without you.'

His eyes narrowed sceptically and then he stepped back and bowed. 'I am sorry, my lady.' He indicated the bedroll lying across the threshold of her bedchamber. 'I am sleeping there.'

Leon woke early. Before rising, he stared at the door that stood between him and Lady Allisende. There hadn't been a sound from her bedchamber all night. She must still be asleep. He stretched and clambered to his feet.

Last night, she'd given him her word she wouldn't

leave the castle without him. Oddly, he believed her. Lady Allisende might have secrets, she might flee into the night to escape a wedding she had no wish for, but he was confident that once this woman had given her word, she could be trusted. Which was just as well, because Leon intended to go the guardhouse to enquire about Simon, the basket weaver's brother. He would break his fast after that.

Half a dozen men were on duty by the gate. The portcullis was raised and through the gap, the approach road was empty. It wasn't surprising so close to dawn.

Nodding a greeting to the guards, Leon climbed the stone steps and entered the adjoining guardhouse. Three men were conferring inside. One of them was Lord Michel's sergeant, Matheu. 'Good morrow, Matheu.'

'Good morning, sir.'

Loopholes in the guardhouse walls gave limited views of the approach road, the moat, and the castle bailey. Leon went to one and peered out. 'All seems well this morning,' he said.

'Yes, it's been quiet.' Matheu looked enquiringly at him. 'Can I help you, sir?'

Leon hid a smile. By now the entire castle would know that their lord had hired him to watch over his daughter. 'I am making enquiries on behalf of Lord Michel. Do you know of a villager, name of Simon?

'Simon? Can't say I do.' Matheu frowned at an arrow slit before stiffening. 'Wait, that's wrong, a Simon does come to mind. Fellow's a pedlar. He's not around much.'

One of the other men cleared his throat. 'Matheu's in the right. Simon's the son of the village reeve. He's a devil with the women, sir.'

'Oh?'

'They adore him.' The guard scratched his chin. 'Can't see why myself.'

'My thanks, that's most helpful,' Leon said. Given the dark hints Lady Allisende was throwing out last eve, she appeared to think that Simon might be responsible for the attack on Sir Claude. It was certainly possible. Village families did sometimes become inextricably entangled with those at their nearby castle, and what Sir Claude had said last eve—*we've all been friends for an age*—suggested this was as true of Galard as it was elsewhere. Simon's anger at Sir Claude was understandable. But to attack the godson of their lord? It was madness. If caught, Simon would pay a high price for his folly.

Realising he needed to know more, Leon returned to the keep. He shouldn't have long to wait. Lady Allisende would soon be up and if she was still intent on visiting Eglantine, he might find answers.

The first thing Leon saw as he entered the great hall was Lady Allisende, sitting at table on the dais, breaking her fast in a gown of deep violet.

He found himself smiling and strode swiftly across. She looked bright and beautiful and her returning smile threatened his peace of mind. And not just her smile—he could barely tear his gaze from her hair. This morning she was wearing a short lavender veil. It was light as gossamer, Leon could see straight through it to the blonde plaits carefully arranged with lavender ribbons at each side of her head. Already a bright strand was unravelling.

Off limits, he reminded himself. Lady Allisende is off limits. He felt his smile fade. 'Good morning, my lady. You're up early.'

'Good morning, sir. When Estelle told me you were

no longer at your post, I thought perhaps you'd had enough of us.'

'I am sorry to disappoint you, my lady, I've been making enquiries at the guardhouse.'

'I have no idea why you think I would be disappointed by your staying, sir. I am quite resigned to your presence.' She waved at a platter of bread and cheese. 'Have you broken your fast?'

'Not yet.'

'Please, be seated and help yourself.' She gave him a direct look. 'Were your enquiries fruitful?'

A pot of ale was set at Leon's elbow. 'It's too soon to say, my lady.'

Lady Allisende seemed happy to walk into the village, but for safety's sake, Leon insisted that they rode. If Simon had knifed Sir Claude, he could still be at large. Further, if Simon had struck because he was aggrieved on behalf of Eglantine, why would he not attack Lady Allisende too? In one respect, Lady Allisende was Eglantine's rival. It wasn't a risk worth taking.

There was no paved square as such, cottages were clustered around a village green that was criss-crossed with sun-baked ruts. A tall oak stood in the centre. In line with many other villages, they probably held markets here. Leon couldn't see a well, which indicated that people drew their water from a nearby stream. Perhaps the same stream that fed the Galard moat.

'Which is the reeve's cottage, my lady?'

Lady Allisende pointed with her riding crop. 'That one.'

The reeve's cottage was neat and well kept. Built in stone, it had a tiled roof and was encircled by a fence. Herbs were growing in pots at the front and a bench sat on one side of the door. There was a rabbit hutch, a straggle of marigolds and a path that led round to the back. Stacks of willow baskets were sheltered by an awning. Out of sight, a pig was grunting. A thread of grey smoke drifted up from the chimney.

Smoke.

Leon's blood chilled and sweat broke out on his brow. Smoke.

Hell, not this again. Not now. Of all the times. Leon knew from bitter experience that he couldn't prevent it from happening, he would have to ride it out and pray it didn't last long. He stared at the smoke like a man possessed as his heart began to lurch about in his chest.

Why now? He smelt smoke every day and it didn't always affect him like this. It made no sense.

The cottage had triggered this. On the surface, it did not resemble his parents' cottage, yet there were similarities. Leon knew how small it would be inside. How dark. Three rooms at most and a ladder to the loft.

Mercifully, he didn't freeze for long, just long enough for a sparrow to fly under the eaves and then the sense of horror began to fade, as it always did. He mastered himself quickly. Dismounting, he turned to Lady Allisende and held out his hand. Thank God, it wasn't shaking. He prayed she hadn't noticed anything amiss. 'Allow me to help you, my lady.'

After she dismounted, Leon secured the horses to the fence and by the time he was following her to the cottage door, he was able to wonder how Lady Allisende planned to deal with Eglantine. Eglantine must see her as a rival. And what about her brother Simon? How was he involved in what had happened to Sir Claude?

A young woman was sitting on a three-legged stool before the fireplace. Flat bread was cooking on a griddle and she was turning it with a pair of tongs. She looked up.

'My lady!' Deftly, the girl flipped the bread, set the tongs on a hook near the fire and rose. 'I trust you are in good health.' She curtsied and looked hesitantly at Leon.

Lost for words, Leon stared. Eglantine was a beauty. She wasn't beautiful in the same way as Lady Allisende, for Eglantine was as dark as Lady Allisende was fair, but beauty she certainly was. Eglantine didn't have Lady Allisende's stature. Apart from her rounded belly, she was small and petite. She had brown, doe-like eyes, and thick, lustrous hair tied back in an old-fashioned plait.

Lady Allisende gave Eglantine a warm smile and took her hand. 'You look well.'

'I am, thank you.' Eglantine murmured. 'It's good to see you, my lady.' She looked as though she meant it. It was yet more evidence of the close bond between those in the village and those in the castle.

Lady Allisende gestured Leon forward. 'Sir Leon, this is Eglantine, the daughter of Isembert, our village reeve. Eglantine, Sir Leon is my escort at present.'

Eglantine gave him a swift, darting glance. 'He is under Lord Michel's command?' she whispered, ducking her head, and mumbling at the floor.

'Aye.'

Eglantine was obviously painfully shy. Leon could barely make out what she said.

Lady Allisende huffed impatiently. 'There's no need to be wary of Sir Leon, Eglantine.' She whispered in Eglantine's ear and Leon caught the words. 'He's not half as fierce as he looks. Come, we were friends before I went away. I am hoping that still holds true.' She glanced at the fire. 'That bread smells done. Take it off the griddle and we can sit on the bench outside while it cools.'

Eglantine did as she was bid, and they trooped back outside. Leon went to stand with the horses and watched his charge from there. What could have been the most awkward of meetings was far from that.

Eglantine, with a final, wary look in Leon's direction, grasped Lady Allisende's hand. 'My lady, how is Claude faring? I heard he was hurt.' Her voice broke. 'Is he well?'

'Claude is fine. He has had a few stitches. He is resting. Be sure he is thinking of you.' She lightened her tone. 'He asked me to tell you that he will not abandon you.'

Shaking her head, Eglantine stared at the ground. 'Whatever he does, he will end up marrying you.'

'Eglantine, do not despair. You must have worked out that I left the castle to avoid the marriage.'

'Yes, my lady.' Eglantine gave a sad smile. 'You left the night before the wedding was meant to take place. I know you tried to avoid it.' She tipped her head to one side. 'You came back though. Why?'

Fleetingly, Lady Allisende's eyes met Leon's. 'Father discovered where I was. He sent someone to fetch me.'

Eglantine put her hand on her belly and gave a faint moan. 'I knew this would happen. The Count will insist the marriage takes place.'

'He can insist all he likes.'

'My lady, in the end your father will have his way.'

'As to that, we shall have to see. I shall certainly speak up for you, Eglantine, of that you may be sure.'

'Thank you, my lady.'

The more Leon heard, the more Lady Allisende amazed him. She was truly the most uncommon lady.

There she sat, talking calmly and openly to a girl who had every reason to loathe her. Another twist of fair hair had escaped Lady Allisende's diaphanous veil, and it gleamed in the sun like spun gold. Leon tore his gaze away. *Listen, man. Focus.*

It was hard though because Lady Allisende was a wonder. Was she frank and open with everyone? It would seem so. He heard her repeat that she would do her best to ensure that Eglantine wasn't left on her own. When the girl lifted her head and smiled back at her, Leon wasn't surprised. Lady Allisende's frankness would disarm anyone.

'My lady?' Eglantine's brown eyes filled with shadows. 'There's something you ought to know. Simon is back.'

Lady Allisende inhaled sharply. From where Leon was standing with the horses, it was barely noticeable, but he was oddly attuned to her every movement.

'Claude did mention him,' Lady Allis said carefully.

Eglantine went pale. 'Simon didn't…? Don't tell me it was my brother who—'

'No. *No*.' Lady Allisende took the girl's hand. 'Claude didn't see Simon when he was struck, if that's what you're thinking, and I don't believe he would hurt Claude.'

Eglantine looked doubtfully at her. 'If you say so.'

'Is Simon staying with you?'

'No, my lady. I haven't seen him. I just thought you should know he's been spotted in the village.'

Eglantine looked, Leon decided, as though she was telling the truth. She hadn't seen her brother. None the less, he felt a flicker of unease. Lady Allisende might be confident that this Simon wasn't behind the attack on Sir Claude—unfortunately his sister didn't appear to agree.

Where did that leave them?

Lady Allisende—as Eglantine's rival—could certainly be at risk. Was the pedlar's return to the village the real reason Lord Michel had hired Leon and his troop?

Leon sighed and wished he were as convinced as Lady Allisende that Simon was innocent of the assault on Sir Claude. As soon as he could, he would have words with Lord Michel.

They rode back to the castle with Lady Allisende's lavender veil rippling in the wind. What an impressive young lady she was. Not only was she the most determined woman Leon had ever met, but she was also kind. Considerate. And refreshingly down to earth.

Allis liked mending things. Hastily, Leon checked himself. To him she was Lady Allisende. He would never have the privilege of calling her Allis for her face. Even Lady Allis was too informal. Then he shook his head. To hell with it, in the privacy of his own head it surely didn't matter what he called her.

For good or ill, in his mind Lady Allisende had become Allis.

## Chapter Eight

Allis and Sir Leon clattered back over the drawbridge and trotted towards the stables. Half a dozen horses were tethered to rings outside. Allis did not recognise them. Visitors. Her first thought was that Claude's father, Lord Robert, had come to see his son, but then her gaze lit on a large black stallion and a chill went through her. Surely not...

'My lady!' A guard ran up. 'Lord Michel asks that you go directly to the estate office.'

Allis nodded. 'Of course.' She jerked her head in the direction of the black stallion. 'Is that Sir Philippe's horse?'

'Yes, my lady.' The guard took Blackberry's bridle and lowered his voice. 'Sir Philippe is in the solar with Lady Sybille. Your father asked me to make sure you speak to him in the office before going up to join them.'

'Very well.'

Sir Philippe's arrival was disturbing. Allis couldn't stand him. Merely thinking about him made her sick to the stomach. She had caught him staring at her on previous occasions, a speculative gleam in his eyes. He had a reputation for cruelty, and she didn't trust him. What brought him here today?

She must have sat there unmoving for Sir Leon was waiting at her stirrup to help her dismount. She scrambled down, took a deep breath, and set off for the steps of the keep. Sir Leon kept pace with her.

'Who's Sir Philippe?'

'Sir Philippe Talmont of Pernes.'

'You don't like him,' he said, as perceptive as ever. 'Why not?'

Allis gave him a look. 'If you keep me company and we encounter Sir Philippe, I think you will see.'

Sir Leon lifted an eyebrow. 'That sounds like an invitation, my lady. I thought you resented my presence.'

'Not at all.' They passed through the great doors and Allis turned to him, cheeks heating. 'I meant what I said at breakfast. I am resigned to your company.'

'Resigned,' Sir Leon muttered, shaking his head.

Conscious she had hurt him in some way, Allis lightly touched his hand. Though the contact was brief it reassured her. Sir Leon was so strong. He didn't judge. Most importantly, he appeared to be completely dependable. Lord, what was she thinking? This man's dependability would only last as long as her father was paying him and not a day more.

'Sir, as God is my witness, I would be happy if you were to spend all day at my side.' Particularly since Sir Philippe was here.

Sir Leon inclined his head. 'As my lady commands.'

They didn't stop to remove their cloaks and were still wearing them as they entered the estate office. Allis received no welcoming smile. Her father was sitting at his table, staring morosely at a beribboned scroll.

'You wished to see me, Papa?'

'Aye. Sir Philippe has brought a document signed by the Rector of the Comtat Venaissin.'

Allis nodded. Their estate lay in the Comtat Venaissin, which belonged to the Pope. The Rector was his administrator. 'What does it say?'

'See for yourself.' Her father nudged the document towards her. 'Be warned, you won't like the contents.'

Allis unrolled the scroll. As she read, a large seal swung gently to and fro.

'Sir Philippe wants to marry me!' She felt the blood drain from her face. 'Papa, it says here that the Rector has granted permission for him to do so. I can't marry that man. He's vile. Besides, I know you dislike him as much as I. However angry I make you, you would never marry me to someone like him.'

'My personal wishes don't come in it.'

Allis tossed the scroll back on to the desk, she'd read enough.

'This doesn't make sense. Papa, the Rector has already given permission for me to marry Claude. How can he hand me over to Sir Philippe? I cannot marry two men.'

'My dear, Sir Philippe has been making noises about a marriage alliance with our family for some while.'

Allis stared. 'You never told me.'

'Why should I? I was confident you'd marry Claude.'

She stepped back, shaking her head. She wasn't sure if Sir Leon had moved closer, but she could feel his warmth behind her. It gave her heart.

'I loathe Sir Philippe.'

Her father glowered. 'You have to marry someone. Sir Philippe is most insistent. I admit I had no idea he was so determined to take you to wife. Since you refuse my godson, I must ask you to consider Sir Philippe. I promised your mother I would look after you.'

'Papa, this isn't about me. This about wanting your holdings to stay in the family.'

'And is that so great a sin?'

'In itself, no. But all Sir Philippe cares for is your land, that, and your ties to Gascony.'

'That is as may be.' Her father scrubbed his face. 'If only you hadn't rushed off to the convent with your sister. Allis, it's not too late to make amends. You could still marry Claude.'

Thinking fast, Allis gritted her teeth. Yes, she could marry Claude. Claude would certainly accept her, and he'd be a better husband than Sir Philippe. Claude would never maltreat her. He could also continue to see Eglantine. 'Claude will never love me,' she whispered.

'And whose fault is that?' Her father's voice sharpened. 'You should have given my godson more attention when he visited. I encouraged his visits to allow the two of you to get to know each other. Instead of which you allow him to become besotted with the basket weaver. How could you?' He thumped the desk. 'Our blood belongs here. All these years I've been training you to take my place as Lady of Galard.'

'Being Lady of Galard is not an end in itself,' Allis said, acknowledging out loud what she'd known for some time. She'd worked hard to learn everything she could about Castle Galard and the village. She could read and write. She'd learned to keep accounts and how to manage servants. It was enjoyable, satisfying work. But only, she recognised, if she was partnered with a husband who thought as she did. A husband who loved her before he loved Galard and the privileges that came with it. She wanted love and she didn't want second-best.

'It's better than the alternative,' her father said.

The alternative. The hairs rose on the back of Allis's neck. 'You're taking Sir Philippe's proposal seriously?'

Her father grunted. 'I have to. Hear me out. We find ourselves in an awkward position. Sir Philippe has obviously informed the Rector of your reluctance to marry Claude. Since I have no male heir, you cannot remain unwed. Allis, I must consider the estate.' He smiled sadly at her. 'You are the most capable of women, but we live in lawless times, a powerful man is needed to govern our holdings here. A woman alone would be prey to attack from all quarters. If you were to marry Claude, my hope was that you would hold the reins and that Claude would grow into his role. Since you've rejected him, we need a powerful man.'

'Papa, that man is not Sir Philippe! You know his reputation. He's cruel. Callous and uncaring.'

'He's more than capable of guarding our lands. Allis, you are a strong woman. If anyone can temper Sir Philippe's nature, it is you.' Her father sighed. 'We are not simply talking about your marriage. This is about land and honour. About privilege and duty. At this point, all I can say is that if you don't accept Claude, you may be forced into a marriage that is even more distasteful.'

Behind her, Sir Leon shifted, and Allis felt a light touch on the small of her back. It was almost, but not quite, a caress. Had it been deliberate? Shamefully, she found herself hoping that it had been. Sir Leon had not said a word, he probably felt he had no right to do so, but it was pleasant to imagine that he was telling her with touch that she was not alone. The impulse to lean against him caught her by surprise. She resisted it. Her father had bought Sir Leon's loyalty, Sir Leon did not understand her predicament. Much as she might wish it, he was not her friend. She stiffened her spine.

'Papa, does the Rector have the power to force Sir Phillipe on me?'

'I wouldn't use the word force,' her father answered. 'Naturally, I had to apply to the Rector when I hoped you'd marry Claude, so the Rector is aware that Claude has first claim on your hand. However, if you don't marry Claude, you may be given to Sir Philippe.'

'Along with your lands.'

'In a nutshell, yes.'

Sir Leon cleared his throat. Conscious of an urge to keep him close, it dawned on Allis that her response was to him was changing. A rush of longing swept through her. Intense, unmistakable longing. She went rigid. Given she and her father were discussing her marriage, her reaction to Sir Leon was scandalously inappropriate.

'Excuse me, my lord,' Sir Leon said. 'Does the Rector have the final say over who Lady Allisende may marry?'

Lord Michel shook his head. 'In this case, some leniency has been granted.' He turned back to Allis.

'Not Sir Philippe.' Her throat worked. 'You won't force him on me.'

'Allis, you can't have read the whole letter. There's more.'

'Oh?'

'In the event you refuse to marry, the Rector has decided Sir Philippe can pay court to your sister.'

The hairs rose on the back of Allis's neck. Bernadette? They were suggesting that Bernadette should marry Sir Philippe? In a trice, she was standing at her father's side, hands clasped together in an attitude of prayer.

'Father, no! That can never be. Bernadette's calling is genuine. She must take the veil.'

Stone-faced, her father shrugged. 'I will do what I

must. Know this. If you refuse Claude, Sir Philippe is waiting. If you refuse Sir Philippe, I trust that your sister will do her duty and accept him.'

Allis felt stunned. She couldn't take it in. Bernadette was so gentle, so self-effacing. The very reason her sister had taken so long to get to the convent was because all she had ever wanted to do was to please people and she knew that her father and stepmother had been reluctant to let her go. Unfortunately, if Bernadette thought Papa was relying on her to further his plans, she would abandon her vocation and be miserable for the rest of her days.

'You would destroy Bernadette's life to further your family ambitions?'

Lord Michel's lips tightened. 'I've been boxed in. It's the only way to ensure that at least some of my descendants live on here.'

'It would be beyond cruel to use Bernadette in that way. Marriage isn't for her. She has a higher calling.'

She was fixed with a withering glare. 'Then it is down to you. For the love of God, Allis, choose. I pray you will do your duty.'

Allis dug her nails into her palms. It was that or hit something. She drew in a breath.

'My lord, I've made it clear I will not come between Claude and Eglantine. The bond between them is a wonderful thing. Not only will Eglantine be devastated if Claude and I marry, but she is bearing his child. A child born of love. As for Sir Philippe…' her voice broke as she glanced at the scroll '… I will consider—consider, mind—marrying him, on two conditions.'

Her father drummed his fingers on the table. 'Continue.'

'Firstly, you must persuade Lord Robert to give Eglantine a gift. One generous enough to tide her through the long days of her grief. One that will ensure your godson's child never suffers want.

'Secondly, I'd like you to dispatch a reasonable dowry to the convent. Bernadette has a true calling and at present is being used as a slave. Her life will be altered beyond belief if you gave her the dowry she deserves.'

Eyes gleaming, Lord Michel let out a gasp of incredulous laughter. 'You don't want much, do you?'

'If you don't send Bernadette her dowry, I refuse to consider this proposal.'

'Very well. Accept Sir Philippe's suit and I'll give Bernadette her dowry. I will also help Eglantine. Hear me out. And don't look at me like that. This is not a punishment.'

'It feels like one.'

Her father's expression softened, he took her hand and gave it a gentle squeeze. 'You are my beloved firstborn and I want you to be lady of Castle Galard. Our family has made a home here. At heart, I know you understand.'

Allis nodded. The trouble was she did understand. She found herself staring at her father's hand. Over the years his knuckles had become more prominent. The skin was thinner. He wasn't immortal and he had no male heir. In order to keep the estate in the family he had to marry Allis to a man she was capable of managing. Claude had been ideal.

Sir Philippe was another matter entirely. Observing him at table on his earlier visits to the castle, Allis had seen he was greedy and self-indulgent. She'd witnessed him striking his servants when enraged. He was a snake. And as for marrying him...

She swallowed hard, tried not think about the marriage bed, and lifted her head. 'On no account must Bernadette come within ten miles of Sir Philippe.'

'That, my dear, is up to you.'

'Very well, Papa. I agree. I shall marry Sir Philippe.'

Lord Michel looked soberly at her. 'Thank you, Allis. I knew you'd do the right thing.'

'You'll send Bernadette her dowry?'

'Aye. And I will speak to Lord Robert concerning support for Isembert's daughter.'

'Thank you, Papa.'

Leon had entered the estate office determined to ask Lord Michel whether he considered the reeve's son, Simon, capable of attacking Claude. As the interview progressed, however, the pedlar was relegated to the back of his mind.

Lady Allisende's distress was tying his insides in knots. He was finding it increasingly difficult to maintain his usual professional detachment. He felt aggrieved on her behalf and every instinct was crying out for him to help her. Realistically, there was little he could do. Lord Michel had hired Leon to watch over his daughter—he had not given him the right to interfere in family politics. The poor woman. It looked as though she would be forced to wed this Sir Philippe. Was he really such a monster?

Leon ought to be impartial. He should treat this commission like any other and maintain his distance. Allis was a noblewoman, and it was the way of things that noblewomen married to further family ambitions. She could hardly have reached her age without realising it, particularly if, as her father suggested, she'd been brought up knowing she would one day be the Lady of Galard.

He shifted to study her profile. That tempting mouth was set in a hard line. There was a small crease between her eyebrows. As he dismissed the urge to smooth it away, it occurred to him that there could be more behind Allis's loathing of her new suitor. Not for the first time, he sensed she wasn't being entirely open. Was there another explanation for her reluctance to marry?

*Her reasons don't matter*, he reminded himself. *Remain impartial. Follow orders.* It was easier said than done. Watching Lady Allis being pushed into an unwanted marriage was ugly. Her bravery was impressive. Most women would use tears to bend their fathers to their will. Not Allis. Even more impressive to Leon's mind was that though she was being forced down a road she had no wish to travel, she found strength to fight for others. Her desire to help her sister fulfil her vocation and to speak up for Eglantine were admirable. Lady Allisende was an exceptional woman. If ever a noblewoman deserved to marry according to her wishes, it was she.

Lord Michel cleared his throat and gave his daughter a strained smile. He wasn't enjoying forcing his first-born into marriage.

'Sir Philippe is waiting to greet you in the solar,' Lord Michel said, quietly.

'Yes, Papa.' Allis stood very straight, hands clenched into fists. Her cheeks were pale. She looked as though she was preparing to face her execution rather than greet a prospective bridegroom. 'I need to compose myself in the chapel before seeing him.'

'Very well.'

She dipped into a curtsy and left the office.

Swearing under his breath, Leon nodded at her father and went with her.

* * *

The chapel lay down a short passage to one side of the great hall. As they approached the door, Lady Allis untied her cloak and placed it on a small table.

'Sir, this is God's house, you may leave your sword here.'

Firmly, Leon shook his head. 'I am here for your protection.' Until he had seen Sir Philippe for himself, and was confident the man wouldn't harm her, nothing would persuade him to remove it.

She searched his eyes and the ghost of a smile flickered across her mouth. 'As you wish.'

Leon unpinned his cloak and put it on the table next to hers.

Inside the chapel, light was filtering through the stained glass in a lancet window, splashing the grey flagstones with every colour of the rainbow. Allis walked towards the altar, pausing to stare at a white marble slab set into the floor. Her eyes glistened, she looked to be on the verge of tears. Gilded lettering was carved deep into the marble. The inscription read: *Here lies Genevieve, Countess of Arles. Beloved wife and mother.*

Allis gazed at it, sighed, and went to a nearby priedieu. She knelt and picked up a prayer book.

Leon's mind was in turmoil. Allis didn't deserve to be forced into marriage with a man she detested. He wanted to comfort her, to tell her that everything would be all right, he wanted it more than he had wanted anything in his life. Yet it simply wasn't true. There was nothing he could say that would improve her lot. Allis, like her father, was trapped.

'My lady,' he spoke softly. 'I am here if you need me.'

'Thank you, sir.'

Her cheeks were pale as death. She clasped her hands and began to read quietly to herself. There was heart-rending catch in her voice. *"'Thou shalt not be afraid for any terror by night; nor for the arrow that flieth by day...'"*

She must be reciting from scripture. It could be a psalm, Leon wasn't sure, he was horribly ignorant about anything to do with Church ritual. Before this, the nearest he'd come to entering a chapel had been when he'd gone to the convent to bring Allis home.

Her voice steadied. *"'A thousand shall fall beside thee, and ten thousand at thy right hand; but it shall not come nigh thee.'"*

*Mon Dieu*, what devastating, violent words. Were they truly comforting her? To Leon's mind, they didn't sound particularly helpful. She was being forced into a life she didn't wish for. However, if she derived strength from such words, who was he to deny her?

Leon tore his gaze from her face and stepped back. She'd told her father she wanted to compose herself and he didn't want her to feel he was crowding her.

The Galard chapel was at least peaceful. As Leon looked about, he realised he wasn't as ignorant as he'd supposed. A statue of Our Lady and the infant Jesus stood on a plinth to the left of the altar, which was covered with an embroidered cloth. Light from the window fell on the cross in the centre. Candlesticks gleamed. He could smell beeswax.

*"'For he shall give his angels charge over thee, to keep thee in all thy ways.'"*

Unable to make sense of what Allis was saying, Leon shook his head. It did seem to be consoling her.

A sudden draught had him turning to the door. Someone was marching purposefully down the corridor towards the chapel. Someone in heavy boots. Spurs chinked. The door opened. Allis took a long, slow breath, closed the prayer book and rose.

'Sir Philippe,' she said coolly. 'There was no need for you to leave the solar, I was about to come up.'

Sir Philippe had cropped, steel-grey hair and dark eyes. Like Leon, he had neglected to remove his sword, the hilt of which was gilded. The pommel was set with a chunk of polished jet which echoed the hard gleam in his eyes. His jacket was crimson. It looked new and far too warm for a day like today. His signet ring was massive, gold with another block of what looked like jet. He had definitely come courting.

Sir Philippe waved dismissively at Leon. 'You. Out.'

Leon glanced at Allis. 'My lady?'

'Thank you, Sir Leon. You may wait outside.'

She hadn't even looked Leon's way. She was watching Sir Philippe as though from afar, gazing at him as one might gaze at a viper. Leon was so reluctant to go, his feet seemed to have turned to lead. None the less, he bowed and left the chapel.

He pulled the door almost shut and stood outside, arms loose at his side. He was determined to hear everything that went on inside. He would wager his last penny he would be needed soon.

'Sir Philippe, this is a most unexpected visit,' Allis said.

There were more ponderous footsteps. 'My lady, this cannot be too much of a surprise.' Sir Philippe's voice was oily. 'I have admired you from afar for years.'

'You have?'

'Indeed.' Sir Philippe cleared his throat. 'When I learned you were unwilling to marry Sir Claude, I realised that my admiration was reciprocated.'

'I am very fond of Sir Claude,' she said.

'Sir Claude is a boy.'

Allis laughed, the brave, foolhardy woman. 'You are not the first person to say as much.'

Leon shook his hands and opened and shut his fingers a few times to get the blood pumping. He massaged his wrists. Soon, he thought. Sir Philippe was about to assault her. The thought filled him with rage.

'I heard the boy was hurt,' Sir Philippe said. 'I trust he will survive?'

'He will. If you wish, I will convey your greetings to him.' Allis paused, adding thoughtfully, 'My father led me to believe you were waiting in the solar with Lady Sybille, yet that cannot be since you are still wearing your sword.'

'Forget the sword,' Sir Philippe said, testily. 'I am not a courtier with airs and graces. You need to know what you are getting. I come to you as a soldier. No coyness, now, I can't abide a coy woman.'

Silence. Leon flexed his fingers one final time. Whatever happened, he didn't want the Galard chapel to be soiled by Sir Philippe's blood.

A slight scuffling was followed by a muffled protest Leon had no difficulty interpreting.

'Unhand me, sir. This instant!'

## Chapter Nine

Leon charged into the chapel. Allis was in Sir Philippe's arms, struggling like a wild cat caught in a snare.

'Get off me, oaf,' she said, frantically twisting her head to escape being kissed.

Reacting on instinct, Leon hooked Sir Philippe about the throat and tore him from her.

As fights went, it was ugly. True, Leon had been paid to guard her, but the urge to pummel Sir Philippe into oblivion was overwhelming. It was more of a brawl than a fight. Leon's fists flew. The chivalric rules of engagement that he had so painstakingly learned at Tarascon were shoved aside. There was no refinement or subtlety in him. Moved by raw rage, a simple thought accompanied each blow.

*Save Allis.*

A satisfying hit to Sir Philippe's shoulder sent her repulsive suitor reeling. The man let out a roar and came back flailing. Too out of control to connect.

*Get her away.*

Leon got in another hit, this time to the side of Sir Philippe's jaw. Growling with outrage, Sir Philippe wiped his mouth with the back of his hand. It came away covered in blood.

'Filthy whoreson,' Sir Philippe spat.

Leon laughed. If this apology for a knight thought insults would stop him, he'd soon learn his mistake. Leon had heard far worse.

'You come to her as a soldier, I think you said?' Leon couldn't resist sneering. 'Let's see how you do in a real fight.'

Eyes blind with fury, Sir Philippe dived at him. Leon twisted aside. Punched.

*Keep her safe.*

The yowl of pain was most rewarding.

From the corner of his eye Leon saw Allis standing to one side, safely out of harm's way. Her delicate veil was torn. A coil of hair had lost its pins and was tumbling over her shoulder, lavender ribbons trailing. She looked so pale. So quiet. A lady to her core, she was everything a man might desire. She did not deserve to be given to this monster. His breath seized and he almost lost focus. His stomach tightened in warning. He must control his feelings. Misplaced emotion was an indulgence he could not afford. His every move must be calculated. Precise. He had the advantage, and he would not lose it. He kept up the onslaught with ruthless efficiency.

*Save Allis.*

Hit.

*Get her away.*

Thud.

*Keep her safe.*

A heavy right hander had Sir Philippe staggering into a prie-dieu. It tipped over with a crash and a prayer book skittered across the floor to stop at Allis's feet.

Her blue eyes were huge and fixed on him. Stooping, she picked up the prayer book.

Sir Philippe chose that moment to remember his sword and snatched at the bejewelled hilt. Leon drew back his arm—it was now or never—and slammed his knuckles into the wretch's face. Sir Philippe toppled like a tree at Leon's feet. Letting out a moan, he went still.

Allis released a fluttering breath. 'Is he dead?' she asked, dread in her eyes.

Leon dropped to his knees, saw the pulse beating in Sir Philippe's neck and the gentle rise and fall of his chest.

'He's alive.'

*More's the pity.*

Allis let out a sob, dropped the prayer book and ran towards him.

Leon wasn't aware of rising, but he must have done, for he found himself on his feet with his arms about her. She was trembling from head to foot. Her veil was gone, and her blue eyes were swimming with tears.

'Thank you, Leon, thank you!'

Wholly absorbed by the feel of her fast in his arms—temptation beyond temptation—it took a moment to realise that her arms had crept up and around his neck. Her fingers slid into his hair. He groaned and she tugged his head down.

'Kiss me. For pity's sake, Leon, kiss me.'

He needed no second bidding. His blood was running too hot for gentleness, and he'd been longing for this for what felt like a lifetime. They came together in a rush. Her lips were warm and soft, and she opened to him with no hesitation. There were no preliminaries. No delicate kisses and tentative nibbles. From the first contact, all was heat and fire. Their bodies adjusted to one another with not a shred of coyness. The longing for completion was instantaneous. Combustible. It was the sort of longing that could destroy a man.

*She is a lady. You inhabit separate worlds.*

The kiss said otherwise. The kiss told Leon that here, now, anything was possible. The thought was dizzying. His legs weakened. She had such passion. Lord, Allis was more responsive and more welcoming than he could have imagined. His lips devoured hers and with a tiny sob, she devoured his. He kissed her throat and gently bit her neck. It took every ounce of willpower to hold himself back. He heard her startled laugh and her husky response.

'Oh. Yes, I like that.'

A scent teased the edge of Leon's awareness. A hint of lavender and warm, welcoming woman. Managing, barely, to rein himself in, he pulled back, smiling. When he cupped her cheek in his palm, that uncoiled length of hair tickled the back of his hand. He felt the contact in his groin.

She let out a sigh. 'I've been longing to kiss you for an age.'

Leon smothered a laugh. She felt the same way as he? No, that would be impossible. A highborn lady couldn't feel the same need, the same craving. An unmarried noblewoman, Allis was innocent. Leon understood the nature of lust, how ephemeral it was. She wouldn't have a clue.

She eased away. Her trembling had stopped. Leon wasn't so sure about himself. He'd never felt so shaky in his life. He wanted her. Badly.

Her hands went to her hair and she flushed. 'I must look a fright.'

*You look adorable.*

He didn't say it, he had no right. He stood there with longing like a knife in his belly as she plaited and reordered her hair. She would never be his.

One thought cut through the pain. *She's in danger at Galard.*

She was trying, not altogether successfully, to set the torn veil to rights. She stooped to retrieve the prayer book from the floor for the second time, glanced at Sir Philippe, lying like a corpse on the chapel floor, and shuddered. 'We had best find my father.'

Leon thought of the horses in the bailey that belonged to Sir Philippe's men and grasped her wrist. 'No. We're leaving.'

Her jaw dropped but she didn't object, so he towed her from the chapel, snatched up their cloaks and marched her down the corridor. By some miracle, she didn't resist. She was probably too shocked.

Ignoring the curious gazes of those in the hall, he strode to a manservant near the doorway. 'Find Lord Michel,' he said quietly. 'Be as discreet as you can. Tell him that his guest is in the chapel. He is indisposed. You will also tell him that I have Lady Allisende. She is at risk here and I am taking her to safety. Got that?'

The manservant looked from Leon to Allis and gave a bewildered frown. 'Lord Michel is bound to ask where you're going.'

'All Lord Michel needs to know is that his daughter will be protected. He has my word.'

Allis was in such a daze—relief mixed with fear over the consequences of what had taken place in the chapel—that she and Leon reached the barracks before she roused herself enough to notice that his grip was like iron. Oddly, rather than protest at such high-handedness, she found it reassuring.

Leon—it was becoming increasingly hard to think of him as Sir Leon—thrust her cloak at her and summoned his captain.

'Othon, I'm taking Lady Allisende to the village.'

'The village?'

Othon looked appalled which, even more oddly, didn't worry her, not one whit. Allis trusted Leon more than she would have thought possible, particularly after so short an acquaintance. She fingered her lips and hid a smile. That kiss…

'The village?' Othon repeated. 'Are you certain, sir?'

'You heard.' Leon raised his voice. 'Look sharp, men. The lady and I need supplies and we need them now. Food for a few days. Ale or wine. Preferably both. Blankets and bedrolls.'

Men scrambled to do his bidding.

Othon massaged his injured collarbone, eyes full of regret. 'I'm not fit for a long ride. Which of the company will you be taking with you?'

Leon shook his head. 'Lady Allisende and I go alone. Have someone saddle our horses, will you? We leave at once. Tell no one where we have gone.'

'Very good, sir.'

Green eyes met hers. 'My lady, do I have your permission to spirit you away?'

'Please do.' Allis glanced in the direction of the keep and shuddered. 'I don't mind where we go, as long as it is far away from here.'

Leon took Allis at her word. Provisions were packed in saddle bags, bedrolls and blankets were strapped behind them. Once they were mounted, he drove them so

far and so fast that conversation was impossible. Allis
assumed the village he had referred to would be nearby.
She soon realised her mistake. They thundered through
field and woodland. They forded streams. They trotted
across bridges and dried-up riverbeds, eventually taking a narrow sheep trail leading up into the hills. The
pace was relentless. Exhausting.

Allis trusted Leon, but as they tore along, she recalled the shock on Othon's face when Leon had mentioned the village. Where on earth was it? If Leon
was happy to take her there, why had Othon looked
so shocked?

The land grew ever more wild, trees stunted and
shrubs spindly. Gorse flared yellow in the afternoon
light. They continued until the horses' pace began to
slacken.

'The horses are tiring,' she said. 'It wouldn't do to
lame them.'

'I'm aware of that. We'll stop shortly.'

Soon after, they reach a spring trickling out of a heap
of rocks. The air was warm and filled with the scent of
thyme. Allis dismounted, sighed her relief, and went to
cool her face in the water. 'Where is this village?' she
asked. 'Is it much further?'

'It's a fair way.' Leon shaded his eyes with his hand
and squinted at the lowering sun. He gave her a crooked
smile. 'I warn you, we won't reach it for a few days.'

Startled, Allis glanced at the bedrolls strapped to
the horses' backs. Where would they sleep? 'We'll be
camping in the open?'

'We may have to.'

The image of making love to Leon under the stars
sprang into her mind. She bit her lip. She ought to feel
shame that her mind had made such a jump. The en-

tire castle must know she had ridden off alone with her father's mercenary knight. She ought to be worrying about her reputation, about the lack of a companion to keep an eye on the proprieties. Far from it.

The thought of making love to Leon allowed no room for anything else. Leon and her in a nest under the stars. Would Leon rush her? She doubted it. Would he lose control and abandon her to agonise about consequences? She did not think he would do that either. Feeling a blush rise, she hastily splashed her face with water.

Her lips tingled. Impossibly, the after-effects of kissing Leon remained with her. She'd never known anything like it. She felt transformed. He wouldn't have to try very hard to make her forget the lessons she had so painfully learned. It was shocking. And marvellous.

She had given up wondering if such a thing would happen to her.

Allis had heard the maidservants talking, she'd listened to the village women, and when they'd mentioned that a smile from a man could weaken their knees, and his touch could make tingles of awareness race up and down their bodies, she'd told herself they were being fanciful. Hugo had never had that effect on her. No one had. This, she realised, was true desire, desire that was more than skin deep. Finally, it had happened to her.

*I want this man.*

Quietly, she studied him. He was loosening his horse's girth, murmuring softly in the great grey's ear. There was no doubt that Leon, with his windswept dark hair, devastating green eyes and broad shoulders, was handsome enough to appeal to almost any woman, but what Allis was coming to feel for him was more than physical attraction.

In the estate office, when her father had reminded her

of his ambition for their bloodline to continue at Galard, Leon had stood at her back. She had imagined a brief caress, a fleeting moment of contact that made her long for his friendship. For his understanding. Friendship and understanding were surely more important than desire.

Blackberry snuffled in her ear. Allis was blocking access to the deepest part of the spring. Thoughtfully, Allis sat back on her heels and moved away so her mare could drink.

Leon unhooked a flask from his saddlebow. 'Do you care for some ale, my lady?'

'Allis,' she said, coming across to take the flask. 'After those kisses, I think we can dispense with formalities.'

Leon handed her the flask and looked down at her, face inscrutable. 'That,' he said carefully, 'might be dangerous.'

'Dangerous? What do you mean?' She laughed. 'I trust you, Leon. I trusted you to help me back in the chapel. I trusted you to take me away from Galard Castle. I trust you now, even though we are alone in a wilderness, miles from anywhere.'

She pulled the cork from the flask and drank.

'My lady, I think you should know that this wilderness, as you call it, is as familiar to me as Galard Castle is to you.'

'Oh?' She looked encouragingly at him, but a shadow crossed his face and his lips compressed. He busied himself with pulling food from a saddlebag. When their eyes next met, he gestured at a flat rock on the edge of the spring.

'My lady, if you're hungry, we can eat there. If we're going to make the most of the light, we should be on our way soon after.'

'Very well.' Allis settled on the rock and accepted some bread and cheese. A pear. She wanted Leon to talk to her. She wanted to know everything about him, though in his present mood, it didn't seem she would get much from him. She contented herself with watching him from beneath her eyelashes as she ate. The way he was insisting on referring to her as 'my lady' was troubling.

Blast the man, he was trying to keep space between them. Was he regretting their kisses? She thought back to the chapel. She hadn't imagined the feel of him pressed so eagerly against her. No question but that he had been aroused. Something else was concerning him and she needed to discover it. Sensing a direct question would be parried, she decided a roundabout approach would be more fruitful.

'Sir, I must thank you for your assistance in the chapel. I dread to think what might have happened if you hadn't been there.'

'You are welcome, my lady.' His eyes narrowed. 'Has Sir Philippe accosted you before?'

'Never like that. But once, at a feast when I was seated next to him, he became a nuisance.' She shrugged. 'It was easily dealt with.'

'What happened?'

'The minstrels were playing, and everyone was distracted. He edged closer and closer. Beneath the tablecloth his hand was everywhere. I'm sure you can imagine.' With a smile, she fingered the point of her eating knife. 'It wasn't hard to keep him at bay. Usually, he accosts me with his eyes, which is remarkably frustrating, as an eating knife cannot be employed for a mere look. And if one complains of being ogled, people assume one is imagining it. Or seeking attention.'

Leon's brow darkened. 'That man is brash beyond belief. And utterly ruthless. For him to have solicited the Rector for your hand, knowing your father favours his godson is unconscionable. Lord Michel must be made to see you cannot marry him.'

'I may have to,' she said, quietly shredding a chunk of bread.

Gently, Leon removed the bread from her fingers and set it aside. A muscle ticked in his jaw. 'For your sister's sake? For Lady Bernadette?'

'Aye.'

He rubbed a hand round the back of his neck. 'Tell me about your sister. How old is she?'

'Bernadette is seventeen. For as long as I can remember she has had religious leanings. She loves the ritual. She knows all the litanies by heart and many of the psalms. Mother died when Bernadette was born, so Sybille is the only mother she has known. Sybille was the one who encouraged Bernadette's spiritual leanings. I think she sensed that they filled the void left by Mama's death. We've often been told how close Mama and Papa were, I suspect that Bernadette feels she is to blame for separating them. I've told her a thousand times that women die in childbed every day. I am not sure she hears me.'

His eyebrows rose. 'You think Lady Bernadette wants to take the veil because she feels guilty. That she's trying to atone for an imagined sin. Is that what you are saying?'

'It seems very likely. Of course Mama's death wasn't Bernadette's fault, but I know it troubles her.' Allis sighed. 'At any rate, when Sybille joined the family, she helped us so much. She is the kindest woman. She notices everything. She saw the comfort that Bernadette drew from her prayers and by encouraging her, gave her a way to exorcise her guilt.'

'You are fortunate in your stepmother.'

'We are. It can't have been easy for her. Bernadette was two when Sybille married Papa, and I was an unruly eight-year-old.'

A dark eyebrow lifted. 'You? Unruly? I never would have thought it.'

'You, sir, are a liar. Put bluntly, I was a monster of a child. I ran wild all over the castle and listened to no one. Papa despaired. Then Sybille took Bernadette and me under her wing and, well, you have seen Sybille for yourself. Because she's so loving and gentle, it's hard if not impossible to cross her. She is such a blessing. And Sybille didn't just help the two of us, she also helped Papa. She taught him that love comes in many guises. I am not sure whether he loved her at the beginning of their marriage, but he certainly does now.'

'They do seem close.' Leon looked away, frowning. 'Bernadette sounds no more suited to Sir Philippe than you are.'

'I wouldn't wish that man on anyone, let alone Bernadette. Marriage to him would kill her.'

'You are a kind woman to rank your sister's welfare above yours.' He was staring at a gorse bush, eyes unfocused. 'Sisters, eh? The trouble they cause.'

Allis went still. Finally, the man was opening up to her. 'You have a sister?'

Leon nodded and began gathering up the remnants of their hasty meal, wrapping what was left of the loaf in a muslin bag and slipping a couple of uneaten pears into his saddlebag. 'I did once.'

Lord, that sounded ominous. Would he think it an intrusion if she asked about his sister? Well, if he didn't want to talk about her, he shouldn't have mentioned her in the first place.

'Leon.' Moving closer, Allis reached for his hand, half expecting to be rebuffed. When his fingers closed convulsively about hers, she pressed on. 'Did she die?'

His mouth twisted. 'All I can say is that like you I suffered a great loss when very young. My sister disappeared when I was four.'

'She disappeared? Whatever happened?'

He looked away. 'I never knew, precisely. One day she was there and the next she wasn't.'

'She vanished without trace?' Allis tried to catch his eyes, but he was looking over her head, looking everywhere but at her. 'What was her name?'

'Blancha.' He released her hand and rose, his eyes stormy. 'My lady, please forget I mentioned her. I was very young, too young to understand what might have happened. Suffice it to say that I had a sister.'

Standing, Allis brushed down her skirts and looked steadily at him. 'I can hardly forget you had a sister, sir. Nor can I imagine what it feels not to know what happened to her. But I can tell you don't wish to talk about it, so I won't, of course.'

'Thank you, my lady, I would appreciate it.'

He turned away, packed what was left of their meal in their saddlebags and they were soon on their way. Their pace was more measured than earlier. Perhaps he had decided that no one was chasing after them. They barely spoke, and Allis didn't mind, she was far too busy thinking. Wondering. Leon's revelation—he had lost his sister—had opened a window into a side of his life that she'd never thought about.

Leon was unlike anyone she had met. He intrigued her. Most knights were filled with self-importance.

Brash beyond bearing, they would boast of their exploits to anyone unlucky enough to be within earshot. Leon could not be more different. He was neither arrogant nor pushy. Despite this, he had an impeccable reputation. He was both honourable and chivalrous. Papa would never have hired him otherwise. Allis might wish Leon was little less reserved, but she liked him none the less. His quiet smile and the amused sparkle in his eyes were incredibly attractive.

The revelation about Blancha was both telling and not telling enough. What about his parents? Where had they been when his sister had disappeared?

Allis ached to ask, but the rigid set of his shoulders stilled her tongue. If he wanted to confide in her, she'd be ready.

As the shadows lengthened and the birds began to fly to their roosts for the night, worry niggled away at her. Leon was so silent. Had she, by encouraging him to talk, pushed him away? He was extraordinarily self-contained. He was open with his men when he needed to be, though much of his authority must derive from his ability to guard his feelings. No soldier respected a leader who bemoaned the cruel twists of fate. Besides, a man like Leon would see no point in reliving his darkest moments. He kept moving.

So, much as Allis wished he would open up to her, she wasn't sure it would happen again. He might not trust her enough. It was a chastening thought.

Chastening enough to make Allis hold her peace until he drew rein beneath a rocky outcropping at the edge of a spindly copse.

'We camp here.'

# Chapter Ten

With the horses watered and safely tethered to a straggly shrub, Leon scouted about for suitable branches with which to set up a shelter. He was all too aware of Allis unpacking the food and drink for their supper.

What had possessed him to mention Blancha? Desire had addled his wits. Leon could think of no other reason for him to behave so unprofessionally. He never talked about his past. Those kisses in the chapel had disordered his mind. Since then, all he could think about was Allis. Of how much he wanted to bed her. Which was impossible. Unbearably so. He was entrusted with her welfare and even if he weren't, he wouldn't harm a hair on her head. For the future Lady of Galard an association with a heretic mercenary would spell disaster.

Why then did he have the nagging feeling that he was at a crossroads, about to take a wrong turn? He didn't understand it. He ached to open up to her. To a noblewoman descended from a line of Merovingian kings. One who was on the verge of marriage, whether he liked it or not, to one of the most unpleasant men he'd had the misfortune to meet.

He picked up a branch. Testing it for strength, he

found it wanting and tossed it aside. *Jésu*, the thought of Allis marrying that man made his blood boil. There must be something he could do to prevent it.

None of which explained why he'd been so foolish as to mention Blancha. Allis had not been shocked, which was heartening, but questions had sprung to life in the back of her eyes. She was longing to know more. Well, he'd said more than enough. For his peace of mind, he must hold his tongue. He admired her, that was the trouble. What he felt for her was impossible to define, but it was far more than desire. Unfortunately.

*Distance, man. Be professional.*

He set about rigging up a shelter, managing not to look her way above a dozen times.

'Is that necessary?' Her soft voice reached him through the twilight. 'The sky is clear. It doesn't look as though it will rain.'

'Best be prepared,' he said, tightening a rope.

Out of the corner of his eye, he saw she'd arranged bread and cheese on a blanket.

'Are you nearly finished?' she asked, wineskin in hand. 'We have a feast here.'

'Start without me.'

'I'd rather wait. We shall eat together, but I shall have a drink.'

She removed the cork of the wineskin, held it aloft and tipped back her head so wine trickled into her mouth. It was a boy's trick. A reluctant grin tugged the corners of Leon's mouth as he wondered who'd taught her. Certainly not the nuns. It was probably Sir Hugo, or her father's godson. Allis truly was remarkable. So down to earth, and yet when she needed them, she had airs and graces too. Their gazes caught. Held.

She smiled. 'Almost ready?'

Leon stopped pretending to adjust the awning and joined her on the blanket. 'You'll feel safer under cover, I'm sure.'

'Thank you.'

She handed him the wineskin and he took a draught, in much the same way as she had.

She laughed and swayed towards him, briefly pressing her shoulder against him. His heart lurched. It was a simple, friendly gesture and it warmed him far more than it should.

'You do that better than I,' she said.

'Not at all, you're an expert. Who taught you?' Leon asked.

'Hugo.'

She swayed again. Leon frowned suspiciously, weighing the skin in his hand. It was not as full as it should be. 'How much have you had?'

'Not enough, I fear,' she said. Imperiously, she held her hand out for more.

Leon hesitated. 'My lady, is that wise? I know you've had a horrible shock, but drowning your sorrows isn't the answer. You'll need your wits tomorrow and if you drink too much tonight, the ride will be hell.'

She eyed him from beneath her eyelashes. It was a strange look. He had the impression she was wondering how far she could push him. The truth was, if it came to a battle of wits between them, Leon wasn't confident he would win. The urge to give her whatever she wished for was astonishingly strong. She was such a brave lady. So desirable. So honourable. The strength of his feelings was alarming. Best not to dwell on it. He pushed the cork into the wineskin and set it aside.

'If you're thirsty, you can drink from the spring,' he said. 'The water's pure and there's plenty of it.'

She smiled, reached across him and took the wine-skin anyway. And Leon permitted it. He sat like a stone, surreptitiously breathing in her scent as she brushed past him. Lavender and Allis and something far more earthy. He would never forget it.

'I prefer wine tonight,' she murmured.

His gaze drifted to her mouth before he managed to check himself. Naturally, she noticed. She was sitting so close she could hardly miss it. She removed the cork and took a long draught.

Was she goading him? Tempting him? Lord, one smile from this woman and Leon's resolutions melted away. He would sell his soul for another kiss. It was undoubtedly best she remained ignorant of the effect she had on him. As an innocent, unmarried lady, she would have no idea of her power over men.

Baffled by his reactions to her, Leon let her drink before holding out his hand for the wineskin. 'You've surely had your fill?'

She slanted a look up at him from beneath her eye-lashes. 'No. Not nearly enough.' With a heavy sigh she shoved the cork back. 'It will never be enough.' Before Leon realised what she was about, the wineskin was in the grass, and she was winding her arms about his neck. 'What I really need is another kiss.'

Allis tugged him towards her, and Leon gathered her to him, groaning in pure relief. Her lips were warm. She tasted of wine; she tasted of forbidden fruit; she tasted of joy and belonging and everything that had been de-nied him for most of his life. She pressed against him, as tempting and as sensual as she had been in the chapel.

At length, when his head was reeling and his hand was sliding inexorably towards her breast, she drew back. Shyly, she touched her mouth. 'Thank you, that was exactly what I needed. I feel much, much better.'

Shaking his head, Leon cleared his throat and tried to ignore the drumbeat of desire that was pounding in his blood. He didn't feel better. Every inch of him was pure want. 'My lady, we should not be kissing.'

'No,' she said, in a dreamy voice. 'I don't suppose we should.'

Her mouth was rosy. Beyond tempting. He was meant to be guarding this woman, not seducing her.

*Control man. Control. Distance.*

Leon shifted away, only meeting her gaze when there was space between them.

Allis stared defiantly at Leon. She didn't need to be told that they shouldn't be kissing. Given her circumstances, it was beyond foolish. A long time ago she had realised she had to look as though butter wouldn't melt in her mouth. It was important everyone believed she was pure. The kisses she exchanged with Leon put everything at risk. Her only excuse was that she had been aching to know whether they would be as incendiary tonight as they had been in the chapel. Had she imagined their power?

Unfortunately, she had not. Tonight's kisses were as overwhelming as before. More, if that were possible.

She could not afford longings like this. Where was her common sense? Kissing was a small step away from unladylike behaviour. Sinful behaviour. She was such a fool. She must never kiss him again. For if she did, she wouldn't have the strength to stop him going further. And if they went further... The consequences were unthinkable. She was not about to go through that all over again.

Her only excuse was that in telling her about his sister, Leon had given her a tantalising glimpse of the man behind the shield. A revelation which, for some reason she had yet to fathom, made her want to know him better.

As if kissing could do that. Certainly, kissing could lead to physical intimacies, but Eglantine's pregnancy was a stark reminder of the perils of chasing down that path. Allis had been lucky where Simon was concerned. Besides, physical intimacy wasn't what Allis wanted, not from Sir Leon of Tarascon. She wanted…

She wanted to know him better. She wanted his trust. She wanted…

'Impossible,' she muttered. 'This is impossible.'

'My lady?'

'Sir, please accept my apologies. My behaviour has been inexcusable. I beg you will forget it.'

His face was expressionless. He inclined his head, painfully, excruciatingly polite.

'Of course, my lady. I understand you are under great stress. Besides, no lady's reputation would stand being sullied by me.'

*No!* Allis wanted to cry. *Never think that. You're worth so much more. More than me, certainly.*

He looked so distant she wanted to hurl herself back into his arms. To soak up his warmth. His strength. 'Thank you, sir,' she said quietly.

A brief spark in his eyes, a slight lift of his lips, and Allis knew that crumb, small as it was, had pleased him. He was worth so much more. And without compromising herself, she could never convince him.

When darkness fell, Leon bedded down several feet away from Lady Allis. He'd given her a blanket to cush-

ion her from the rough ground and left her staring up at
the awning of the shelter. He was looking at the stars,
far enough away from her to ensure there would be
absolutely no touching, no accidental rolling together.
She'd made her wishes plain.

It was just as well she had. *Mon Dieu*, how could so
much temptation be wrapped up in one woman?

Leon hadn't been prepared for her to kiss him again,
though perhaps he should have been. Given what had
happened in the chapel and her reaction then...

He must avoid touching her. For a heady moment
it had felt as though he was coming home. There was
a feeling of inevitability about kissing Allis, it was as
though their being together had been ordained from the
beginning and was not to be questioned.

The sense of belonging was a delusion. It was a painful reminder of how Leon had felt as a child, in those
long-ago days before the Inquisitor arrived in Monteaux
and destroyed everything. Happiness and contentment
were invariably followed by devastation and despair.

He knew that. Meeting Allis was making him hope
that the world might be different. She was muddying
his mind. Making him long for a life that could never
be his. His troop depended on him. He was not about
to throw away everything he had achieved by chasing
a reckless dream. Lady Allis was a noblewoman. Off
limits. He must never forget that the feeling of belonging, of knowing one's place in the world, was *always* a
delusion. Tantalising, to be sure. But a delusion.

Nothing lasted for ever and he would do well to remember it.

Sir Leon had retreated behind his shield again, and
much as Allis wished otherwise, she told herself it was

for the best. They spent the next few days riding towards
the village. By common consent, conversation was kept
to a minimum. Allis ought to be thinking about her father and his plans for her to become Lady of Galard.
She ought to be thinking about Bernadette and Sybille.
But concern for her family was lost behind the need to
unravel the mystery that was Sir Leonidàs of Tarascon.
He was fast becoming an obsession.

The ground rose and fell and rose again. The air was
thin, and the terrain harsh. The track became so narrow it was little more than a rabbit run. Allis didn't see
anyone else, though a couple of times she heard a bell.
And once, sheep bleating. It was a wonder Leon knew
the route. But he pressed confidently on. At one stop,
he disappeared into the wilds for a full hour. When he
returned, he must have found someone, for he had re-
plenished their dwindling stock of food.

They rode on. And on. To think she had accounted
herself a horsewoman. Her legs ached. She was saddle-
sore. But she had time aplenty to think about Leon.
She'd been much struck by the revelation that he'd lost
his sister. She couldn't imagine what that must be like.
Perhaps, when they finally reached this village, he
would tell her more. The thought kept her going.

Then came the evening that he pushed them harder
than ever. Allis had reached the stage when she couldn't
feel her legs. She had gone numb. She was famished.
Eyeing the lowering sun with some misgiving, she
turned his way. He was glowering at a pile of stones
and what looked like a worm-eaten pile of timber.

'Leon, I can't feel my toes. May we stop? Please?'

When his eyes met hers, her stomach sank. For a

moment it was as though he couldn't see her. Then he blinked, smiled politely, and drew rein.

'We're here.'

'This is the village?'

'Aye.'

'No one's about,' Allis said, puzzled. She hadn't been sure what to expect. She'd guessed that with it being so out of the way, the village would be humble. But this— where were the houses? There was no sign of life whatsoever. It was possible they were standing on what had once been a path through a village, though it was hard to tell. Instead of cottages lining the path, all she could see was charred timber. Thistle and juniper were growing up around scorched beams. Whatever this place had once been, nature had reclaimed it long ago.

Warm though she was, goose pimples rose on her arms. There wasn't a single building that she would call a house. This so-called village hadn't been inhabited for years, possibly decades. She gestured at the nearest pile of beams. 'Was that a cottage?'

'Aye.'

The bleakness in Leon's voice made her shiver. His eyes were glassy. They held a world of pain, so much naked emotion, she was forced to look away. It hit her when she looked back at him and saw his gaze caught by that chaotic pile of timbers. His jaw was set. His fists were clenched on the reins, and he sat in the saddle as thought turned to rock.

'I wasn't sure I'd remember where it was.' His voice was little more than a croak.

The agony in his eyes brought tears to hers. This was a place of horror for him. Of dread and death. Chilled to her core, Allis had a strong suspicion that he'd wanted her to see this. Seeing him so overcome, she decided to allow him a few moments to gather his thoughts.

A hill rose up on their right hand, Allis focused on what had been a wall near the top. That had surely been a window. A door. The lintel was cracked but a more substantial building had once stood there. It was surrounded by rubble. Rubble that had fallen in such a way that Allis, the daughter of a nobleman, had no difficulty interpreting. The clumsy ribbon of stones had been a curtain wall. Cautiously, she looked at him.

'That was a castle.'

'A small one.' Leon cleared his throat. 'It would never match your father's.'

She risked another sideways glance. His expression was stoic rather than relaxed. None the less, it was an improvement on a moment ago.

'It's obvious something terrible happened here. This isn't just any village, is it? It was *your village*.'

Glittering green eyes bored into hers. Leon jerked his head in agreement and his throat convulsed.

Uncertain how best to proceed, Allis brought Blackberry to a stand and dismounted. He'd come here on the spur of the moment, ostensibly to keep her safe. Seeing this place—Leon's village—didn't make her question his motives. He was still protecting her, she didn't doubt that for a moment. But why bring her here?

She caught her breath. Could Leon want her to know where he came from? He must do. For him to have brought her here when there were surely other places of safety far nearer to Galard...

He trusted her. Allis felt a glimmer of hope, which she immediately squashed. Hope was the last thing she should feel in connection with this man. She couldn't deny that she felt it though. He had brought her here because he wanted her to know his history. It was a gift. A high honour. He was opening up to her. If his pain was too raw for speech, she was content to wait. She mustn't rush him.

Leon could not be in the habit of baring his soul to others. A commander must rise above his emotions. It was plain as a pikestaff that he'd never come to terms with the devastation associated with his village. She yearned to help. But how? She could try giving him a practical task—a small distraction while the painful memories tore through him. Yes, that might serve. Turning away, she led Blackberry through the twilight, picking her way down the path between the ruined cottages.

Behind her, she heard the creak of leather and the crunch of riding boots on stones. Without turning, she allowed herself the tiniest of smiles. Ever protective, Leon had dismounted.

'My lady, you shouldn't wander off alone. Outlaws have been known to camp here.'

'Outlaws?' She looked back and met his gaze. Yes, he would find this—whatever it was—easier if he began by focusing on something other than grim memories. 'I doubt any outlaws are here today.'

'You never know.'

'I'll be careful, I'll stay close. What's the village called?'

'Monteaux.'

Monteaux. So there was water here. Well, that was something. 'Where's the best place to camp?' she asked in a matter-of-fact voice. 'I'm ravenous.'

That glimmer of hope flickered. Surely she had won Leon's trust.

The sun was sinking fast. Shadows filled the spaces between the thistles and the half-burned timbers, and they had yet to set up camp. Leon's heart felt as though it had been ripped apart. After that night of terror all those years ago, he'd returned to the village a handful of times, sometimes with the men, sometimes alone. Each time it became harder. This time, with Lady Allis, he realised he had made the most dreadful error. What had he been thinking, to bring her here? Had he truly thought Lady Allis would be interested in his past?

He stared at her back as she calmly negotiated what had been the village's main street, gracefully skirting a rock here, a heap of charred wood there. Most ladies would be berating him for taking them to what must seem like a hellhole. Allis seemed to take it all in her stride.

By now she would have worked out why he'd brought her here. His thoughts were jumbled. As chaotic as the scorched village. There was no need for alarm, he'd brought her here because he wanted her to know him.

This wasn't about lust, though there was no doubt he wanted her. A man could lust after many women. It meant nothing. What he was coming to feel for Allis was different. He wanted her friendship. That didn't mean he had the right to burden her with his past. Allis was open and warm-hearted enough to offer friendship without that.

He scrubbed his face. He was bone-weary. Truth to tell, he'd not been thinking straight since he'd dragged Sir Philippe off her. Now that his blood had cooled, he couldn't believe he'd brought her all this way. Monteaux, for pity's sake. He was being absurd.

He would compose himself. He would find a smile and set up camp. They would eat and rest. In the morning, with a little luck his thoughts would have ordered themselves and he would find a way to redeem himself in her eyes. He let out a breath. He ought to take her back to Galard. She didn't belong here.

Abruptly, she faced him. 'Leon, I have to ask. Your parents died, did they not?'

'My lady, you are as relentless as your father.'

'Don't be evasive. It won't work. Leon, please. It's my belief you need to tell me. You brought me to your village because you wanted in some way to free your soul from the past.'

His lips twisted. 'I am not acquainted with Lady Bernadette, but that sounds just like something a novice in a convent might say. I have no idea what you mean.'

'Leon, you want to tell me. You need to. What happened to your parents?'

'They were killed,' he said softly. 'Along with most of our neighbours.'

Once started, it was as though a dam had burst. Leon couldn't stop. Those huge blue eyes invited further confidence and the words he'd locked inside for most of his life poured out, a bitter torrent of grief and anger. 'My father was a shepherd, as were many of the villagers. Most were Cathars.'

Allis blinked. 'They were heretics?'

'Cathars are not devils, my lady. Nor are they godless. They were the kindest, most hospitable, and hardworking people you could imagine.' His mouth twisted. 'Sadly, the Inquisitor did not view them in that light.'

'The Inquisitor?' Allis looked appalled. 'I have heard vague stories about the might and ruthlessness of the Inquisitor. They were so horrifying, I dismissed them as exaggeration.'

A muscle tightened in Leon's jaw. 'He came to Monteaux with the intention of rooting out heresy. As you can see from what remains, it was a small village. I can't imagine how anyone here posed much of a threat to the might of the Church. None the less, the Inquisitor decided to grace us with his presence. That man is none other than His Holiness the Pope.'

Allis's hand flew to her mouth. Her eyes were wide with shock. 'The Inquisitor who destroyed your village is now Pope? How is that possible? And how is it that I know so little about it?'

'It happened when you were a child.'

'But over the years someone should have mentioned it. Leon, why did it happen?'

He sent her a strained smile. 'Perhaps our village was an easy target. Perhaps the Inquisitor was looking for advancement. The details are lost to me, I was too young. All I can tell you is that one day I woke before dawn to find the village ablaze. I ran away and hid with a group of other children. Young boys mostly. There were only a few of us left. One of them told me he'd seen every adult, including some of the older children, taken prisoner. We never saw them again. I learned later that most were convicted of heresy. They died at the stake. Others died in prison awaiting trial.'

Allis swallowed, reached across and she squeezed his arm. '*Jésu*, Leon, this is the worst tale I have ever heard.'

'I only wish it were a tale.' He paused. 'The one crumb of comfort was that one of the boys mentioned seeing my sister. He thought she may have escaped.'

'But you never found her.'

'No.' His fingers interlocked with hers. 'I've been searching for Blancha for years. Hoping.'

Allis swallowed. 'How old were you when this happened? I recall you mentioning you were four when your sister vanished.'

'Aye.'

'How did you survive?'

'Luck, mostly. Initially, shepherds from another village took us in. We worked, and we were fed. We didn't work, and we went hungry. It was as simple as that. We wandered from place to place, never stopping for long in case…in case—'

'In case the Inquisitor found you.'

'Just so. In time we found ourselves at Tarascon. I found work in the stables and eventually became a squire.'

'And then a knight.' Allis put in. She gave him a troubled smile. 'You are the most remarkable man. Have you been dreaming of revenge since you were four?'

'I did at the beginning.'

She released a slow breath. 'And now?'

Leon looked at her. His mind was so full it was a struggle to find words. Now? All he could think was that he would shortly be leaving Galard and this wonderful, remarkable woman could well be marrying Sir Philippe. 'Revenge is the last thing on my mind, my lady, believe me,' he said drily, adding swiftly, 'I have my men to think of. Our troop has a reputation to uphold. It would do irreparable damage if we allowed the past to interfere with new commissions.'

'Oh, Leon.' Her brow cleared. 'That is a relief. You looked so severe I was afraid you were going to take a wrong turn.'

Leon grunted. He didn't trust himself to say any more.

The following morning Allis woke to find Leon had vanished. The food bag was balanced on a nearby boulder with what appeared to be a bottle of small ale. A bucket of water stood nearby. Allis hadn't seen a stream when they'd ridden in, but the name of the village told her there was water somewhere. Leon would know his way about.

He reappeared leading the horses after Allis had refreshed herself and eaten. His brow was dark as thunder and he was so tight-lipped, she scarcely recognised him. One look told her that he regretted talking about his childhood. Well, she wouldn't press him. She had secrets she didn't want to talk about. Didn't everyone? It was hard to be completely open. She would simply reserve further questions for a more opportune moment.

'Have you broken your fast?' she asked, gesturing at the bread. Sybille had often told her that Papa was more approachable when his belly was full. If Leon ate something his mood might improve.

'I ate earlier,' came the curt reply.

'Very well.' Allis gathered up the half-eaten loaf. 'I'll pack this away to keep it safe.'

'My lady?'

Irritated that he had reverted to using her title, especially after those kisses, she took her time to look up. 'Sir?'

'I apologise for dragging you here. It was a mistake. We start back to Galard this morning.'

Her mouth slackened. Was he serious? They'd only just arrived, and he must have more to tell her. Heavens, the horses were saddled up, ready to go. 'You'll surely show me the village first?' Leon looked blankly at her and she gestured at the ruins on the hill. 'I'd like to see the castle.'

'There's nothing to see. A few blackened stones. Come, my lady, your father will be worried.' His expression was unyielding, he was determined to leave.

'Very well, sir, if you insist. I'm aware I must return,

not least to spare Bernadette from being forced into marriage.' She sighed. 'Frankly, I'm dreading it. After what happened with Sir Philippe, it seems entirely possible that my father will never forgive me.'

'There are bound to be repercussions, but Lord Michel will forgive you,' Leon said, his expression softening fractionally. 'You are his firstborn. He loves you dearly.'

She shot him a startled look. That she hadn't expected. 'You are an expert on love, sir?'

Beneath his summer tan, he flushed. 'You know I am not. That doesn't mean I'm blind. Your father both loves and respects you.'

'I know whose interests he is serving when he asks me to marry Sir Philippe.'

Leon made a swift negative gesture. 'You're wrong. He is trying to serve your interests. He wants to place you in the setting he believes you deserve. He wants to protect you.'

Rising, Allis put her hands on her hips and glared at him. 'I thought you were on my side! If you think marrying Sir Philippe will serve my interests, you're not the man I thought you were.'

His green eyes were thoughtful. 'My lady, I agree that marriage to Sir Philippe is an appalling idea. Thankfully, I very much doubt that your father will match you with him. It has occurred to me that Lord Michel could be using Sir Philippe to help you realise that marriage to Sir Claude is the least bad option.'

Allis bit her lip. A similar thought had struck her in the middle of the night. Her father was nothing if not calculating.

He stepped closer. 'My lady, your concern for Eglantine and her unborn child is laudable, but it's blinding you to the obvious course.'

'Which is?'

'Marry your father's godson. It need not end his liaison with Eglantine.' He took her hands, mouth softening, and Allis found herself wanting to rest her head against him. She resisted. 'To my mind,' he continued, 'the key thing is that Sir Claude would not abuse you. You would be safe with him.' His mouth quirked into a smile. 'And you would be Lady of Galard. Your father is relying on you. It is a great honour.'

On the ride back to Galard Castle, Leon did his best to ensure her well-being while keeping his distance. It wasn't easy.

'My lady, are you weary? There's a good stopping place a mile away.'

'My lady, do you care for some ale?'

*Mon Dieu*, it was hard work, holding himself back. It was hard seeing those pretty, kissable lips pursed with worry. Hard knowing that when they reached Galard, they must part. Likely, she would marry Sir Claude. While he…

He would leave and find another commission. He'd accepted this one against his better judgement. Never again. Next time, he'd find work more suited to his nature.

So, for the few days it took to reach the village huddled next to the walls of Galard Castle, Leon tried to remain aloof. It helped that Allis made no secret of her displeasure. He'd disappointed her. She assumed he approved of her father's machinations. She didn't seem to have noticed that he hadn't said he approved, merely that he understood her father's motives.

It was just as well. Lady Allis and he had no future. Even something as innocent as a friendship between them was impossible. The very idea of a friendship between a lady descended from Merovingian kings and a lowborn mercenary was laughable.

It would never work. He was not capable of looking at her without yearning for more, far more, than friendship.

# Chapter Eleven

*Castle Galard*

No sooner had Leon and Allis ridden into the bailey than they were ushered, worn and weary, straight to the solar.

'Allis!' Lord Michel strode up and grasped his daughter's hands, relief writ large on his face. '*Dieu merci*, you are well.' He kissed her on both cheeks and lifted an eyebrow at Leon. 'Sir Leonidàs. Where the devil did you take her?'

'My lord, I apologise for worrying you. Lady Allisende was quite safe, I assure you.'

Leon would have said more but Lady Sybille had sprung up to embrace Allis. Hugs and kisses were being exchanged all round. It didn't escape him that Allis, despite the smiles and greetings, was uncharacteristically subdued. Her father's strategies had upset her past bearing. Not to mention that Leon had been too harsh on her, expecting her to ride at such a pace.

'Welcome home, dear. I am so happy to see you.'

'Thank you, Sybille.'

Lady Sybille turned to Leon, shooting him a glance

so chastening he immediately revised his opinion of her. This lady might appear to be all sweetness and light, but she had teeth. He made a note to remember it.

'Sir Leon, I hope you realise my lord was worried sick. As were we all.' Turning back to her stepdaughter, Lady Sybille wrinkled her nose. 'My dear, the state of you! Your violet gown will never be the same, just look at that tear! A bath is called for. Come along, I will assist you myself.'

Allis hung back. 'A moment, if you please. I need to speak to Papa.'

Leon's stomach dropped. This was it. She was going to demand that her father dismiss him. He'd dragged her into the wilds of Languedoc. He'd subjected her to appalling conditions and filled her mind with the horrors of his childhood. And to what end? His defence—that the moment he had seen that lout's hands on her, his one thought had been to get her away—would be dismissed out of hand. His actions had been unacceptable. Impertinent.

Lord Michel had paid Leon to guard his daughter, so Leon was unlikely to be accused of assaulting a guest in the family chapel. However, he had no wish to witness Allis denigrating his character and behaviour.

'I can wait outside,' he said.

'That won't be necessary, sir,' Allis said coolly. 'Papa, before I encountered Sir Philippe you promised to send Bernadette her dowry. Have you done so?'

Lord Michel drew his head back. 'I have not. And there's no need to look daggers at me, hear me out. I am not a mind reader. If you recall, I agreed to send Bernadette her dowry because you undertook to marry Sir Philippe. What was I to think when you fled with Sir Leon?'

Allis lowered her head. She was biting her lip and gripping her hands together so tightly Leon could see the white of her knuckles. His stomach churned with the need to comfort her.

'I am sorry, Papa.' Her voice was so low it was barely audible. 'Sir Philippe caught me by surprise. I was praying and he marched into the chapel and lunged at me. I had to get away.' Her voice strengthened. 'Next time I shall be less faint-hearted.'

Her father's eyebrows lifted. 'You, my dear, are anything but faint-hearted.' He frowned. 'Are you saying you'll marry Sir Philippe?'

'If I have to. Although you must know that he only wants to marry me because of our land and the family connections with France.'

Lord Michel scrubbed his chin. 'You could change your mind about my godson.'

'Papa?' Allis exchanged glances with Leon. 'Did you encourage Sir Philippe to ask for my hand?'

Beneath his beard, Lord Michel went red. He made a choking sound. 'How could I? You saw the Rector's letter.'

She stood before her father, straight-backed and determined. 'True, and at the time I thought it odd that the Rector was encouraging Sir Philippe's suit when everyone expected me to marry Claude. Admit it, Papa. You asked the Rector to write that letter hoping that I would see that Claude is the better choice.'

Lord Michel stood very still, stroking his beard with an appreciative smile playing about his lips. 'I wondered if you'd realise. Allis, my dear, I would not see you married to Sir Philippe if he were the last man on earth.'

Leon let out the breath he had not realised he had been holding. Relief. Of course, his relief was tainted with the thought that Allis would be marrying Sir Claude. She would be safe with the boy, he told himself. She would be cared for. His job here was done.

An ache had taken hold in the region of Leon's chest. He must leave. Quickly. Galard Castle had a way of giving a man wild dreams. Of making him believe it was somewhere he and his men could leave their devils behind them and finally settle down. Find peace. Not that there would be any peace for him if he had to watch Allis wedding Sir Claude. He would have to go elsewhere.

Allis looked enquiringly at her stepmother. 'Speaking of Claude, Sybille, how is he?'

'He is fine. Lord Robert came to see how he was, and after a few days Claude had recovered enough for them to leave for Carpentras together.'

Allis stared. 'Claude's gone home with Eglantine so near her time?'

'Yes, dear.'

'What about Eglantine?'

'She's at the cottage with her father.'

Allis stepped closer, blue eyes intent. 'Has the baby arrived?'

'Not yet.'

A brief silence fell as Allis stared pensively through the window. Leon could have sworn he heard her mutter. *'First things first.'* He couldn't be sure. Then he heard it again. *'First things first.'*

She smoothed her gown and lifted her head. Her face was weary and her clothes travel-stained, but she was every inch the dutiful lady. The passionate woman Leon had kissed in the chapel and en route to Monteaux had vanished. It came to him that he was never likely to see that Allis again. His heart clenched. Lord, he would miss her when he left.

But for a short time. Part of his attraction to her was desire, pure and simple. And desire, overpowering though it invariably appeared when it had one in its grip, never lasted. He would get over it. The wanting, the unfamiliar sense of belonging that he felt whenever he was with her, would start to fade when he got his next commission. In a year's time, Lady Allisende would be a weak memory. A ghost.

'Father, if you insist, I will marry Claude.'

'No!' Leon blurted his denial before he'd had time to think.

Lord Michel and Lady Sybille exchanged startled glances. Allis didn't react, it was as if all joy and life had been sucked from her. Which was, Leon realised, exactly what would happen to her if Sir Claude became her husband. Lord Michel looked so dumbfounded Leon recognised he could scarcely make matters worse. It was irrelevant anyway. He could hold his tongue no longer. This commission was ended.

'My lord,' Leon said. 'I'll be blunt. Both you and I know that Sir Claude would make a lousy husband for Lady Allisende.'

Lord Michel's mouth worked. Bright splotches appeared on his cheeks. 'Sir, I can draw my own conclusions. I pay you to guard my daughter, not to advise me.'

'My apologies, my lord, but I cannot remain silent.'

Lord Michel spluttered, but he waved Leon to continue. He was listening.

A rustle of skirts gave Leon pause. Allis was by his side, looking up at him. 'Please, sir, say no more.' She gave Leon a warm smile such as he hadn't seen in days. He had little time to bask in it though because she immediately turned away. 'Papa, you must forgive Sir Leon. He means well. He is a kind man, as was proved by how much Sir Philippe's eagerness disturbed him.'

'Eagerness?' Having pushed his way into this family conference, Leon would not be silenced. 'That man used violence against you and deemed it his right. It is no man's right to use force against a woman.'

'Thank you, Sir Leon, those are noble sentiments,' Allis said quietly. 'If I may speak for myself?'

Dismally aware that in truth he could do nothing, Leon subsided. As a hired man, he had no power here. None whatsoever.

Out of the corner of his eye, Leon saw Lady Sybille raise a knowing eyebrow at Lord Michel. What might that mean?

'Papa, I accept the matter of my wedding is important to us all. If I swear to marry, will you permit me to visit Bernadette? She needs her dowry. Allow me to take it to her. Please.'

Frowning, Lord Michel drew his head back. 'I should have thought you'd done enough jaunting about. If I agree to send Bernadette her dowry, there's no need to drag yourself to Saint Claire's. Hugo can take it.'

'You're missing the point, Papa. I'd like to see her.'

'Be reasonable, Allis, you are worn out.'

She stiffened. 'Nonsense. All I need is a bath as Sybille suggested, and a brief rest.' She sent Leon a veiled glance and her voice softened. 'Sisters are important. I miss her. We've never been apart so long before.'

'I'll think about it,' the Count said, waving a dismissal. 'Sybille, set Allis to rights, will you? She looks beyond unseemly.'

Papa thought Allis looked beyond unseemly.

Allis wasn't party to the conversation that followed

between Leon and her father, but she had known that her disappearance from the castle might cause Leon difficulties. She and Leon had been together for several days with no female companion. There hadn't even been one of Leon's men to stand as witness that nothing untoward had occurred. In truth, all they had done was exchange a handful of kisses. Even so, her father would be appalled. Her stomach felt hollow. Sadness. It wouldn't be wise to pursue a friendship with him. She was a young, unmarried lady and her conduct should be exemplary. She must always appear pure and innocent. She must push those kisses from her mind.

It wouldn't be easy, particularly since Leon had trusted her enough to reveal his painful family history. She could see the small boy that he'd been wandering about the scrub with a handful of other children, struggling to survive. Leon had mentioned not understanding religion. After the trials he'd endured that wasn't surprising. What was surprising was that he'd built a life for himself and his men. Leon's troop were renowned for their *esprit de corps*—their loyalty to one another as well as to their leader. Sadly, these insights into his character somehow made it more impossible to forget him or his kisses. He was a remarkable man.

Apart from those kisses, no harm had been done. She prayed her father would believe it. She was hopeful he would because Leon didn't strike her as impulsive by nature. Papa would surely have reached the same conclusion. The idea that Leon's reputation might be affected by a momentary lapse didn't sit well with her.

Fortunately, at supper time, Leon and her father strode into the great hall together and there was no sign of awkwardness between them. As before, Leon was partnered with her for the meal, yet another indication that all was well between him and her father. When everyone was seated, Allis leaned towards Leon and lowered her voice. 'I trust you and Papa remain on good terms?'

He inclined his head. 'Aye.'

She waited for Leon to enlarge and when nothing was forthcoming, she nudged him in the ribs. 'What happened?'

'I gave your father my report, reassured him that you had been safe the entire time and offered to resign the commission.'

'You did what?' Cold to her bones, reeling at the thought that Leon was about to leave, Allis stared. When he said nothing more, she kicked him under the table. 'And...?'

His smile was crooked. 'The Count was kind enough to ask me to stay a while longer. As he doubtless wishes to tell you himself, he will allow you to take your sister's dowry to the convent.'

Allis was so relieved this wouldn't be Leon's last night at the castle, that mention of Bernadette's dowry sailed right over her head. 'You're staying?' She craned her neck to catch her father's eye. 'Thank you, Papa.'

Her father saluted her with his goblet, took a draught and set the goblet down. 'I knew the only way to ensure peace in this castle would be to let you take Bernadette her dowry.'

'Bernadette's dowry?' Allis blinked. 'You're saying I can take it to her?'

'Do pay attention, didn't I just say so?' Her father sighed. 'Sir Leon will escort you to Avignon with a contingent of his men. You may go as soon as you feel you have recovered.'

'Thank you, Papa.'

Her father fixed her with a look. 'Mark this. Upon your return, I expect a serious discussion about your future. There will be no more delays.'

Allis gave a jerky nod and bit her tongue. She would say nothing to jeopardise Bernadette receiving her dowry. That was more important than anything. Bernadette's calling had to be honoured.

She forced a smile and stared blankly at her trencher. If only it wasn't so hard to ignore the rebellious thoughts simmering away inside. If Bernadette could find her own path, why couldn't she? Was it selfish to think this way? Was it wrong to wish that Papa, having agreed to honour Bernadette's wish to become a nun, might honour her wishes too?

*I want to choose my husband.*

Why was that not possible? Allis knew Galard every bit as well as her father. She loved the people. She loved every stone. Papa must realise she would never pick a man who would bring it to rack and ruin.

Yet as a woman she must live under her father's thumb. Why? Why did women have to do so much obeying? All she wanted was the freedom to choose her husband. A husband who was strong and reasonable. A husband who was passionate and honourable. A husband who...

Allis wasn't looking at Sir Leon, but she might as well have been, for his face took shape in her mind. Those penetrating green eyes were looking directly at her. And his mouth, that clever mouth that wreaked havoc with her senses, was smiling that crooked smile.

'My lady?'

She turned to him. It was hard holding down her blush, but she tried. 'Sir?'

'I assume you will want to go to Avignon tomorrow.'

He knew her too well. She nodded and found her tongue. 'I should like to set out after breakfast, if that is agreeable.'

Leon nodded easily. When he transferred his attention to a platter of chicken in wine sauce Allis breathed again.

Leon went to the tiltyard shortly after sunrise and took up a post on one of the stands. Peire had been practising and he wanted to observe his squire's progress. The quintain had been set up and Peire was charging down the lists, lance at the ready. At the last moment, his squire's lance wavered, and he missed his shot. A volley of swearing rose into the air.

Hiding a grin, Leon beckoned him over. 'No need for gloom, lad. That's an improvement on last time. You're still seated.' He made his voice stern. 'Where's your helmet?'

'Sorry, sir, I forgot.'

'Don't forget again. A mistake like that could cost you dear.'

Peire gave him a reluctant nod. 'Yes, sir. Do you need me for something?'

'Aye. I'm escorting Lady Allisende to Saint Claire's this morning. Ask the grooms to ready the horses.'

Peire's eyes lit up. 'You'll need an escort. Can I come? I'd like to see that place again.'

'You may come if you wish. Please alert Vézian and Stefe.' Leon went on to list a handful of his most loyal men to make up the full escort and when he had finished, Peire dismounted. 'Got that?' Leon asked.

'Yes, sir.' Peire paused. 'Is this part of the plan? Are you going for vengeance? When this commission is finished, I mean. The men are prepared to die for you.'

'They're prepared to die?' For a moment Leon's mind went blank. Then it dawned on him, Peire had fixed on the ageing Pope as the cause of past ills. He wanted retribution for his lost childhood. Leon understood that all too well. Revenge had once coloured his every thought and deed, it had been his driving force. It was a shock to discover his squire still thought of little else.

'Peire, you must remember that the Pope was not implicated in the despoiling of your village. That was a clash between local lords. Revenge achieves nothing except cause more pain and misery. Our troop must look to the future. If we mire ourselves in the past, we have no future.'

Peire grunted, bending to snatch up a bow and a quiver of arrows that lay on the grass at the edge of the lists.

Leon was surprised to see them. 'You've taken to archery? I thought you aspired to be a knight. A bow isn't usually a knight's weapon.'

'I like to keep my eye in, sir,' Peire said.

'Very laudable, I'm sure. Peire, you are not the only one to have had a difficult past. You must leave it behind. Thoughtless action can have devastating repercussions. Our troop would suffer. Comrades who have become loyal friends might die. Others certainly would. What really matters—'

Leon broke off as he spotted what really mattered. She was standing on the opposite side of the lists, watching him. Allis. Up early, as ever, in a cherry-coloured gown and light cloak, she had her riding crop in hand. That irrepressible twist of golden hair was already working free of its ribbons.

'Lady Allisende!' Leon vaulted the barrier and strode towards her, calling over his shoulder to Peire as he did so. 'Enough of this. Alert the men and ready the horses. We leave at once.'

'Aye, sir.'

Leon's heart was heavy. The ride to Saint Claire's would be bittersweet. He couldn't stay at Galard for ever. His departure shouldn't be upsetting, he'd been leaving places all his life and had been resigned to it from the start. The difference this time was that he was moving on because he couldn't stand idly by and watch Allis married to a boy not much older than Peire. A boy who was in love with someone else. Leon had never felt so torn. Today was likely to be the last time they would speak together. He must make the most of it.

In the bailey, Leon ensured Lady Bernadette's dowry was wrapped securely and strapped to the back of his saddle. He would ride out at Allis's side amid the troop.

Her gaze flickered to the chest strapped to Titan's back. She lifted an eyebrow. 'I assume that is my sister's dowry.'

'Aye. With so many men, it is quite safe.'

She nodded and her gaze settled on his helmet, strung from the side of his saddle. 'So, we are once again riding out on official business.'

'Yes, my lady.'

'You're not concerned we might be attacked?'

'My lady?'

'You're not wearing your helmet.'

'We won't be attacked.' Leon was all too aware that he had set his helmet aside because he felt closer to her without it. He managed a smile. 'I seem to recall you objecting when I wore it to escort you home from the convent.'

'You were hiding from me.' Allis looked at him from

beneath her lashes and lowered her voice. 'You're no longer in hiding.' Then she looked him full in the face, and his pulse thudded.

Her eyes danced, flirtatious and teasing. It was impossible not to look at her mouth, impossible not to be reminded of the way she fitted perfectly into his arms. The way she made him feel they belonged together. Kissing her had been the worst mistake. Except—that simply wasn't true. Kissing Allis had been perfect. Perfect. If she could have remained in his arms, he would have died a happy man.

And therein lay the problem. This woman drew him like no other. No one else would match up to her. Ever. When he was with her, Leon felt like an untried lad. Parting with her—a cold lump formed in his stomach— was going to be grim. Allis enjoyed touching him. Holding him. Which only made it worse.

'What's the matter?' She was biting her lip. 'Something troubles you.'

Leon forced another smile. 'Not at all, my lady, not at all.'

'Liar,' she said, a hint of challenge in her eyes. 'Leon, there is something I must ask you. Did you accept my father's summons because you knew his commission would take you to the Pope's city?'

He stared. 'No, my lady. When I first arrived at Galard I had no idea I would be sent to Avignon.'

'Are you thinking of your sister?'

He stared. 'My sister?'

Faint colour stained her cheeks and she shrugged. 'At the lists, I overheard your squire say something about vengeance. I assume it relates to your sister's disappearance.' She shot a glance at Peire riding behind them, and her tone became confidential. 'You hope to find her.'

Hiding a resigned sigh, Leon stared ahead. So much for their last ride together being happy. This was Allis. He'd told her about his bleakest moments and, being Allis, she was not likely to forget them.

'I would rather my past was not a subject for discussion.'

She shook her head and that irrepressible tendril of hair waved in the breeze, like a golden pennon. 'Leon, please. We've moved beyond this. You're out of hiding, remember?'

Heart cramping, Leon simply looked at her. He'd misjudged her. This wasn't curiosity, this was concern. It made his longing for the impossible even more painful. She was killing him.

The wind was brisk and northerly, and they had no choice but to ride with it blowing directly in their faces. From time to time it tugged on Allis's veil like a naughty child. It reminded her of the mistral, but this wasn't the mistral, thank heavens, it was too early in the season for that. Riding into the teeth of the mistral would have been a nightmare.

As it was, Leon's dark hair was whipped about every which way. Allis blinked grit from her eyes and gave him a sideways glance. His face was calm, as impassive as ever, and his mouth was set in stern lines. She'd never met a more guarded man. His harsh childhood had taught him self-reliance. It had enabled him to survive. No, she was doing him a disservice, Leon hadn't merely survived. He'd thrived. And he seemed to have no notion of how remarkable he was.

'Sir Leon?'

'My lady?'

'I realise watching over a woman isn't usual for a

man of your standing. Do you find it very tiresome?'
It was an intrusive question Allis probably shouldn't be
asking, and she wasn't sure he'd answer.

'Tiresome? Not at all, my lady. It's certainly unusual
for me to be present at intimate family discussions.
Awkward though that has been, it's certainly given me
insight into family politics.'

She laughed. 'Watching Papa at work is not always
as straightforward as it seems.'

'So I have observed. However, money is always welcome, provided it is honestly earned. I'd be a poor commander if I didn't find opportunities for my men.'

'That's true. I have been wondering what happens if
a trooper is gravely injured or can no longer fight? Do
the men set money aside for lean times? Do you? Have
you given thought to your future?'

Green eyes met hers. 'My future, my lady?'

'Aye. What are your plans for when you are too old
to fight?'

The stern set of Leon's mouth eased. He was almost
smiling. 'You have a never-ending supply of questions.'

'You find me impertinent?'

'Not at all. You have a quick mind, and you are interested in everything.'

*I am certainly interested in you,* Allis thought before
she could stop herself. Though he didn't make it easy.

'So?' she persisted. 'Do you have money set aside?'

'Aye, we all do.'

'Who looks after it for you?'

He laughed. 'No one, we look after it ourselves.'

Just then, some golden hair blew into her eyes, so
she sat back in the saddle and twisted it loosely behind
her. 'You're surely not saying you keep it with you?'

'Certainly.'

She leaned towards him, asking softly. 'All the time?'

'Aye. We like to know where it is. When our days of soldiering are ended...' His voice trailed off. 'To be honest, Alli—my lady, I try not look too far into the future.'

That hollow feeling appeared in the pit of her stomach. Leon was saying that he didn't look into the future, because he didn't believe he had one. It was so wrong. An honourable man like Leon should have more to look forward to than living like a nomad. Of course, she reminded herself, coming from a family of shepherds the nomadic life must seem natural. She would hate it.

'What if you were robbed? Your future could be snatched away in an instant. It's horribly precarious.'

He let out a bark of laughter. 'We won't be robbed. There's safety in numbers.'

'You have made a home with your troop.'

'Aye.'

She looked earnestly at him. 'Leon, Peire has me worried. Please reassure me that you have turned your back on all thoughts of revenge. It would be such a waste of life.'

A muscle flickered in his jaw, and he drew in a slow breath. 'I know it. My lady, it's been years since the Lions have sought vengeance.'

'Your squire disagrees.'

'Peire's a bloodthirsty lad. I shall convince him otherwise. My lady, it might help to know that not all the troop come from Monteaux. Others joined us at Tarascon, more men later. The newer recruits have no interest in revenge. They hold the others in check. If I have any say in it, my men won't be dying in a ditch. They're decent men. Brothers in arms who are reliable and true, and they've earned enough to pay for a reasonable retirement.'

Allis smiled. 'I'm glad. So, in the near future, what are your plans?'

'After we leave Galard?' he said, calmly.

Allis froze. She forced her lips to move. 'You are not leaving yet, I hope.' Inside, she wanted to weep. Leon took pains to appear unemotional, but that was a front. His kisses told her that he was the most passionate of men. Leon of Tarascon had emotions. Unfortunately, life had taught him to hide them. He was past master at that. Well, two could play at that game. She swallowed hard. She did not want to think about Leon leaving Galard, but she would if she must. 'What will you do?'

'Find a new commission.'

The words burst out. 'Leon, I shall be so sorry to see you go.'

His mouth went up into that lop-sided smile. 'No, you won't, you will rejoice to see the back of me. And you shouldn't be calling me Leon. It's too intimate. You are a lady.'

Allis gave him a lofty look. 'I shall call you whatever I like.'

He grimaced. 'No, my lady. I'm a mercenary. I've been paid to watch over you and you must never forget it.'

It felt like a slap in the face. Sending a covert glance at the boy riding behind them, she managed to respond softly. 'And those kisses? Am I to forget those too?'

He gave a brusque nod. 'Assuredly. Think of them as minor intimacies that should never have happened.'

'Minor intimacies?' She caught her breath. She would dream of his kisses until the end of her days.

'No need to look like that, my lady. For your own good, you must see that I—a mercenary—could never be more than an acquaintance.' His tone lightened. 'Just think, you can look forward to leaving your bedchamber in the morning without having to clamber all over me.'

Although he spoke in jest, Allis couldn't bring herself to smile. Everything hurt. She felt bruised inside. 'Say what you like. I shall miss you, Leon. I hope you will miss me.'

He looked away sharply. 'You do me too much honour. My lady, it's plain that this commission is serving us both ill. When we return to Galard, I shall see your father and explain that my troop will be decamping as soon as may be arranged.'

Allis felt a prickling at the back of her eyes. Blinking rapidly, she frowned. 'I don't want you to go. I'd like you to consider staying a little longer.'

'I am sorry, my lady, we have to move on.' He gave her a wry look. 'Galard is too close to Avignon for my peace of mind.'

Allis swallowed. 'You suspect Peire might do something rash.'

Leon nodded curtly. 'It's possible. I'm glad you understand.'

Allis gripped her reins and looked away. Pain. She didn't want him to go, but what could she do? A tear rolled down her cheek. She felt empty inside. A shell.

## Chapter Twelve

Leon was uneasy about Peire, but he had no wish to admit that his main reason for needing to move on was Allis herself. Working for her father, constantly being thrown into her company, was more than he could stand. Lady Allis was bringing parts of him to life that were best left alone. If he stayed much longer, he'd be totally in her thrall.

The narrow street outside Saint Claire's wasn't as busy as it had been on Leon's previous visit, and they rode down it guarded by several of his men. The convent door was swiftly opened and, having arranged to join the men later at The Crossed Keys, Leon himself took Lady Bernadette's dowry chest in. He stood by the wall while the elderly nun twittered with excitement.

'Lady Allis, it is so good to see you,' she said, warmly squeezing Allis's hand. She eyed the dowry chest in Leon's arms. 'Is that what I think it is?'

'I believe so,' Allis answered, smiling. 'Please alert my sister and Mother Margerie.'

'Of course, of course.' The nun fumbled with the keys and secured the door. 'They will both want to speak to you. Wait here, if you please.' She scuttled through the arch and into the cloisters.

\* \* \*

Mother Margerie appeared with shameless speed. Her severe features were for once relaxed, and to Allis's astonishment she swept into a deep curtsy. 'Lady Allisende, this is a pleasure.' Her gaze passed over Leon as though he were invisible and fastened on the dowry chest.

'As you see, Mother,' Allis said in a neutral voice, 'we have brought my sister's dowry.'

Mother Margerie's thin lips formed a smile. Until that moment, Allis hadn't been certain she'd ever see the woman give a genuine one. 'God bless you, my lady. You are doubtless aware we hoped to see it sooner, but this will cement Lady Bernadette's position in the convent.'

Cement? The word grated. Bernadette wasn't a statue, she was a warm, loving, flesh and blood woman. Allis was readying herself with a tart response when she caught the gleam in Leon's eyes. He gave a slight headshake and cleared his throat. 'Excuse me, Sister, is there a strongroom?'

Mother Margerie stiffened. 'This is a convent, sir, not a fortress.'

'Where would you like me to put it?'

Beady eyes glittered avariciously. 'I assume it's heavy.'

'Aye. It's much too heavy for a lady to carry.' Face inscrutable, Leon offered Mother Margerie the casket. 'I suppose you might manage it. Do you care to try?'

At best, his question was a veiled insult and when Mother Margerie's jaw dropped, Allis had to bite the inside of her mouth to stifle her laughter. Leon merely lifted an eyebrow. 'I thought not. So, where shall I put it?'

'My office, if you would. Follow me.'

They left the narrow courtyard. Shortly afterwards Bernadette ran in, eyes bright with pleasure.

'Allis, you came!' She flung herself at Allis and gave her a joyful hug.

Allis responded in kind, bending to kiss the top of her sister's veil. She held in a gasp. Bernadette felt even thinner than she had been when Allis had left the convent. '*Mon Dieu*, do they never feed you?' She laid a sisterly hand on Bernadette's ribs; she could count each one. 'You are thin as a rail.'

Bernadette laughed. 'They will feed me now, I assure you. Sister Teresa says you brought my dowry. Is it true?'

Taking her sister's hand, Allis nodded towards the arch. 'Leon is carrying the chest to Mother Margerie's office.'

Brown eyes looked at her. 'Leon?'

'I told you about him, remember? Papa hired him to take me home.'

'Sir Leon of Tarascon,' Bernadette murmured, nodding. Taking Allis by the hand, she drew her through the arch and into the cloister. 'Let's sit on the wall and wait for them, you won't be allowed to stay long. Are Papa and Sybille in good health?'

'They are very well, Papa particularly,' Allis said drily, thinking of her father's manoeuvrings to get her to accept the idea of marriage to his godson. She stared at the well head. 'He has persuaded me that it is in everyone's best interests that I marry Claude.'

'But, Allis, when we last spoke you were set against it. Do you think you can be happy with him?'

Tears stung at the back of Allis's eyes. She shrugged. Saint Claire's didn't encourage visitors and she didn't want to upset Bernadette on what might be one of the last times she'd speak to her. 'Happiness must, it seems, take second place to duty.'

'And Eglantine?' Bernadette asked softly. 'Has the baby arrived?'

'Not yet, I think she may have a few weeks to wait. I am hopeful that Papa will offer her his help. And Claude does love her. He is not cruel by nature, so it must be possible to arrange something for her and the child.'

'I shall pray for them,' Bernadette said. Footsteps sounded elsewhere in the cloisters. Leon and Mother Margerie were almost upon them.

Bernadette leaned in, planted a firm kiss on Allis's cheek, and sprang to her feet, becoming in an instant, the demure novice she so wanted to be. Only Allis heard her sister's final whisper. 'Most of all, Allis, I shall pray for you.'

On their return to Castle Galard, Leon enquired after Lord Michel and was directed to the solar. He went up with a heavy heart. Despite his gruff manner, Lord Michel was an easy and likeable man. However, as much as Leon had enjoyed working for him, he couldn't stay a day longer. It had become too painful.

As he anticipated, the Count was sitting on a settle, deep in conversation with his Countess. Best get it over with quickly, Leon decided. With tact. The last thing he wanted to do was to cause offence.

'Welcome back, sir,' Lord Michel said, rising. 'I trust Bernadette has been given her dowry?'

'Aye, my lord.'

'You found her in good health?'

'I wasn't given the opportunity to meet Lady Bernadette properly, my lord. Lady Allisende took the chance to speak with her in the cloisters, she will doubtless tell

you more. On the ride back, she mentioned that her sister seemed very happy. The dowry was well received.'
Leon decided to say nothing of the way it had been spirited into Mother Margerie's office for her to gloat over while Lady Bernadette hadn't had a glimpse of it.

'Well received? I'll bet it was,' the Count grunted sourly.

Lady Sybille looked expectantly at the door. 'Where is Allis? I wanted to ask if Bernadette was eating.'

'Lady Allisende is talking to Sir Hugo. He was asking that very question.'

Lady Sybille frowned. 'Oh, dear. I do hope Bernadette is doing the right thing. I wish she'd come home.'

'As do we all,' the Count said testily.

'My lord, before Lady Allis returns, I need to speak to you concerning the contract between us.'

Lord Michel looked sharply at him. 'Go on.'

'My lord, I have enjoyed working for you, but I believe our agreement has run its course.'

'What the devil are you talking about?' Lord Michel's mouth tightened. 'Do you want more money?'

'No, my lord. You have paid us handsomely.' There was disappointment as well as shock in the Count's expression, and Leon realised a pat explanation was not going to suffice. What could he say? If he even hinted that Lady Allis was fast becoming an obsession, he would likely be gelded. 'My men are not used to remaining in one place for long, my lord. It's best we decamp.'

Lord Michel pulled on his beard. 'In heaven's name, why? Your men are welcome here. They have lived up to their reputation. They are well disciplined—not one of them has put a foot wrong. Furthermore, Sir Hugo tells me their involvement on the practice field has energised his entire guard. I was hoping your troop—with you as their leader, of course—would consider becoming a permanent part of the Galard garrison.'

'My lord, the men do indeed like it here. However, I am sorry to disappoint you, but—' Leon shrugged, dimly conscious that with every word he seemed to be digging a bigger pit for himself. It would be unbearable watching Allis make an unsuitable marriage, yet it was impossible to say so without placing her in an awkward position. The Count would realise that Leon lusted after Allis.

Lady Sybille tipped her head on one side, her expression was every bit as puzzled as her husband's. 'Sir Leon, I too am surprised by your wish to leave. You and Allis deal well together, far better than we initially expected. I thought you liked it here.'

Surprised and flattered by their reaction, Leon shoved his hand through his hair. 'I do, my lady, of course. However, we do not wish to outstay our welcome.'

Lady Sybille left the settle and came towards him. A gentle, ladylike hand was placed on his arm. 'Sir, I ask you to reconsider. While you were away with Allis, your men gave every sign they were glad to be here. My maidservant informs me that they are regular customers at the village tavern. In short, they have made friends in both village and castle.'

They had? Leon thought quickly. It was possible. Peire aside, his men did seem less edgy. Othon had been impressed by Lady Sybille's care for his collarbone, and to a man they enjoyed the food, which was plentiful and nourishing. Now he came to think of it, they all seemed more relaxed. They understood the Count and his retainers thought well of them and were responding accordingly. Was it possible his men had found somewhere they could call home?

Leon held in a grimace. If that was so, he could

hardly drag them away. The troop might soon tire of life at Galard. Equally, they might decide to stay. What kind of a leader would he be to deny them the chance of a secure future? 'The men are undoubtedly grateful for your hospitality,' he muttered. He was stalling and he knew it. As a good commander, his men's well-being must come before his misguided obsession with the Count's daughter. *Jésu*, since meeting Allis, confusion seemed to have become his bedfellow. He was no longer certain what to think. Nothing was clear.

The Count looked him in the eye. 'Stay for a few more weeks, sir,' he said. 'Good men are rarer than hen's teeth. God knows we could use you here.'

Quick footsteps sounded on the stair and the latch lifted. Leon knew without turning who it was. He turned anyway. Allis. Her beautiful blue eyes were full of questions. Questions and concern. The jolt inside him was a painful reminder—not that he needed it—that he wasn't ready to bid her farewell. She wanted him to stay. So be it.

'Is all well, Papa?' Allis asked. Though addressing her father, she was looking at Leon. This question was directed at him.

Leon bowed. 'My lady, your father has asked the Lions to consider settling at Galard. I have decided we shall give it a trial.'

The Count clapped him on the arm. 'Excellent. What do you say, Allis? Shall we ask him to give us a month?'

Her eyes went wide. 'A month might not be long enough.' Her lips curved into an entrancing smile. 'Perhaps we should make it two.'

From that day on, Leon was rushed off his feet. Sir Hugo Albret, whom Leon already knew was a close family friend, took to consulting him on everything.

Generally, it began at breakfast, when Allis was, since the seating arrangements remained the same, sitting next to him. 'Sir Leon,' Sir Hugo would say. 'There's a horse fair in Arles today. A couple of our animals are being put out to grass and we need to replace them. I would value your opinion. Would you care to join me?'

With Allis's warmth at his side, Leon paused before answering. Her family seemed to assume that the threat against her had gone. Leon was not so sure. The mystery surrounding the attack on her so-called fiancé had not been resolved and he felt bound to act as her personal guard, even with distractions such as horse fairs in Arles.

Leon turned to Allis. 'Lady Allis, will you come with us?'

'I would love to.' She smiled warmly at Hugo. 'I will be glad to help.'

Hiding a sigh, Leon resigned himself to the peculiar torture of being with Allis and having to watch her easy manner with Sir Hugo. The fellow was obviously dear to her.

The following morning, again at breakfast, Sir Hugo was interested in hearing Leon's ideas about re-ordering the armoury. Again, Allis joined them. Leon was both startled and impressed by her unladylike knowledge of arms and weaponry.

The day after that, Lord Michel invited Leon and Allis to ride into the village. The Count wanted Leon's views on whether it would be worth paving the village green. As they drew rein outside the tavern, Leon, who was doing his best not to look at Allis, glimpsed Stefe and Othon sitting just inside the door. A feminine laugh floated out. Leon shook his head. He was preparing to dismount to speak to them when Lord Michel held out his hand to stop him.

'You mistake the matter, Sir Leon.'

Leon lifted an eyebrow. 'You expect my men to be drinking at this time of day, my lord?'

'Since I charged your captain with overseeing clearance of a clogged ditch, I am not surprised,' the Count said. 'They are simply refreshing themselves.'

Through the tavern door, Leon saw a serving girl talking with great animation to Stefe. Lady Sybille was, apparently, correct. His men were making friends. About to glance at Allis, he checked himself.

'Sir Leon, about the green,' Lord Michel said. 'As you are probably aware, we use this area for weekly markets. In winter, cartwheels wreck the turf, and it becomes a sea of mud. It would be quite an expense to pave. Not to mention that the villagers won't thank me for taking them from their fields so near harvest time.'

'I did notice the ruts,' Leon replied. 'My lord, I have seen villages where the square is partly paved. I assume you are not planning to fell the oak in the middle?'

'Oh, no, Papa, you cannot fell the oak,' Allis put in. 'In high summer the shade is very welcome.'

'I wouldn't dream of it, my dear. The oak stays.'

So it went on, day after day. A week went by. Then another. Each day, Leon saw yet another instance where the lives of his men were intertwining with those of retainers and villagers.

For Leon, the torture did not let up. He reminded himself that he was glad to watch over Allis. Keeping her safe had become far more than work, it had become a necessity. On the other hand, being with her from dawn to dusk was an immense challenge. His thoughts veered this way and that like clouds in a storm. It was utterly baffling. In one sense it was a blessing they were never left alone. They had no chance to speak privately. Regrettably, his carnal longings showed no sign of fading. It seemed they never would.

Then came the morning when Lord Michel caught his eye at table. 'Sir Leon?'

'My lord?

'It's over a month since we last discussed terms. My wife and I should like to speak to you about our arrangement. Please join us in the solar when you have finished breaking your fast.'

The bread Leon was chewing turned to dust in his mouth. Washing it down with ale, he got to his feet. Allis would have done the same, but her father shook his head at her. 'Just Sir Leon, my dear. You may wait here.'

Leon left the great hall and went upstairs.

'So, Sir Leon, I hope you have enjoyed these past weeks?'

'Very much so,' Leon said, awkwardly. If being tortured night and day by close proximity to the woman of his dreams could be called enjoyment. He racked his brains for something positive to say. 'I have learned much about life at Galard. The people are fortunate to have you as their lord.'

'It is kind of you to say so.' Lord Michel smiled at Lady Sybille. 'My wife and I have a new proposition to put to you.'

Leon looked enquiringly at the Count. 'A new proposition, my lord?'

'Aye. We have been thinking about you and Allis.'

Leon felt his face go blank. 'My lord?' Had the Count and Countess realised he'd taken liberties with Allis?

How on earth had they found out? Had they been watching him? He was conscious that his gaze continually strayed towards her. As soon as he noticed it happening, he took care to look elsewhere, particularly when they were in company. He tried not to look at her.

'Sir Leon, as you have yourself doubtless observed, my daughter isn't an easy woman to handle. When we first hired you, Lady Sybille and I were concerned as to how she would take to you. I must say we are pleasantly surprised. You seem to have her measure.'

Leon almost choked. It was impossible not to think of the many ways he had taken Allis's measure. He knew the span of her waist and he had imagined cupping her breasts in his hands. He knew her taste, her scent...

He mumbled something about it having been a pleasure and felt himself flush. Guilt.

The Count cleared his throat. 'As I said, my wife and I have another proposition for you. Before I give you the gist of it, I must stress that we shall not take offence if it doesn't appeal. All you have to do is say if it is of no interest and we will say no more about it. Understood?'

Cautiously, Leon let out a breath. There was no anger in Lord Michel's tone. The Count was regarding him in such a friendly manner that he couldn't possibly be aware that anything improper had taken place between Leon and his daughter.

'Understood, my lord.'

'Sir Leon, you many have noticed that my eldest daughter is wilful and often argumentative. She and I have come to blows—not literally, you understand— on many an occasion. That will not change. I love her dearly.'

Lord Michel paused and looked questioningly at

Leon, who had no idea what he was expected to say. 'That is understandable, my lord,' he managed to answer.

'Quite. I hoped that would be your response. What I am working round to say is that I wish Allis to have the best of marriages. The best. Allis has shown me that Claude is, in very many ways, unsuited for her. He's a lovely lad, but he lacks your strength. Sir Philippe certainly has strength, but he has no idea how to use it and his morals are questionable, to put it kindly. I've no wish to see my lovely Allis beaten into submission. That isn't my way, and I don't believe it's yours.'

Leon's heart missed several beats and then started to race. What on earth? Where was this going? The Count surely wasn't heading towards a conversation about marriage between him and Allis?

*Impossible. I am lowborn. Nobody. Not a drop of noble blood runs in my veins.*

Paralysed by an excruciating rush of hope and fear, Leon could say nothing. Fortunately, Lord Michel was in full flow.

'Sir Leon, I'll be blunt. I have no male heir and it is my dearest wish that Allis should become Lady of Galard when I am gone. One way or another, my bloodline belongs here.' He looked earnestly at Leon. 'Well, sir? Will you have her?'

Leon's heart was thundering so loudly he barely heard what the Count said. He must have misunderstood. This couldn't be happening. Couldn't. 'My lord?'

'Would you care to marry my daughter?'

An image took over Leon's mind. He was lying entwined with Allis in a vast baronial bed. Lord, the woman disrupted rational thought as easily when she wasn't with him as she did when she was. Her skin was smooth and silky, and her hair was trailing over him as she pressed kisses everywhere. *Everywhere.* He returned the favour, naturally. In his mind, the mattress was soft and the linens fragranced with lavender.

Would he care to marry the woman of his dreams? His mouth dried. What a question.

Despite his longings, it wasn't easy to answer, for that question prompted a thousand new ones. What would happen to his men? Was it possible for him to truly be lord of Galard? Or would he be expected to act as a caretaker for any children he and Allis might have…

It didn't matter. None of it mattered, except…

'My lord, I would be honoured to marry Lady Allisende. Above all things,' he heard himself say. Quickly. Slightly incoherently. Before he could talk himself out of it. It was, after all, the only answer he could give. Honoured?

He'd be delighted. Thrilled. Terrified. He wasn't prepared to marry. *Mon Dieu*, what was he doing? If this went wrong…

The Count's face broke into a broad smile, and he clapped Leon on the shoulder. 'I thank you, sir. Thank you, indeed.' He reached for the handbell. 'I shall send someone for Allis and we can tell her as soon as she appears.'

Leon grimaced. 'I wouldn't do that, my lord. Allis— Lady Allisende—won't care to be told.'

Lady Sybille rose and looped her arm through her husband's. 'Sir Leon is in the right, my love. Allis would like to be asked. Grant her that pleasure.' She rested her head against her husband's arm, adding wistfully, 'I'll always remember the day you proposed to me. It was spring and you brought me a posy of forget-me-nots tied with a satin ribbon. You'd tied a betrothal ring on to the ribbon, and I didn't notice it at first.'

The two of them exchanged long, loving glances. Leon watched them through a haze of shock and disbelief. If Allis accepted him, he would marry into her family and it would become his. The Count and Countess of Arles would be his relations by marriage.

His mind raced. Originally, thanks to the Count's insistence that Allis should marry first his godson and, failing that, the execrable Sir Philippe, Leon had assumed the Count was a stickler for hierarchy. He'd taken it for granted that Lord Michel was doing his utmost to find Allis a nobleman and that he'd push her into a distasteful marriage, irrespective of her wishes. He'd already learned that was not the whole truth. The Count was a brilliant tactician and here was yet more proof.

Leon had misjudged both the Count and Countess of Arles. Badly. Unless...

Did they know of Leon's humble background? The hairs rose on the back of his neck. Leon took it for granted that the world knew he came from nowhere. Perhaps Lord Michel and his wife were giving him this chance because they didn't know...

He cleared his throat. 'My lord, before I propose marriage to Lady Allis, I must make it clear that my background is, well, humble. I am not noble.'

The Count dismissed his objections with an airy wave. 'You're the best warrior in the district. Your men are well disciplined, it's obvious they respect you. And my daughter, so my wife assures me, likes you very well. As far as I'm concerned that makes you more than eligible. Go to it. Find Allis and ask her.'

## Chapter Thirteen

Allis was sitting morosely on a bench in the hall by the solar stairwell. She fixed her gaze on the door arch and allowed herself to feel the sadness welling up inside. She'd been fighting it too long. These past few weeks, Leon had been holding her at arm's length. He was probably telling Papa that he could stay no longer. Once gone, she would never see him again. She longed to be up in the solar, not to witness Leon making his adieus, but while he was here, she wanted to be with him as much as possible.

For over a month, her stomach had felt hollow. Since delivering Bernadette's dowry, Leon had been duty itself. Not once had he let his guard slip. She hadn't had a single kiss. She'd caught the odd smile, but that was all. The man she'd come to know in Monteaux was back behind his shield.

She felt devastated in a way that would have been unthinkable in the spring. How could this be? She'd not known Leon long yet the thought of life without him was unbearable. He'd made it plain there was nothing here for him.

Stupid man. Could he not see that she loved him?

Saints, where had that come from? Stunned, Allis gazed blindly across her father's hall.

She loved Sir Leonidàs of Tarascon. Of course she did—it was impossible not to not love him.

Misery filled her. Inescapable, implacable misery. He was a hireling while she was an aristocrat. Noblewomen weren't permitted to fall in love with mercenaries, even honourable ones. In Allis's world, it seemed that ladies weren't meant to fall in love at all. What could she do? There must be something, there had to be. She couldn't let him walk away.

Papa liked Leon. If he failed to persuade him to stay, perhaps she could. She would be willing to do anything. Anything. Despite his recent control, she knew Leon was as physically attracted to her as she was to him. She would never forget the sparks in his eyes, the slight tightening of his lips whenever he hid a smile. He couldn't fool her. He felt the fire between them.

If he weren't so honourable, she could use that knowledge. Knowing Leon, if she braced herself and invited him to join her in an illicit liaison, he would probably counter her by saying that he had no wish to rob her of her innocence.

There was nothing for it, the only way she could keep him, even for a little while, would be to confess to having already indulged in the most unladylike behaviour imaginable. She would tell him that she was no longer innocent. He would be outraged, of course, but it might rid of him of his scruples. Then they could indulge in a glorious, sinful affair.

And afterwards? It couldn't last for ever. Allis didn't care, or rather she did, but there didn't seem to be anything she could do about that. She had never felt this strongly for any man, and she never would again. She loved Leon and he thought he was going to leave. The dolt.

She bit her finger. What else could she do to delay his departure? Leon cared for his men, she could use that. She could bribe Othon to say that his collarbone was not healing. She would pronounce him unfit to ride. She would…

A brisk step sounded on the stairwell. Leon. She didn't want to deceive him, but she would, if it kept him with her a while longer.

Leon came straight over. 'My lady.' He captured her hand and bowed over it. 'Would you care to walk with me?'

Swallowing hard, Allis nodded. 'You've spoken to Papa?'

'Aye.'

'Is everything arranged?'

'Not quite.' Leon guided her deftly past the stacked trestles towards the far end of the hall.

Her heart lifted. 'Father has asked you to stay, and you have agreed?' That would be the perfect outcome, she thought. It would give her time to put her plan into action.

Leon looked at her, face inscrutable. 'That depends.'

Allis stopped dead. 'Are you being deliberately obtuse?'

'Patience, my lady.'

He continued down the hall, drawing Allis with him. They passed through the great double doors, went down the steps and entered the bailey. It was, as usual, full of noise and activity. Stable boys were shovelling old hay into carts. A ring of people had gathered around what seemed to be an impromptu wrestling match. As shouts of encouragement rose up, Allis glimpsed Peire in the thick of it, throwing a punch at another squire. The clink of coins told her that wagers were being made. She half expected Leon to intervene, but he didn't seem to have noticed the squires were fighting.

'Is there no quiet corner in this castle?' he muttered.

He towed her past the outbuildings and into the herb garden and was brought up short by the sight of two gardeners, teasing out weeds that had taken root between the marjoram and the thyme. They were using hoes. Never again would Allis see a hoe and not think of Bernadette in Saint Claire's. He swore.

'Leon, whatever's the matter?'

'Is there nowhere we can be alone?'

'The chapel?'

'That won't do. You'll be reminded of that man.' He laughed. It wasn't a happy laugh. 'It would cast a pall on proceedings.'

Wondering what was eating him, Allis looked past the herb garden and pointed. 'There's no one in the vegetable plot.'

'Very well then, the vegetable plot will have to do.'

When they were standing on the turf next to a bed of onions, Leon released her hand.

'My lady, this is hardly ideal. I must apologise for the hasty nature of this.'

Watching him thrust his hand through his hair, she realised what was wrong. Leon was nervous. 'Whatever's happened? Leon?'

'Your father's given me permission to court you.' His gaze caught hers, intent and unwavering, despite his apparent unease. He heaved a sigh. 'I find myself woefully unprepared, and for that I apologise. You deserve better.'

He sank to his knees, watching her all the while with

that intent green gaze. Allis was so astonished, she said not a word.

'My lady, Lord Michel has given me permission to ask you to marry me. Please say you will. My lady?'

'Father has agreed? Truly?'

He laid his hand on his heart. 'Truly. My lady, if you accept me, I shall be the happiest man on earth.'

*And I,* Allis thought, *will be the happiest woman.*

She began to smile. It was impossible not to.

He smiled back, his crooked, charming smile. 'I expect you need time to consider.'

'I don't need time. Of course I'll marry you!' She laughed, a laugh of pure joy. 'Tomorrow, if you like.'

'Thank God.' Leon surged to his feet and before the astonished gaze of the gardeners, swept her into his arms. He gave her a searing kiss that banished all doubt. 'Thank God,' he muttered, breath hot in her ear. He eased back, eyeing her with a rueful grin, even as his fingers closed firmly on hers. 'I warned you I was ill prepared. You deserve flowers and tokens of my enduring esteem. Today, all I have are assurances. My lady, I will honour you until my dying day. I will never force you to do my will, in any way.'

She snorted. 'We're bound to argue.'

His eyes gleamed. 'I look forward to it. We will learn to accommodate each other. Be assured that I will protect you with all that is in me.' He looked at her mouth and Allis didn't need to be told that he had kisses on his mind, just as she did.

She leaned in, but, with a meaningful glance over his shoulder at the gardeners, he simply took her hand.

'You have questions, I am sure.'

Allis laced her fingers with his and a rush of warmth raced through her. She couldn't stop smiling. 'I can't believe it. I was braced to bid you farewell and now we're to be married. How did you persuade Papa?'

He grimaced. 'My lady, about that—'

'Since we are to be married, you must call me Allis.' She was dazed with excitement. This handsome, honourable knight, the man she loved, was to be her husband. 'Leon, I am so very, very happy.'

'So am I. I never dreamed such good fortune would be mine.'

'Mmm.' Allis barely heard him. Her mind was brimming with questions. 'What about Claude?'

'Lord Michel said that you have convinced him that Claude was unsuitable.'

*'Dieu merci,'* she muttered, shaking her head. 'Leon, when will we marry, do you know?'

'Soon, I believe, though there will be much to organise. First your father needs to know that you have accepted me. After that, he will send to the Rector to inform him of his wishes.'

'I hope the Rector agrees.'

'You father seems confident that he will.' Leon crooked his arm at her. 'He and your stepmother are in the solar, anxious to hear your decision.'

'We'd best go up then.'

Allis took Leon's arm, prey to conflicting thoughts. She loved him, but he wouldn't thank her for confessing as much. He would be embarrassed. She must be sensible. It was obvious that for him their marriage was one of convenience. He was marrying her for status. For security. If she wanted his love, she was going to have to fight for it.

Leon had no idea so much was involved in arranging what he heard Lady Sybille refer to reassuringly as a simple, straightforward wedding. He'd fondly imagined that once the betrothal was agreed that he would be able to see Allis whenever he wished. To his intense frustration, this didn't happen. Unfamiliar duties piled up with alarming speed, and he found himself wrestling with them from dawn to dusk.

Lord Michel was the most exacting of men. He seemed to have thought of everything. The day after the betrothal he provided Leon with his own office, an extravagance Leon had never aspired to. He had stood in the doorway with a bemused smile on his face as Lord Michel motioned him in. The desk was grey with dust and there was a faint smell of must in the room. On a shelf behind the desk lay half a dozen yellowing parchments. There was a sturdy-looking chair and a cross-framed camping stool. And, thankfully, a tall lancet window. Leon hated being shut in.

The Count tramped to the desk and peered disparagingly at the surface. 'Apologies for the grime. As you may guess this was a storeroom. It will be cleaned.'

'You are beyond generous, my lord, but it's not necessary.'

He received a penetrating look. 'Marrying Allis will be no sinecure, lad. Do you have much experience of estate management?'

'None whatsoever,' Leon admitted, a twist in his guts as he recognised his shortcomings. 'I have much to learn.'

'Precisely.' Lord Michel grinned. 'Allis aside, there will be plenty to keep you busy.'

'I'm sure. My lord, I must tell you that while I can read, writing is beyond me.'

The Count grunted. 'That's irrelevant. It's a blessing you can read. As to writing, frankly, I have an appalling hand, which is why we have scribes in Galard. Alert Hugo whenever you need one.'

'Thank you, my lord.'

After a few days, Leon was surprised to discover he rather liked having an office. It left him free to think without interruption, which was a new luxury. He certainly appreciated that Lord Michel was doing his utmost to make him feel at home.

Still unable to credit his good fortune, he set his mind to clearing a path to his marriage. Acquiring the agreement of the Rector to the match was not his responsibility. Lord Michel had that well in hand. Leon's first responsibility was to negotiate terms for his men. Given his recent observations of the way his men were settling in, he believed most of them would stay.

In the event he was satisfied with what the Count offered. Every man in his troop could, if they chose, have a place in Castle Galard. No one would be turned out. Once this was set down in writing, some of Leon's doubts began to melt away.

As to the tricky issue of estate management, Lord Michel made it plain that help would be at hand.

'Any questions, Leon, come to me. Failing that, ask Hugo. He knows everything.'

'Thank you, my lord.'

Which made it rankle all the more when three days later Leon was sitting at his desk, wondering why the only time he saw Allis was when they were at the supper table, in full view of the entire household. It wasn't the same as talking with her when they were on their own. That spark he loved so much was dimmed.

In fact, now he came to think about it, he and Allis hadn't been alone since they'd stood in the vegetable plot, plighting their troth and even then, two gardeners had been watching them. Was she avoiding him? Or had Lady Sybille, for some reason, decided to keep them apart until the wedding day?

At supper that evening, Leon made sure to arrive early in the great hall. When Allis arrived, she was wearing a gown he'd not seen before. He didn't have to be a merchant to know that the cost of the fabric must have been breathtaking, for the weave was extraordinary. As she came towards him, the gown seemed to shimmer, appearing first blue, then green. A plain gold ring shone softly on her right hand. He hadn't seen it before and was immediately reminded that he had yet to find a betrothal gift. He would be sure to remedy that on the morrow.

He accompanied her to her seat. 'It is good to see you, my lady.'

An eyebrow rose. 'Leon, I've told you before, since we are betrothed, you may call me Allis.'

Beneath the table, he reached for her hand. 'You look very well tonight, Allis, that gown makes you look like a princess.'

'A princess?' Shaking her head at him, she smiled. 'I have a number of gowns. You've not seen them all.'

'You look like a princess in this one. The pink gown you wore on your first night back from the convent… that made you look like a rose.'

She laughed out loud. 'A rose? Heavens, Leon, you're beginning to sound like a troubadour.'

'It's true. Mind, you are beautiful whatever you wear. Even in those ghastly rags you wore in the convent.'

'Flatterer.'

'It's not flattery if it's the truth.' He lifted his hand to his lips. 'I am the most fortunate of men.'

Her blue eyes darkened and she looked even more beautiful.

'I looked for you this morning,' he said, softly. 'As I looked for you on other mornings. Are you trying to avoid me?'

'Why would I do that?'

Allis withdrew her hand from his to reach for the goblet. Seeing it empty, Leon beckoned a servant over and waited until her favourite wine had been poured before speaking again.

'Allis, where were you?'

'I walked to the village. I've been there most mornings.'

A knot formed in Leon's gut. His betrothed was a headstrong woman and all her life she'd been used to going into the village. 'Allis, please take care. Remember the attack on Sir Claude. I trust you took an escort?'

She took a sip of wine and set the goblet down. 'Of course I did. Papa insisted. I went to see Eglantine. Her time is very near.'

'She's well?'

'Apart from pining for Claude. She was devastated when he went back to Carpentras without her.' She let out a huge sigh. 'I blame myself. When I told her I would speak up for her, I think she began to hope.'

'It's not your fault.' Leon looked intently at her. 'Eglantine and Claude come from different walks of life. She must have known from the outset that there was little chance that they'd be permitted to live as man and wife.'

Briefly, Allis leaned against him, and he felt a rush of affection for her that was almost painful in its intensity. 'You're in the right,' she murmured. 'Not everyone is as fortunate as I.'

His heart gave a little jump. 'Fortunate?' Was this her

way of telling him that she was glad they were marrying despite the difference in their stations? She was so lovely. So poised. So ladylike in that shimmering gown. Was he wrong to deny her a marriage to someone of her own class? By rights, she should be marrying someone trained from the cradle to negotiate with importunate lordlings chipping away at the estate boundaries. Well, at least he could deal with the military side of things. What he was less confident about was whether he'd ever find his way around a set of estate accounts.

She looked earnestly at him. 'Leon, I am incredibly happy.'

This time Leon leaned into her. He lowered his voice. 'I am glad to hear it. I was beginning to think you'd decided you couldn't marry a fellow who didn't know how to keep a proper tally of estate revenues.'

Firmly, she shook her head. 'Far from it. I've been busy, that's all. I feel for Eglantine. I know she has her father, but she's bereft without Claude.'

'If you wish to see her tomorrow, I will be your escort. And we shall ride rather than walk.'

Her eyes lit up. 'Thank you, I would enjoy your company.' She reached for the goblet. 'By the by, if you need help with the accounts, I trust you know you may call on me.'

His eyebrows lifted. 'You can keep accounts?'

'Of course. Papa taught me.'

It was at that moment that Leon realised he wouldn't simply fight dragons for this woman. He would learn to keep the estate accounts and he would enjoy it.


Dawn was edging round the shutters when Allis woke. Today, she was going to marry Sir Leon of Tarascon.

As she had done these past few mornings, the first

thing Allis did was to hold out her hand and admire her betrothal gift. Leon had done her proud—a large cabochon ruby was set in the most beautiful gold ring. The ruby was highly polished, it glowed like dark fire in the early morning light. He couldn't possibly have found it in the village. Had he sent back to Avignon for it? Perhaps it came from further afield. Well, wherever it came from, Allis liked it very well. Smiling, she pushed back the bedcovers. It was their wedding day.

And their wedding night…

The flutter of nerves—sharp and intense—caught her by surprise.

Would Leon be disappointed with her? She didn't think so. Whenever they kissed, their passion seemed to be equally matched. Which meant she would have to take care to control her responses to him. Leon thought he was marrying a lady. She fingered the ring, smiling ruefully. She mustn't disappoint him. She must do nothing to make him think he'd got the wrong end of the bargain. Leon was saving her from an unsuitable marriage. To be sure, he was also marrying her for the rise in status, for his future and that of his troop.

She sat on the edge of the bed, frowning at the ruby. She was marrying for love.

'What am I to you, Leon?' she muttered. 'Can you learn to love me?'

The door rattled. Estelle entered with Allis's gown over her arm, a flowing river of green silk, the colour of Leon's eyes. The instant Allis had seen the fabric, she'd known it would make the perfect gown for their wedding.

'Good morning, my lady, what did you say? I didn't quite catch it.'

'Nothing,' Allis said, hastily. 'Nothing at all.'

So much hung in the balance. It would help if she were not so apprehensive about their wedding night. Leon was a kind man, she reminded herself. It would be all right.

The ceremony took place in the family chapel. Allis entered on her father's arm, the green gown hushing about her feet like sea foam. Her hair was bound loosely with ribbons, and she was wearing a chaplet of flowers.

She had not gone more than two paces when she saw that everyone had been keeping secrets from her. Towards the front of the chapel, next to her stepmother stood Bernadette. She was wearing her grey novice's habit and the most enormous smile.

'Bernadette!' Abandoning all dignity, Allis rushed forward to give her a fierce hug. A silly flood of tears almost blinded her. 'It's wonderful you're here. How did you find out?'

Bernadette grinned. 'Papa, of course.'

'I'm amazed Mother Margerie allowed you to come. Did she make a fuss?'

'She tried to. Papa dealt with her, but you must know I wouldn't miss this for the world. I wish you every happiness.'

'Thank you.' Allis wiped her tears away.

Bernadette stepped aside and there was Leon, green eyes gleaming. He held out his hand. Quaking inside, Allis moved towards him. He looked remarkably handsome and more imposing than usual in a jacket fashioned from blue silk and dark hose. Someone, probably Sybille, had embroidered the tunic neck and sleeves with gold thread. He looked like a lord, so much so that she was slightly intimidated as he gazed down at her. She thrust her misgivings aside.

*This is Leon. He is probably as tense as I. Thank God, I am marrying him,* she thought. *Thank God.*

The chapel was filled with Galard's most favoured knights and retainers. Hugo was there with a few of the castle guard. Several of Leon's men—Othon, Vézian and Stefe—were among them, grinning from ear to ear. All come to witness Lady Allis and Sir Leon exchange their vows.

With a final smile for Bernadette, Allis stood before the altar and put her hand on Leon's arm. The warmth of his hand covered hers, the priest bowed his head, and the ceremony began.

When the formal proceedings were over, the wedding party processed to the great hall.

Allis and Leon sat in places of honour at the centre of the board on the dais, where they were expected to stay for hours, the still centre of a magnificent feast which swirled around them like the ever-changing sea.

Huge platters were heaved in front of them, piled with meats and pastries. Bunches of grapes had the morning dew still upon them. The air filled with rich scents—cinnamon and cloves, wine and ale. Cheese. Too tense for hunger, Allis picked at her food, she could hardly taste a thing. It was as though she were in a dream. Nothing seemed real.

The platters were removed, and Leon leaned back with sigh. Allis saw him looking longingly towards the stairwell.

'How long will this last?' he muttered.

A tiny muscle was flickering at the side of his mouth. He looked nervous. No, that could not be right, she must be misreading him. Like all men, he would be impatient for the bedding.

'We can't go upstairs yet,' she whispered. 'There's more ritual to get through. Dusk will be falling by the time it is ended.'

'Truly?'

'Truly.'

Even as she spoke, the tall doors at the far end of the hall were flung wide. The villagers trooped in and were greeted with servants offering ale and wine. More pastries appeared. Noise levels rose. Someone gave a crack of laughter and half the hall joined in.

Leon and Allis stayed in the places of honour as servants and villagers filed up to offer their well-wishes. Gifts and sprays of flowers piled up on the table in front of them. A posy of daisies from the village children, a bright chaplet of ribbons for Allis's hair, a braided bookmark. A glorious vase filled with yellow roses came from Hugo. And for Leon, some beautifully wrought studs for Titan's bridle, and three bleached linen shirts, worked no doubt by Sybille. More flowers. Sweetmeats. A willow basket. A rack of hooks from the blacksmith.

They were surrounded by smiles throughout. Heartwarming though it was, as the last of the villagers bowed away, Allis released a quiet sigh.

'You're exhausted,' Leon observed.

'My face aches with so much smiling.'

'Mine too.' He took a firm grip of her hand and leaned towards her. 'I have agreed with your father that we may slip quietly away. I hope you don't mind, I took the liberty of telling Estelle that you had no need of her services.'

Allis held down a blush and gave a jerky nod. With a brief kiss for her father and stepmother, and a final hug for Bernadette, she slipped out of the hall and began winding her way upstairs. Leon followed close behind.

'I never realised that sitting at table accepting gifts could be hard work,' he said. 'I swear it's more tiring than competing in a tourney.'

Recognising that edge of humour in his voice, Allis laughed. They had reached her bedchamber door.

Leon lifted the latch and bowed her in. 'My lady.'

Allis dipped into a curtsy. 'Thank you, sir.'

# Chapter Fourteen

For the first time, Leon stepped fully into Allis's bed-chamber. It smelt of beeswax and summer. The shutter was closed, and the wall sconces lit. Three candles burned in the hearth. The bedcover was sprinkled with rose petals and posies decorated the bed hangings.

Allis was gazing at the bed with what looked depressingly like apprehension. He took her hand. 'Allis, what's wrong?'

Quickly she shook her head. 'Nothing.' Her smile was strained.

'I am not about to fall on you like a ravening beast. Allis, I know you are innocent and likely as surprised by this turn of events as I.' He tugged her towards him, and those great blue eyes looked up at him. 'I'd hoped you were pleased.'

'I am pleased.'

Even though she was smiling, Leon heard doubt in her voice. It was up to him to dispel it. 'You're nervous.' He shrugged and pressed a chaste kiss to her cheek. 'I am too.'

'You? How can that be?' She gestured at the rose-strewn bed. 'You have surely done this many times?'

He shook his head, took her with him to the bed and sat down, drawing her with him. 'I have never bedded my wife. If fortune favours us, we will have many years together. I don't want to hurt you or do anything to jeopardise our relationship.' Allis sighed and laid her head against his chest. Leon cupped her cheek and smiled ruefully down at her. 'When your father asked me if I would care to marry you, I was honoured beyond belief. I want this to be perfect.'

She jerked and lifted her head, blue eyes intent. 'Father asked you to marry me? I thought...' Her voice trailed off.

'What? What's the matter?' Leon's heart sank. She was suddenly as stiff as a board. Worse, she was no longer meeting his gaze.

'You don't really want me.' She gave a harsh laugh. 'I thought you'd asked for my hand. I thought you'd stepped into the breach to save me from Claude.'

Leon took her chin, insisting she looked at him. 'I tried to tell you that the idea was your father's when we were in the garden.'

'Did you? I don't recall.' She shrugged. 'Never mind, it has become irrelevant. We're married.'

Leon stared helplessly at her. 'Allis, I *wanted* to marry you. If I hadn't thought your father would toss me out on my ear, I would have asked—'

'But you didn't.' She pulled her hand free.

Resolutely, Leon reclaimed it. He wasn't sure quite how it had happened, but it appeared he had blundered. Badly. All he could think was that he must be frank. The truth was always best. 'Allis, think about it. Until these past few days, I had no reason to imagine that Lord Michel would look kindly on my asking for your hand. Allow me to explain. Your father said that he would be pleased if I offered for you, and I jumped at the chance. I didn't even think.' His voice went husky. 'I just knew that I desired you above all things.'

'Well, marriage to me has certainly solved many of your problems.'

The resignation in her tone was troubling. 'Meaning?'

'When we took Bernadette's dowry to the convent you spoke of your future, of the constant uncertainty that surrounds you and your men.' She pushed to her feet, strode to the fireplace, and stared at the candles in the hearth. 'Marrying me has ended that uncertainty, hasn't it?'

Rising, Leon went to join her. 'Stop this. Allis, I want you as I never wanted any woman.'

'Lust,' she said scornfully. 'In my experience, that is all men think about.'

'Actually, no. You're wrong. I know lust and what we have is certainly no such thing.'

She tipped her head to one side, an arrested expression in her eyes. 'What do we have?'

'We are drawn to each other. You cannot deny that.'

'No, I cannot,' she said quietly.

'We have respect. And until now, I would have said we had a fair understanding of each other's characters.' His lips quirked. 'I enjoy your company. I would swear there is affection between us.' He reached for her and when she made no move to shy away, took her firmly in his arms. 'I don't want to quarrel.' He kissed her cheek. 'This is our wedding night.'

She sighed, a faint whisper of sound and laid her head against him. Leon's chest ached. He had disappointed her, but that that was surely a gesture of trust and acceptance. 'I honour you, Allis,' he murmured. 'I always will.'

'I honour you, too.'

He smiled. He'd never expected that, not from a titled lady. 'Will you allow me to seduce you tonight?'

'I will.'

Unable to suppress his smile, he scooped her into his arms and carried her to the bed.

Leon set Allis carefully on her feet next to the bed. He was frowning. Not at her, thankfully, but at the silken coverlet. Made from oyster-coloured silk, it was thickly embroidered with birds and flowers.

'Those birds are bright as jewels,' he muttered. 'Allis, this is too fine to lie on.'

'It is beautiful,' Allis agreed. 'Sybille made it for me after she married Papa. I've always liked it.' Aware that the opulence she was used to must seem alien to Leon, she leaned forward and whisked it back. Rose petals flew in all directions. 'We can pull it over us, later.'

Later. She swallowed and gave him a shy smile. His eyes were dark with what she recognised as desire, and she had no idea how to proceed. This was the husband she had never thought to marry, the husband of her heart. She would enjoy his seduction and pray that there would be no recriminations after.

'Allis.' He drew her to him. 'My wife, my beautiful wife.'

The kissing began gently, featherlight touches as his lips grazed hers. He moved on to her cheek, covering it with soft kisses before groaning and returning to her mouth. Each kiss sent a whisper of need streaking through her. He was being far too gentle. Inside, Allis burned with impatience. She wanted to tear the blue jacket from him and haul him into bed. She wanted to indulge in the most unladylike behaviour imaginable.

As he kissed her, he was stroking her back and the curve of her buttocks. She wanted more. Much more. She curbed her impatience for as long as she could. She was a lady. Leon expected innocence.

His breathing was unsteady. Hers was too.

She finally broke when he started caressing her breasts. She let out a gasp. A moan. By now her breathing was definitely fevered. Fortunately, so was his. Allis ground herself against him and the kisses stopped. He was looking down at her, eyes cloudy.

'You're not afraid.'

It wasn't a question. Slightly shamefaced, Allis shook her head. There was little point in pretending. It had to be obvious she was far from afraid. She only prayed he hadn't guessed the rest. 'Leon, kissing you, doing this with you, is the greatest of pleasures. How can I be afraid?'

His lips curved. And then his mouth and hands were back at work again. It was glorious. Dazzling. Her entire body was aflame. She looped her arms about his neck, matching him kiss for kiss and sigh for sigh. Leon's mouth and hands became increasingly insistent. He tugged at her skirts. Silk whispered, and an instant later he was caressing the skin of her thigh.

Allis pulled at the fabric of his jacket. 'I want to kiss you everywhere.'

'Everywhere?' Leon laughed, his voice was rough with need. 'You don't know what you are saying.'

'Show me. Show me everything.'

Allis could hear nothing but her breathing and his. Boldly, she reached for his belt. Her mouth dried and her fingers became thumbs. She laid the belt on a coffer. The faint click sounded loud in the quiet. Cloth whispered as their hands collided to toss his jacket aside.

At last, candlelight was gleaming on Leon's body. Allis tried not to stare, but truly, she had never seen a man so well formed. He had the odd scar, which was to be expected, he was a warrior after all. All that toned muscle was astonishing. And he was hers to command. Or was he? She would soon know.

'My turn,' she murmured and reached up to loosen her hair.

His fingers were there before her. Gilt hairpins fell in glittering arcs and tinkled on the floor. Her chaplet of flowers was tossed aside. He made short work of her buttons and lacing. It could have been her imagination, but she rather thought his fingers were trembling. Thank goodness. It helped to know that he was as nervous as she. It meant that he cared, at least a little. Her green gown floated away, and she was naked before him. What had happened to her shoes and undergown? She had no idea. It didn't matter. Leon was looking at her as though she was the most beautiful thing he had ever seen. Desire, she reminded herself. He desires me.

'Allis,' he breathed, carefully arranging her hair about her shoulders. 'You are the loveliest woman in creation.'

He was naked. So handsome and so attractive, that looking at him weakened her knees. She leaned against him, dazed.

'Leon?'

'Hmm?'

'Did you take off your clothes or did I?'

'Lord knows.' Laughing, he nuzzled her cheek. 'You smell of heaven. Heaven and joy.'

They kissed again, tongues playing, hands teasing and caressing, and were on the bed before she knew it. She had no idea how they got there. It was as though the world was lost. Her whole being was focused on Leon, lying skin to skin next to her. This was glorious. He was glorious.

The kisses drew out, with Allis giving as many as she received. Before this man, she had been kissed, but until Leon she had never kissed from her heart. This was what kissing should be. She kissed new places… places she had never dreamed of kissing. His chest was wonderful, with all those muscles and that light sprinkling of curls and that welcoming scent that was pure Leon. She kissed scar after scar.

'Allis, that…' His groan went right through her.

She lifted her head. 'Good, I hope.'

'Bliss,' he said, even as Allis found herself lying on her back. They were practically fighting to kiss each other.

He focused on her breasts, using lips and tongue just as she had with him. It was a new sensation—both sensual and, if she didn't know better, loving. Helpless with need, confused by the strength of her longing, Allis wriggled and groaned.

'Leon?'

He looked up. 'Hmm?'

'I'm melting inside.'

His eyes gleamed. 'You're ready.' He kissed her nose. 'I will do my utmost not to hurt you.'

'I know.'

Leon shifted over her, and it happened almost without thought. Just as Allis feared it might. It wasn't that she forgot that she must act the lady, but as he moved over her, she slid her arms about his waist and tugged him to her. That was all it took. He was home and it felt wonderful.

'Allis, sweetheart, forgive me.' Leon looked stricken as he attempted to ease back. 'Did I hurt you?'

Allis had wrapped herself about Leon, keeping him exactly where he was. He had no complaints there but...

'Allis? Have I hurt you?'

'Not at all.'

Leon's wife—would he ever become used to the thought that this incredible woman was truly his wife?—gave an embarrassed laugh and he allowed himself to relax.

'You made me melt,' she added. 'Perhaps that helped.'

Leon searched her face and broke into a smile. *'Dieu merci.'* He leaned his forehead against hers. He'd had no experience in bedding innocent ladies, and the ease with which they had joined had come as surprise. A pleasant one, naturally. 'I would hate to give you pain.'

The urge to move became a compulsion and gradually he surrendered to it. He watched her intently, alert for the slightest sign of distress. Thankfully, she breathed his name and pressed closer.

Charmed by her innocent enthusiasm, enthusiasm that had captured him from their first kiss, he covered her lips with his. A murmur of acceptance spurred him on. He nuzzled her breast and she muttered encouragement. He found a spot beneath her ear and kissed that too. Licking, giving her the gentles of nibbles. She gripped him closer, her every response making it clear that she wanted more. Allis wanted passion, all of it. Scarcely able to believe this was going so well, he started to lose control. Still being careful. Still conscious that he must not hurt her.

His lady's hands streaked fire along his flanks. Her eyes closed and, as her legs wrapped around his calves anchoring him in place, Leon wondered if she was even aware of what she was doing. There was passion here, such passion. It would have been wasted on Claude, absolutely wasted.

Words blurred in his mind. Thoughts were tenuous. This…with Allis…

Leon was losing himself as never before. He had never known the like. An overwhelming tension was winding inside him. It grew tighter and tighter, drawing him into unchartered territory. Her eyes opened, dark and lustrous. Briefly, she touched his cheek. The gesture was devastating. Heartbreaking. Loving. It seemed so real.

'Leon.' She smiled. 'Husband.' Her arm slid round his neck and he felt her reach her pleasure. With an inarticulate murmur she covered his neck with kisses.

The fiery rush of his release took Leon by surprise. It was more powerful than he'd dreamed possible. Bedding Allis was a revelation. She made him believe that two could truly become one, that the words mercenary and lady, and male and female had no meaning. With Allis, such distinctions no longer existed. He sagged against her, shaken and dazed. Weak with love.

Love? His breath stopped. *Love?*

It shouldn't be possible. It wasn't possible. Leon didn't have the first idea about love, although he had to admit that Allis had entered his life like a whirlwind. Dressed in convent rags, her beauty had dazzled him. Knowing that beauty was superficial, he had set about ignoring it and instead he'd found himself captivated by her mind and nature.

Allis was loyal and loving. So loving that she would fight to the death for her family. His lips twisted. Why, she would even have married the loathsome Sir Philippe to save her sister and fulfil her father's wishes concerning their bloodline.

His chest hurt. Could this be love? Was that what he felt for her?

She was threading her fingers through his hair, that lovely face still lost in his neck. He had the impression she was breathing in his scent, which he found incredibly moving.

'Allis?' He shifted on to his side. Though tall, his wife was a slight woman, and he had no wish to squash her.

She looked at him, cheeks aflame, eyes dreamy. 'Aye?'

'Thank you,' he said, simply. It was all he could think of to say. He could hardly say, *Allis, I have no notion what love is about, but I believe I love you.*

She smiled. 'It is I who should be thanking you.' She ran her fingers down his shoulder, a question in her eyes. 'Leon, the pleasure of it—I had no idea. Is it always like that for you?'

'Not always. In truth the pleasure you have given me is unsurpassed.' He caught her hand and kissed it. 'We are fortunate. It seems we are matched in passion. Not everyone is.'

She looked at him through her eyelashes. Leon waited, wondering what she would come out with next. While he waited, he admired the golden fire in her hair as it flowed across the pillows. She bit her lip and, intriguingly, went bright red.

'Leon, how often will we…?'

He laughed. 'As often as you like. Though I expect not tonight, you are bound to be sore. I dare say we should wait until tomorrow.'

'We really have to wait that long?' She sighed, and her breasts shifted enticingly against him. 'I am not in pain.'

That sounded like an invitation. Leon felt himself stir. He wrapped a strand of hair round his wrist and brought her a shade closer. 'No?'

'Not in the least.' Her lips curved and she gave a slight shrug. 'I couldn't help noticing though, that what we have just done must be tiring for the man.'

'Making love,' Leon heard himself say. 'We made love.' What he had just experienced had been more, far more than a simple bedding. He found himself almost biting off his tongue in a desperate effort to hide his feelings. He'd never felt this way. Hadn't known it was possible to feel so much.

'Leon, it's obviously far more strenuous for the man. You must be exhausted.'

He hardly heard her. He was too busy watching her mouth. She was asking for a kiss. Begging for one. He held off. He loved this woman. He was sure of it. That didn't mean he should get carried away and declare himself. She probably wouldn't believe him. In any case, she might not want his love. However, it wouldn't do to disappoint his wife on their wedding day...

'Allis, I'm not exhausted. Not in the least.' He lifted an eyebrow. 'Besides, there are many ways a man and a woman can take their pleasure of each other. Some are more tiring than others.'

'Many ways,' she said thoughtfully. 'Really? Will you teach me?'

'It will be my pleasure.'

Her eyes sparkled as she reached for him. 'And mine too, I am sure.'

The bedcovers had slipped to the floor when Leon woke, Allis fast in his arms. Judging by the light creeping round the shutter, morning was half over. His wife slept on.

Smiling, he disentangled his body from hers and eased out of bed. Allis muttered and shifted but did not wake. Her blonde hair lay in a glorious tangle about her face. Carefully, he brushed it away, fingers lingering on her cheek. She would need her rest this morning.

As he bent to straighten the bedcovers, curiosity had him glancing at the mattress. Last night he'd expected there to be a little blood. However, he'd been so intent on giving Allis pleasure, he hadn't really looked for it. It was odd, though, he was pretty certain he would have noticed had there been any.

He frowned and looked closer. No blood. He shrugged. He'd never bedded a virgin before, but shouldn't there be some?

Puzzled, he padded to the wash bowl. As he pulled on his clothes, he found himself glancing back at her. He'd heard that many ladies lost their virginity when riding and Allis was a keen horsewoman. Most likely she'd lost her maidenhead when riding.

On the other hand...

It had been so good between them. So much so, that in the cool light of day Leon couldn't help but wonder if she'd been rather too knowing. What had she said? 'You make me melt, perhaps that helped.'

A lump formed in his throat. Allis had known what to expect! She'd caught his rhythm entirely too quickly for an untried maid. And he'd been so dazzled, he'd failed to notice. It had, after all, been incendiary. There'd been no pain when he'd entered her. None. His mind wouldn't leave it. Allis had not been innocent.

Did Lord Michel know? He must, Leon realised, with a sinking heart. All that talk about the Count respecting Leon and choosing him for Allis because of his sense of honour was simply flattery. Leon felt like kicking himself. A flare of white-hot fury shot through him. He mastered it with difficulty. With reason.

A nobleman who discovered that his supposedly innocent wife was nothing of the kind was likely to be enraged. Such a woman would be considered spoiled. Tainted goods. The best she could expect was to be set aside until it was proved that she wasn't carrying another man's child. A child who, if it happened to be a boy, might be named heir.

Lord Michel had chosen Leon because he imagined he was in no position to make a fuss when he discovered Allis had lost her maidenhead before her wedding. Could she be with child?

Leon stared at her, heart thudding. When had she last lain with her lover? It must have been before she had gone to the convent. How long had she been there? Had she been with child all along? She was so slim it couldn't be possible. Could it?

He found himself praying—him of all people, actually praying. He prayed that Allis and her lover had parted several moons ago.

That must be true. It had to be. Allis would not have married him if she were carrying another man's child. She had too much integrity. She would have told him. His heartbeat slowed. The shock was beginning to dissipate. Where was her lover? For the man to have vanished so completely, he must only care for himself. Either that or he was dead. Furthermore, whoever he was, the way Allis had responded to Leon last night told him that she wasn't pining for the fellow. There was no love lost on either side, which was excellent news.

Leon wanted Allis for his wife more than anything. Naturally, he hoped that they would have children and that one of them would inherit Lord Michel's holdings, but his heart was telling him that he wanted Allis more than he wanted his heir to inherit the Galard estate. Even so, disquiet had him curling his fingers into fists. Allis herself was the prize, but he was human enough to wish—to pray—that she wasn't carrying another man's child.

If only she had been straight with him from the outset. Smiling grimly, he thought back over the previous night, to the moment her body had first tightened around his. She had been surprised when she reached her pleasure. The way she had gasped his name and looked at him, starry-eyed and dreamy. So beautiful. He would swear that he had been the first man to please her in such a way.

Last night he'd been swept away by the stars in her eyes. He'd been flattered because she was generally so matter of fact. So cool and capable. And last night the idea that he had been the only man to put that looked of sated bliss in her eyes had been an unexpected delight. That still held true, he would take his oath on it. He'd given Allis pleasure, and it had been the first time.

Whoever her lover had been, he had not taken care with her. Who had it been? Not Sir Claude—that boy was obsessed with his Eglantine. Was it someone here in the castle, one of Lord Michel's knights? That didn't seem plausible either, the household knights were loyal to a fault. Who could it have been?

Returning to the bedside, he picked up a strand of golden hair and rubbed between his fingers. So soft. So lovely. Allis was a delight in so many ways. Passionate and caring and—to add spice to the mix—wilful and stubborn.

Where had her lover gone?

Allis sighed, opened her eyes, and smiled. 'Good morning.'

'I thought you'd never wake,' Leon said, recognising with a wrench that whatever had happened in his wife's past, he couldn't help but be pleased with her. He was enraptured. Even with hurt but a heartbeat away, he was helpless with love and utterly in her thrall.

She held out her hand. 'Come back to bed.' Her voice was husky. Inviting.

Confused and wounded, he shook his head. Much as he ached to tumble back into her arms, he needed to think. And he would think more clearly away from her. He wanted her too much. He loved her too much. And he had no idea what to do with the knowledge that she hadn't come to him a virgin.

'I ought to get to work,' he said. 'There's much to do.' A discussion of her innocence or lack of it on their wedding night would achieve nothing. What counted was that Allis had flowered in his arms. With luck, once she had rested, she would flower again. He kissed her cheek, closed his ears to her sigh and headed for the door. She wanted him. Good. Last night he'd been braced for pain and virginal tears. This was better. It had to be.

If only she'd been candid with him about her lost virginity. He rubbed the back of his neck. It was no use reminding himself that she'd been brought up among men who valued their womenfolk for their innocence. If Leon had been a real nobleman, the purity of his bloodline would have been all. As matters stood, he had no bloodline to think of. His family was dead. Even if they'd been alive, they had no claims to nobility. Still, it stung to discover that she hadn't trusted him enough to be honest. It stung.

At best it was an insult. As the latch dropped behind
him, he hurried down the spiral stairway. Anger carried him into the near-empty armoury. As he called for
someone, anyone, to arm him, hurt roared in his ears.
Allis had misled him. She didn't trust him.

Titan was saddled in no time. Conscious he was bel-
lowing like a bull, Leon rode to the tiltyard and snatched
up an axe. 'Get a sack on that quintain!'

Sir Hugo appeared and leaned on the railing. 'Good
morning, Sir Leon. Beautiful day.' Noticing the axe,
Sir Hugo raised an eyebrow. Fortunately, the man had
the wit to say no more.

Leon slammed down his visor. Titan, ever responsive to his commands, charged down the lists. Allis
didn't trust him. He sliced through the sack at the first
charge and galloped to the opposite end. Titan turned,
the world span, and Leon found himself staring bemused at the straw spilling from the ripped sack. What
the devil was he doing?

She didn't trust him.

Except... That was not wholly true. She had trusted
him in bed. She had trusted him with her body. It was
a beginning. If he treated her well, he could build on
that. Allis would learn to trust him with her heart. With
her mind and soul. He would win her.

Sir Hugo straightened. 'I've not handled a battle-axe
in a while. If you'd care for a little competition, I'd be
happy to join you.'

After a brief bout with Sir Hugo, Leon's emotions
were under control. Thank God. Lack of control could
be lethal. He would not allow it to wreck his marriage.
Handing Titan over to Peire, Leon headed for his office, collecting a tankard of ale on his way through the

hall. He would think of his marriage as a campaign. A campaign he had no intention of losing. He would win her. He set down his ale. Some office work would be the perfect distraction.

Several scraps of parchment lay on the desk, weighed down by a brass handbell. Lord Michel's signature was scrawled at the bottom of the top one. Leon drew it from the pile. It was a note asking him to speak to the blacksmith about fashioning a new backplate for the solar fireplace. As he read, his smile faded.

Questions remained, they circled in his mind, like crows over a corpse. Did Lord Michel know his daughter had lost her virginity? When the Count claimed to have chosen Leon as a husband for Allis because he and Lady Sybille thought they were suited, it had seemed plausible. Leon had wanted to believe that Lord Michel had seen qualities in him that he hoped for in his son-in-law. It had been so very flattering. Was it the truth?

He set his jaw. He must turn this to his advantage. He would prove his worth to Lord Michel, just as he would prove his worth to Allis. He would give neither of them reason to regret his alliance with their family, unorthodox and ill starred though it might appear.

As to the question of Allis's lost virginity, Leon's lowly background worked in his favour. Until now, he'd never quite realised how far his views diverged from those of a nobleman, but this was a rare instance when he was blessed by his lack of breeding rather than cursed. He had won Allis because of it. Though saddened that she'd not trusted him enough to tell him all, Leon would not condemn her.

A short laugh escaped him. He himself was no innocent, it wouldn't be fair to blame her.

Rubbing the bridge of his nose, he frowned at the

other scraps of parchment awaiting his attention beneath the handbell. All of them oddly shaped pieces cut from larger ones that still had use in them. Most of them had been scraped clean so many times they were almost worn away.

Duty called. He went to his chair and began sorting through the pile.

## Chapter Fifteen

Allis lazed against the pillows, smiling. She was certain her father would not object if Leon spent the whole morning with her instead of working. Still— she stretched luxuriously—she could laze in bed and dream about what had passed between them. She had much to think about.

Finally, she knew what it was like to lie with the man she loved. Idly, she twisted her hair about her finger. She ached to know what Leon thought of her in his heart. He had called her beautiful. He seemed to admire her, though he'd never mentioned love. He hadn't even come close. None the less, she couldn't wish for a more considerate lover.

Except—Allis scowled at the door—why on earth had he left her, when they could spend the day together? He was too diligent for his own good.

After rolling this way and that, she realised she wasn't going back to sleep. Leon had kept her awake half the night, but she wasn't tired. Besides, bright lines of light were forcing their way past the rim of the shutter. It must be almost noon. This was her first day as a married woman and she wasn't about to waste it. She tossed back the bedcover, went to the window, and opened the shutter. A slash of white light fell starkly across the bed, seeming to cut it in two.

A sense of disquiet curled in her belly. She found herself frowning at the band of sunlight on the bed. At the rumpled sheets. It took a moment to pin down the reason for her disquiet. That sheet, it was something to do with...

No blood. While crumpled, there was no blood on the sheets.

Her mind leaped back to the way Leon had left the chamber and her breath seized. He had smiled, but the spark had gone from in his eyes. He had worked out that she had not come to their marriage bed a virgin.

*Leon knows and he is offended. I should have told him.*

She flew to the door and peered into the corridor. 'Estelle?' she called. 'Are you there?'

A floorboard creaked and another door opened. 'Here, my lady.'

'Please fetch water and help me with a fresh gown. I'm joining my husband.'

'Would you care for breakfast, my lady?'

'Thank you, Estelle, a pastry will do. Please hurry.'


Allis knocked briefly at the door of Leon's office and walked straight in. He was talking to Hugo. She caught something about trying out a new style of helmet when they were next in the lists, but he broke off as she entered.

'Come in, my lady.' Leon spoke so formally her heart twisted. 'I didn't think to see you this morning.'

Allis felt herself flush. 'Leon, I apologise for interrupting, but I need to talk to you.'

'If you wouldn't mind, Hugo,' Leon said, 'we can continue this later.'

'Of course. I'm headed back to the lists. You can find me there.' Hugo gave Allis a sharp glance before squeezing past her. 'If you will excuse me?'

Allis nodded and then she and her husband were alone. She took his hand. 'I have disappointed you.'

'You could never disappoint me.'

His voice was firm. Allis searched his face, hunting for the doubt she had seen when he'd left the bedchamber. Green eyes studied her, he had not pulled his hand away, but...

*He knows.*

A slight sob escaped, she had to be open with him. 'I am sorry, Leon. I didn't tell you and I should have done.'

His eyebrows shot up. 'Tell me what, exactly?

She lowered her voice. 'That I was no longer a virgin.'

He released her hand, crossed his arms and simply stared. She rushed on, conscious she was babbling but she couldn't help herself. 'I should have been frank with you. I'm sorry I wasn't. I came to apologise.' When he didn't respond, she swallowed. 'I pray this won't ruin our marriage.'

His expression softened. 'Ruin our marriage? Don't be ridiculous.' He smiled wryly. 'It might surprise you to hear that I was no virgin either.'

Blinking, she let out a choked laugh. 'You don't mind?'

He shrugged. 'I wouldn't say that, but a little reflection made me see that I wanted you as my wife more than I wanted you to have saved yourself for me.' His eyes were kind, his expression earnest. 'Allis, you're my wife and that pleases me very well.'

'I wish I'd told you.'

'You've told me now.'

She caught his hand and wove her fingers into his. 'Do you think Papa knows?'

Leon grimaced. 'I suspect that he might.'

A cold stone lodged in Allis's belly. 'That would explain it.'

'Explain what?'

Allis hesitated. She'd been hurt when she'd realised that her father had offered her to Leon, rather than Leon asking for her hand. However, she'd reconciled herself to it because she cared for Leon, and she assumed her father had chosen him for his skills as a warrior and commander. If that wasn't so, if her father suspected Allis had lost her virginity, he might well have decided to offer her to someone like Leon. Someone who, though noble to his core, didn't have a drop of noble blood in his body.

'I am not sure how to phrase this,' she said carefully. She didn't want to add fuel to the fire by offending him more than she had already.

'Allis, I need to know your mind. Be as blunt as you like.'

'Very well. Leon, Claude would never have objected to my lost maidenhead, all he truly cares about is Eglantine. Most noblemen, however, would certainly have objected.'

Leon nodded. 'You think Lord Michel chose me for my lack of breeding, that he thought me less likely to kick up a fuss.' He shrugged. 'It's possible.'

'I'm sorry, Leon. I hope you don't feel insulted.'

Releasing her hands, he caught her by the waist and aligned her body with his, green eyes suddenly aflame.

'Allis, you and I are a match,' he said fiercely. 'Breeding doesn't come into it.'

Allis stared. Was she imagining it or was there a disturbing edge in his tone when he used the word breeding? Heavens, did he think she was carrying another man's child?

'I am not with child,' she said. 'If that's troubling you, you may dismiss it from your mind.'

'It did occur to me,' he admitted. He gave an odd laugh. 'Although I must say it wasn't my main concern.'

Her eyes widened. 'It wasn't? I find that hard to believe. Most men—'

'I am not most men. As I've already told you, I am happy you are my wife. I gave this some thought earlier. How long were you in the convent?'

'Several weeks.' Her cheeks warmed. She wasn't in the habit of having conversations like this with a man, even if he was her husband. 'In any event, my liaison ended months before that.'

'I assumed as much.'

She laid her palm on his chest. 'I haven't seen that man in an age. There's no way I am carrying his child.'

A gentle finger ran down her cheek. 'So I concluded. There is no need to explain. I understand you married me for expediency. My love, there are worse reasons to marry.'

Allis's heart gave a little leap. Leon had called her his love. It was just a turn of phrase. It didn't mean that he actually loved her. Still, it gave her hope. He was giving every sign he valued her, despite her less than pure past.

'Who was he?' he asked.

She stared at his neck. 'He was a mistake, a stupid mistake. I hope I never see him again.' She shuddered.

'Things got out of hand. I think we forgot ourselves and then suddenly it was too late.'

She could see the pulse beating in Leon's neck. His eyes were like ice. 'The man forced you, is that what you're saying?'

'No. Leon, you must not think that. I regret what happened, but he did *not* force me. I dare say I encouraged him for all the wrong reasons. I was attracted to him, I was curious.' She paused. 'It took me a while to understand this, but mostly I was furious that Papa did not respect my lack of interest in Claude.'

Leon held her gaze, mouth quirking slightly. 'You, my love, are a strong-willed woman. It sounds as though anger drove you into that man's arms.'

'Regrettably, that is probably true. Thinking back, it's hard to see why I found him so appealing. It started off with kisses. I quite liked those. But I didn't realise how far it would lead.' Her cheeks burned and she had to look away. 'When you and I kiss, I begin to melt inside. He didn't make me melt.'

Leon grunted. 'You don't need to tell me that. It is obvious he didn't please you.'

'He most certainly did not.' She lowered her voice. 'You, however, pleased me very much.'

Leon's mouth curved into a smile that bordered on smug. He sobered quickly. 'Where's the fellow now? Does he live in the castle?'

'It wasn't Hugo, if that's what you're thinking. All I did was kiss him.'

'That's a relief. And your so-called lover? I mislike the idea that I might run into him unawares.'

Allis felt her face fall. She didn't know what to say. Claude had mentioned Simon after he'd been knifed.

He hadn't blamed Simon outright but mentioning him in the context of the attack had been strange.

Simon's most endearing quality had always been how much he adored his sister. Claude had got Eglantine with child. Simon could have hoped that Claude would relent and marry her. Why then would he attack Claude? It was such a tangle. Until Allis knew more, she refused to jump to a conclusion.

Leon was watching her, a line between his eyebrows. 'Allis? If the man's not in the castle, where is he?'

'He never stays in one place for long, he might have left the district.'

'I hope to God he has.'

Anxiety had her biting her lip. Theirs wasn't a love match. If Leon became obsessed with the idea that her former lover was watching him, gloating over the fact that he'd taken his wife's virginity, the strain on their marriage could become unbearable.

'He doesn't live in the castle.'

'That's a mercy.' Leon smiled, but it seemed a little forced.

Desperate their marriage shouldn't sour when they had only just begun it, Allis pressed close and drew his head down. 'I need a kiss.'

He obliged, though the kiss was brief. Reserved. Well, she would have none of that, not after last night. She wound her arms about him and ran her hands up and down his back. Up to his impressive shoulders and down over his buttocks.

'Allis, what are you doing?' The hoarseness in his voice was promising.

'Cuddling my husband.'

'Why?'

'Because I wish to.'

'In broad day?'

She went on caressing him. Kissing his jacket over his heart, gripping his narrow waist...

'Allis?'

'Hmm?'

'What if someone comes in?' Leon shifted against her, smothered a groan, and she knew that desire had him in its grip.

'I care not. Kiss me, Leon.' Winding her fingers into his hair she pulled his head down. 'A real kiss,' she murmured against his mouth. 'One that makes me melt.'

The kiss deepened and his body moulded itself to hers. Their breathing quickened. Loud boots tramped past the door. Leon looked at her, eyes shining green fire. 'Like last eve, eh?'

She nodded.

'In that case, we are in the wrong place. My lady, you look fatigued, allow me to escort you to our bedchamber.'

'Thank you, sir.'

As they hurried upstairs, a prayer took form in Allis's mind. *Let our marriage become a true marriage. Please God, let Leon learn to love me.*

They were surely a match. And, provided Leon learned to love her as she loved him, all would be well.


The day after their wedding, Lady Allis and Sir Leon had hidden away for much of the day. They didn't appear at supper. Estelle left a tray outside their bedchamber door. The following morning however, they were up early as usual.

At breakfast, Allis nudged Leon in the ribs. 'We must start the day by thanking the villagers for their gifts.'

Leon had already noticed that Allis was wearing a ribbon bracelet made by one of the housewives. He nodded agreement. 'Naturally.'

They were soon riding towards the village green. After greeting several people, Leon reined in before the tavern. He was about to suggest they ordered refreshments when Allis frowned.

'Leon, did you hear that?' A low groan floated across the green. Allis's gaze followed the direction of the sound, and she caught her breath. 'That's Eglantine's cottage! The baby's coming. Leon, I need to check the midwife is there. You'll wait for me?'

Leon had barely nodded his assent before Allis jumped down from Blackberry and tossed him her reins. She hurried past the tall oak and vanished into the cottage.

It was rare for an unmarried woman to be present at a birth. Despite this, it wouldn't be the first time Allis witnessed a lying in. She had shocked Sybille by attending quite a few and knew what to expect. Eglantine was a petite woman, which meant she might take her time delivering the baby.

Happily, when Allis walked in, she saw that not only was the midwife present, but that Eglantine was smiling between birth pangs. It was a good sign.

For Eglantine's lying in, an alcove to the side of the chimney had been turned into a bedchamber. The birthing chair was positioned next to the bed and, since ancient custom dictated that babies were born more easily when the mother's hair was loose, Eglantine's hair was flowing over her shoulders.

Time passed. Eglantine alternated between being propped up in bed and walking about, holding her belly. Occasionally she sat on the birthing chair, gripped the handles, and allowed the midwife to examine her.

Eglantine's father Isembert was nowhere near as calm. White as whey, he wrung his hands and winced at his daughter's every moan.

After a while, Allis and the midwife exchanged glances.

The midwife sighed. 'Isembert, you are distracting Eglantine. It's best you wait outside.'

Isembert dragged himself outside and Allis followed. The pacing and handwringing continued. 'What will become of Eglantine when I am gone, my lady?' he muttered. 'She will become an outcast.'

'Nonsense. Eglantine is too well loved for that.' As the words left her, Allis wondered whether that was true. Eglantine was indeed loved, but the villagers could be narrow minded. In his role as reeve, Isembert was a man of some importance, but he didn't have the influence of a nobleman. Did he have the authority to overcome the prejudice his daughter might encounter?

Allis looked across at the tavern. Hours earlier, she had run out to suggest that Leon return to the castle. He'd promised to send a couple of his men to watch over her. In case, he had said, you find you need assistance. Sure enough, Stefe was seated outside with Vézian, Leon's sergeant. They were laughing uproariously with Flora, one of the serving girls. Catching Stefe's eye, Allis nodded his way. At once, he rose and hurried towards her. They met in the middle of the green, beneath the oak tree.

'Is all well with Eglantine, my lady?' Stefe asked.

'I believe so. You know her?'

Stefe jerked his head towards the tavern, and faint colour darkened his sun-burned cheeks. 'Not personally, my lady. Flora was concerned. Eglantine is friendly with Flora.'

Allis lifted an eyebrow. 'I see.'

Stepping back a pace, Stefe saluted. 'If you need anything, please be assured we'll be at the tavern.'

'Thank you, Stefe.'

Thoughtfully, Allis walked back towards the cottage. Never had she been so conscious of the many blessings she had received. Chief among them that her father had seen Leon's potential and allowed her to marry him. She'd also been fortunate in that Simon hadn't left her with child, but even if he had, her status would have given her some protection. Papa, though strict, was kind. Allis felt her mouth tighten. Was it right that her father's status meant she would never have to deal with the difficulties Eglantine might face?

Her mouth tasted bitter. It wasn't right. It wasn't just. Nor was it something Allis could ignore. She had to help Eglantine.

Outside the cottage, the reeve was still tense and white-faced. He looked bleakly at her. 'My lady, not everyone is as accepting as you are. The child will be illegitimate. It will have no name, no status whatsoever.'

'Isembert, I promise I will aid you.'

'That's kind, my lady, though I fail to see what you can do.'

'Have faith, Isembert. I will think of something.' It was a vow Allis intended to keep. Knowing Eglantine was in safe hands, she kept Isembert company until, finally, they heard the reedy cry of a newborn babe and rushed inside. Eglantine was lying against the pillows, a small bundle fast in her arms.

'Father, come and see,' Her face was alight with love. 'She is the most beautiful baby.'

Isembert stumbled to his daughter and held out his arms.

Allis sank thoughtfully on to the stool by the fire.

Two hours later, Allis and Isembert were sitting on a wall bench in the Galard family chapel. Allis kept a wary eye on the door. Papa and Sybille were due any moment. Meanwhile, Isembert was clutching his new granddaughter and staring at her like a man in love.

When the chapel door swung open, Allis held her breath. She had no idea how her father would react. Still, she had an ally in her stepmother and she wasn't surprised Sybille reached Isembert first.

'Isembert, what a gorgeous child! Do let me hold her.' Sybille cooed and smiled and displayed the infant to her husband. 'Look, Michel, she has the look of Claude.'

Allis's father grunted. 'Can't see it myself, babies all look the same.'

'Never say so. Look at her nose. And the shape of her eyes.' Sybille gave her husband a wistful look. 'I believe we should send a letter to Carpentras. Claude needs to know that he's a father.'

Lord Michel made a sound that was neither agreement nor disagreement. Watching him frown pensively at the baby, Allis sent up a swift prayer. She'd been hoping that sight of his godson's tiny daughter would move him in a way that words and arguments never could. She crossed her fingers and prayed.

'Robert is a grandfather,' Sybille added softly. 'We must write to him too.'

'Write? Hmm. Perhaps.' Lord Michel nodded at Isembert. 'Your daughter is well?'

'Thank you, my lord, she is.'

'Glad to hear it. Is she well enough to travel to Carpentras tomorrow?'

Allis and Sybille exchanged conspiratorial smiles. Most village women worked soon after their babies were born. Eglantine would be no exception. She was certainly well enough to travel.

Isembert's eyes bulged. 'Carpentras, my lord?'

'Aye. You shall escort your daughter,' her father said. 'I'll be sending a letter to Lord Robert, make sure he gets it. And for pity's sake, stop looking so nervous. My wife spoke the truth. That child does indeed have the look of my godson.' He paused. 'I take it you'll go? With your daughter and grandchild, of course. Mind, I can't say how you will be received when you get there.'

Isembert searched his lord's face and a wary smile dawned. 'Thank you, my lord. Eglantine will be delighted to have the chance to meet Sir Claude's father. We'll take the risk.'

'Fine. I assume you won't need long to pack?'

'No, my lord.'

'Very well. A cart will be sent to your cottage, the three of you can travel in that.'

Allis rose, looped her hand in her father's arm and kissed his cheek. 'Thank you, Papa. Thank you.'

Leon was in his office, working steadily through what seemed to be a never-ending list of tasks, when someone rapped on the door.

'Enter!'

A guard stood there, scroll in hand. Leon repressed a sigh at what would undoubtedly mean more desk work when he needed to exorcise a few more demons with a bout on the field with his men. 'From Lord Michel?'

'No, sir.' The guard handed the scroll over. Unusually, it was addressed to Leon himself. Even more unusual, it had no seal. It was tied with string. 'A carter brought it.'

'A carter?' How strange.

'Aye, he brought a consignment of wine for Lord Michel. Your letter came with it.'

'My thanks.'

The guard went out and Leon untied the string. The handwriting was neat and small. He didn't recognise it, which came as no surprise.

*The Convent of the Sisters of Saint Claire, Avignon*
*Michaelmas, the Year of Our Lord 1341*

*To Sir Leonidàs of Tarascon*

*Greetings, Sir,*
*I hope this letter finds you in good health.*
  *What I am about to disclose will undoubtedly come as a revelation to you, indeed I can scarcely credit it myself. Permit me to introduce myself.*
  *I am a nun at Saint Claire's Convent, and my name is Sister Catharine. I arrived as a refugee and have been here for nigh on twenty years. I took my profession sixteen years ago and the convent has become my home.*
  *You will, I am sure, be wondering at my presumption in writing to you. I beg you, bear with me. I will be as brief as I can. I am hiding in the scriptorium as Mother Margerie has no notion I am writing to you. Indeed, she would doubtless give me a penance for each bead on my rosary should she discover I have done so without her permission.*
  *Yesterday, I overheard our novices talking in the cloisters and what one of them said amazed me. As I understand it, sir, you might have met her, for she is the youngest daughter of Lord Michel Galard, Count of Arles. Her name is Bernadette. Rather unusually, Mother Margerie gave*

*Novice Bernadette permission to return home to attend her sister's wedding.*

*Imagine my astonishment when Novice Bernadette mentioned that her sister's husband is none other than Sir Leonidàs of Tarascon, the leader of a band of warriors who has forged a great name for himself and his men. I understand your troop are known as The Lions of Languedoc.*

*Sir Leonidàs, your reputation does you proud.*

*I spoke to Novice Bernadette and asked her to describe you. I apologise if you feel this was intrusive, but I have good reason to do so.*

*Before I joined our Order I had a younger brother named Leon. The last time I set eyes on him I had seen nine summers and my brother four. My brother had green eyes and dark hair.*

Leon forgot to breathe. Had his sister Blancha written this letter? No, it was surely impossible. Why would Blancha take refuge in the very city which had become home to the man who had destroyed Monteaux? And why become a nun when the Church had declared their people heretics?

He spread the scroll on the desk, weighed it down with the handbell and an ink pot, and continued to read.

*We lived with our parents in a small hamlet in the foothills of the Pyrenees. My name in those days was Blancha. We were a family of shepherds, as were most of the villagers. Our lives were simple. We didn't have much, but until the arrival of the local bishop we were content.*

*Please understand that for the sake of discretion I am omitting much.*

*After Papá and Mamá were taken I looked ev-
erywhere for my brother. When I couldn't find
him, I fled. I have thought of him often. I prayed
for him to survive. If, as I hope, you are he, I beg
you to come the convent. I long to see you and
will do my utmost to meet you.*

*As to the rest, it can keep until I see you. Nov-
ice Bernadette mentioned that the wine merchant's carter is an honest man, so if you are not
my brother and are unable to come you might en-
trust your reply to him.*

*Please keep this letter close. Should I be mis-
taken, and you are not my brother, I would appreciate a message to that effect.*

*God keep you, Sir Leonidàs. I wish you well in
your marriage. God bless you.*

*Sister Catharine*
*The Order of Saint Claire, Avignon*

Leon stared in disbelief at the letter. His heart was
thudding and his hands shaking. He reread every word.
He stared at them until the letters blurred and whirled.
Then, Blancha's letter firmly in hand, he went to find
his wife. A maidservant told him that Eglantine's baby
had been born and though Lady Allis had come to the
castle with the reeve and his new granddaughter, they
had all returned to the village.

## Chapter Sixteen

Leon rode to Eglantine's cottage. A cart was positioned outside, and as he dismounted Stefe and Vézian staggered out bearing a travelling chest. They heaved it on to the cart. Flora emerged next, a basket of linens in hand. She handed the basket to Stefe and as she did do, Leon saw her run her fingers over Stefe's. Stefe flushed to his ears.

'Stefe, Lady Allis says they will leave on the morrow,' Flora said. 'She asks that you find a suitable cover to protect everything from the dew.'

Stefe grinned. 'As my lady commands.' Stefe noticed Leon and straightened. 'Sir Leon. Do you need me, sir?'

'Not at present.' Leon waved a dismissive hand and dismounted. 'Carry on.'

He went inside. Allis was sitting on the edge of Eglantine's bed, the babe in her arms.

'Leon, welcome. I thought you were in the office.'

'I was.' Leon smiled at Eglantine. 'Congratulations on the birth of your daughter.'

'Thank you, sir.'

Allis handed the child back to her mother.

'Allis, I have received a letter from Avignon. I'd be glad if you read it.'

'Certainly.'

As soon as Allis had reassured herself that Isembert was content to oversee the loading of the cart, Leon took her to a table outside the tavern, ordered small beer for them both and pulled his letter out of his tunic. Allis read in silence. Frowned. She shot him a penetrating glance and went back to the letter.

'Sister Catharine refers to the local bishop of your village,' she said softly. 'Is that who I think it is?'

Lean nodded, replying equally softly. 'The Bishop of Pamiers. Formerly Jacques Fournier.'

'Now known as Pope Benedict the Twelfth.' Allis studied the letter. 'I see she writes the words for mother and father in the Occitan style.'

'Aye.'

'Leon, this is very convincing.' Allis looked at him, eyes troubled. 'Do you think Blancha—I mean Sister Catharine—is in danger in Avignon?'

Lean curled his fingers into a fist before allowing them to relax. 'I do not believe so, particularly since she has taken vows that tie her to the Church. So much time has elapsed. Most massacres aimed at the annihilation of my people took place years, if not decades before the destruction of Monteaux. I've come to see that many of them happened for political rather than religious reasons.'

'They were about claiming land, you mean?'

'Yes. They were about sovereignty. About wealth and power.'

Allis covered his hand with hers. 'The other day I asked Papa about the Cathars—don't be concerned, I mentioned no names—and he said that poor people were pawns in a much larger game.'

'That's it. And what happened in Monteaux has not been repeated.'

'It's over then?'

'I believe so.'

Her hand tightened on his. 'You'll want to see Sister Catharine as soon as possible. It's too late this evening. We'll go tomorrow.'

Heart swelling, Leon lifted Allis's hand and kissed it. 'Thank you, *chérie*.'

At dawn the next morning, Allis woke to a loud rapping on their bedchamber door.

'Sir Leon!' It was Othon's voice. 'You are needed downstairs.'

Leon groaned. Unsurprisingly, he had been preoccupied last night. He had listened to Allis's account of Eglantine's lying in and of Papa agreeing to write to Lord Robert, but it was obvious he wasn't hearing her. In the end, understanding he could think of little but his sister and what it would be like to greet her after all these years, Allis had fallen silent.

The doorlatch rattled. 'It's urgent, sir.'

Allis poked him in the ribs. 'That's your captain. You must get up.'

Leon stumbled out of bed and when he had gone, Allis summoned Estelle. While she dressed Estelle filled the silence with chatter.

'I think it's wonderful that your father has sent Eglantine and the baby to Carpentras, don't you?'

'Aye, Estelle, it is indeed.'

'Do you think Sir Claude will marry Eglantine?'

Allis murmured something non-committal about Lord Robert having a say in the matter and as soon as her hair was plaited and pinned, she left Estelle to her speculations and hurried down to the hall.

Leon was standing with her father and Othon by the high table. Her father's colour was alarmingly high. Voices were strained. The three of them were obviously in the midst of an intense and frank discussion.

'My lord,' Leon's voice was clipped. Professional. 'Peire is like a son to me, I must go after him. Othon says he's not been gone long. God willing, I can catch him before he does any damage.'

'What the blazes is he doing charging off to Avignon?' her father growled. 'The blasted boy's a hot-head. One of the grooms heard him muttering about vengeance. I hope to hell no one else in your troop thinks as he does.'

Peire had gone to Avignon? Allis recalled various remarks that the boy had made concerning revenge. She also remembered his savage expression when he had reminded Leon that the troop were looking to him to provide satisfaction for past wrongs.

Leon had called the boy bloodthirsty. Without doubt, Peire's decision to go to Avignon was troubling. Leon must be worried beyond reason. He was clearly fond of the boy, yet this turn of events put Leon in an awkward position. At present, he looked determined. Calm and competent.

'My lord.' Othon stepped forward, interrupting her train of thought. 'Not long ago many of us would have agreed with Peire. Coming to Galard has changed us.'

'I hope to God that's true, Captain,' her father said, irritably. 'There is enough discord in this world without the Lions making matters worse. The last thing we need is for someone to stir up long-forgotten prejudices against the Cathars.'

Allis froze. No wonder everyone looked so tense. Leon had clearly told her father everything.

A muscle twitched in Leon's jaw. 'My lord, my men

have always fought for justice. Our commission here, together with the trust you placed in us, has strengthened our determination to abandon all thought of reprisal.'

'Except, it would seem, for your squire,' Lord Michel said drily. 'To what end, I ask? An early grave?'

'Rest assured, my lord, I shall find Peire before damage is done.'

Leon was wearing his leather gambeson and his riding gloves were tucked into his belt. He glanced briefly at her, eyes so remote Allis knew he was about to ride out. Had she not come down so swiftly, he would have gone without her. A chill stole over her. Leon was a proud man. She had already hurt him by not telling him soon enough about her lack of innocence. She wasn't about to permit Peire's folly to drive another wedge between them.

She turned to Othon. 'Captain, Estelle is in our bedchamber. Ask her to bring me my cloak, riding boots and purse. Tell her I shall be in the stable. Please hurry.'

She ran down the steps and into the bailey, calling for a groom to saddle Blackberry. Though it was warm, the sky was overcast, a dismal grey that promised rain.

Estelle ran up as Blackberry was led out. She eyed the assembling men. 'Where are you all going, my lady?'

'Avignon.' Allis kicked off her shoes, dragged on her riding boots, and secured her purse at her waist. Leon was already at the gate, at the head of a small contingent. She told herself that it was a good sign that Leon was taking so few men. If he expected serious trouble, more of the troop would surely be going with him. And he would be wearing his helmet.

She mounted swiftly. A worm of doubt gnawed at her as she kicked Blackberry forward. 'I won't be left behind,' she muttered. She knew Leon heard her because he lifted a dark eyebrow. She could read nothing from his expression, the infuriating man. He might be a little thankful, she was trying to support him.

'We will ride hard,' Leon said to the troop at large. He gestured at Vézian. 'Sergeant, if my lady drops behind, be sure to stay with her.'

Allis swallowed down a rush of anger and swore to keep up if it was the last thing she did.

Leon was true to his word, he set a brisk pace. A light drizzle soon darkened his gambeson and those of his men who, like him, were but lightly armed. His sword was strapped at his side and his helmet and shield were looped over his saddlebow. He was not wearing full armour for the same reason he was only taking a handful of men. He had no wish for his party to be conspicuous.

His wife displayed her usual fighting spirit and when the walls of Avignon appeared, jutting out here and there along the city boundaries, she was still at his side. Her cloak was dark with damp and her veil was sticking to her cheeks. Blackberry's flanks were heaving and lathered with sweat.

'Where do you think to find him?' Allis asked. 'Near the Papal Palace?'

'It's largely a building site,' Leon said. 'But it's a good place to start. That lad can climb like a monkey. It's my guess he'll be up on those workmen's walkways hunting for a way in.'

Allis closed her eyes. 'I hope to God he doesn't succeed.'

Puddles glistened outside the Papal Palace. As Leon had mentioned, most of the palace walls were lost behind a network of wooden scaffolding.

'The square is unusually quiet,' Allis murmured. 'There are no workmen up on the platforms.'

Leon narrowed his eyes on the scaffolding. 'It's probably slippery up there. Perhaps they are waiting for the ladders and walkways to dry out.'

'Showers don't usually stop them. It's very strange.'

They rode on, rounding a corner. A hooded figure was squatting like the most miserable of gargoyles at the far end of a walkway. It was Peire, no question.

'Leon,' Allis whispered. 'Do you see him?'

The boy obviously saw them at the same moment, for he flung back his hood and shot to his feet. 'Sir Leon!'

Leon set a hand to his hip. 'What the devil do you think you are doing? Come down this instant!'

Rather to Allis's surprise, Peire did as he was told, scrambling down with some dexterity.

'You seem to have developed a hump,' Leon said coldly. 'Show me what's under your cloak.'

Shame-faced, Peire fumbled with his cloak and pulled out a bow. A quiver of arrows was strapped to his back.

Eyes hard as stone, Leon shook his head. 'What did you think to achieve?'

Peire stared sullenly into a puddle. 'I reckon you know what I hoped to achieve, sir.'

'Peire, it's true your family were wronged, but what happened to them had nothing to do with the Pope. You cannot use him as a scapegoat.' Pointedly, Leon looked about. 'It's quiet as the grave here. What happened?'

Peire shrugged. 'Nothing. The Pope's away. I asked why it was so quiet and was told he's ailing. He's gone to the country.'

Allis and Leon exchanged relieved glances.

'And your horse?' Leon enquired.

'At The Crossed Keys.'

'Very well. Hand me that bow. We intend to dry out at The Crossed Keys and you, my lad, can do some explaining.'

Peire wiped his nose with the back of his hand. He looked close to tears. Utterly miserable and impossibly young 'I dare say you won't believe me, sir, but when I arrived and found the devil was away, I was actually relieved.'

Leon leaned on the pommel of his saddle. 'Oh?'

'I can't explain it. I no longer wanted to kill him.' He gulped. 'I couldn't stop thinking about what you would say.'

'And what would that be?'

'Killing the old and vulnerable is never honourable. Never.'

Imperturbably, Leon nodded. 'You have caused a great deal of trouble and you will be disciplined.'

'I am truly sorry, sir.'

Leon grunted. 'Come, everyone is soaked, we need to dry out.'


Peire had his other weapons seized and when they reached The Crossed Keys, he was put under guard. Then, having given Vézian strict orders to ensure the boy didn't move as much as a finger, Leon was able to contemplate taking Allis to meet his sister. As his wife didn't hesitate to point out, her presence would guarantee Leon's entry to Saint Claire's. Allis would, she told him, ask to see Lady Bernadette, leaving Leon free to talk to his sister alone. When their visit was over, Leon and Allis would rendezvous with the troop at the inn and return to Castle Galard as one party.


Leon approached the convent with a dry mouth. He dismounted and went to ring the bell, hoping most fervently that Sister Catharine would turn out to be Blancha. It was fortunate he wasn't in full armour. It wouldn't do to meet his sister for the first time in over twenty years as a faceless warrior. His rain-soaked gambeson was probably off-putting enough.

In her letter, Sister Catharine had mentioned knowing he was a soldier and from the little he recalled of his sister, she had been a sensible girl. If Sister Catharine was indeed Blancha sight of him in full military attire should not truly alarm her. However, he'd never forget Allis making a point of informing him that she preferred to see his expression as they talked. Leon wanted his sister to see him as a man, not a faceless warrior.

He rolled his shoulders and sent Allis a tight smile. Realising that Blancha might yet be alive had turned what he knew of the world on its head. If Blancha was here, all these years he hadn't been alone. He had had a sister, even if she had retreated from the world.

While they waited for a response from inside the convent, he smiled grimly to himself. 'Allis, Mother Margerie has your sister's dowry—will we be forced to resort to bribery to gain entry?'

'I don't think there will be any difficulty. We should be welcome until Bernadette has taken her vows.' With a grin, his wife patted her purse. 'Nevertheless, I like to prepare for all contingencies. I have coin with me. If need be, we can appease her with a donation to convent coffers.'

The shutter behind the grille in the door rattled and opened. The face of an elderly nun appeared in the gap. She was vaguely familiar.

'Good day, Sir Leonidàs.'

'You remember my name?'

A brief smile added more creases to the nun's cheeks. 'Sister Catharine warned me that you might come calling.'

The shutter closed. The key grated, bolts were shot back, and the door creaked open.

Leon smiled. 'As you see, Sister, my wife is with me.' He gestured at Titan and Blackberry. 'We cannot leave our horses unattended in the street.'

'Welcome, my lady,' the nun said, before glancing back at the horses. 'Very well, bring them in. There's a ring in the wall.'

They led the horses into the narrow courtyard while the nun meticulously closed and secured the door.

'Sir, since it might rain again,' the nun said, 'you may wait in the lodge while I fetch Sister Catharine. Lady Allisende, I assume you would like to see Novice Bernadette. Please, come with me.'

Allis and the elderly nun went under the arch and shortly afterwards another nun came running across the courtyard, her grey habit swirling around her ankles.

'Sir Leonidàs, bless you for coming.' The nun came to an abrupt halt at the lodge entrance and stared up at him, shaking her head. 'Save for your eyes, I would not have known you.'

'Nor I you,' Leon murmured, searching for Blancha in the features of the comfortable-looking nun before him. He held out his hands and Blancha—Sister Catharine—stepped forward, tears in her eyes. Brown eyes. His sister had had brown eyes.

'You are so large,' the nun murmured. Then she tipped her head to one side and winked. 'Little Leon has grown so tall.'

Leon's stomach lurched as the years fell away. This was Blancha, he had no doubt. That wink, that slight tilt to her head. The warmth in her eyes. Goose pimples raced over his skin.

'Blancha.'

'Leon.'

He flung his arms about her and briefly the portress's lodge was lost behind a prickle of tears. A maelstrom of buried feelings roared up inside. Tearing loss. Agonising pain. Blind terror. Releasing a shuddering breath, he watched his sister wipe her eyes with the edge of her veil.

She gave a shaky laugh. 'What a miracle you are safe,' she said, waving him to the chair by the table. She pulled out a stool for herself and glanced back at the courtyard. 'Leon, we must speak quietly. No one in the convent knows where I come from.'

'I understand.' He gestured towards the cloisters and lowered his voice. 'What I cannot understand is how you came to enter a convent when our parents were killed as heretics. You joined the very Church that destroyed our family. Why?'

'I took the veil because I decided a convent would be the last place the Inquisitor would look for a Cathar. Of course, I had no idea that he would be made Pope and would soon follow me to Avignon.'

'That must have been a blow.'

Her brows lifted. 'That, Leon, is an understatement.'

'Yet you stayed?'

Blancha shrugged. 'Aye. After the horrors, I found that the contemplative life suits me. I have no need to leave the convent. I stay within these walls.'

'All the time? You're never tempted to venture into the city?

'Never. But that is enough about me.' She gripped his hand. 'Tell me how you escaped.'

'When the village was burned, I looked everywhere for you,' he said softly.

'How much do you remember?'

'When the fires started, I hid in the scrub with the other children,' Leon said. 'I crept back to the village a few times, hoping to find someone a little older. I searched all over. Scratched around to find food.'

'After Mamà and Papà were taken, I came back to look for you too,' Blancha said.

'I'm sure. It wasn't surprising you didn't find me. I took care to remain hidden.'

'Leon, you were so small. How in heaven's name did you survive?' She looked him up and down and sent him a faint smile. 'I see you found food.'

Leon lost track of time as he and Blancha talked. Not wishing to distress her, he passed swiftly over the hardships of his childhood and went on to speak of his time at Tarascon.

'So that is how you became a knight,' she said, when he had finished. 'It's strange to think you command your own troop. I've heard they are known as The Lions of Languedoc.'

He shrugged. 'I was lucky.'

Blancha shook her head. 'You must have trained incredibly hard. You have talent. Leon, I am proud of you. Now tell me the rest, if you please.'

'The rest?'

'You're married, or so Novice Bernadette said. I want to hear about Lady Allisende.'

'Aye, I'm married.'

'She makes you happy?'

'Very much so.' Leon felt himself smile. The sense of certainty was terrifying. 'I love her,' he said softly, trying the words out on his tongue. 'I love her.'

'Leon, that is marvellous.'

Marvellous indeed, Leon thought. And it would be even more marvellous if Allis found it in her heart to love him back. He was filled with an urgency to tell her. He had blundered his way through his proposal by not confessing immediately that her father had suggested they marry. She had forgiven him and, despite his disappointment when he'd learned about her previous lover, her swift apology and obvious desire to make a success of their marriage was promising. 'We cross swords occasionally, but we talk about everything,' he said. 'That has to be a good sign.'

'I am sure it is.' His sister looked earnestly at him. 'Leon, you may not remember, but Mamà and Papà crossed swords sometimes. They talked about everything too. It's natural. I hope you don't doubt her.'

'Allis? Never.' The shrewd look in his sister's eyes told him that she understood his feelings ran deep. 'Would you care to meet her? She's somewhere in the convent talking to Novice Bernadette.'

Blancha's eyes lit up. 'I'd love to meet her, of course.' She jumped up from the stool. 'Where did they go?'

'I am not sure. They went through that arch into the cloisters.'

'They're probably in the visitors' lodge. Wait here, I'll fetch them.'

As Leon stared through the arch towards the cloisters, he became aware of an unusual warmth in the region of his chest. He'd never understood what was meant when someone said their heart was singing. Today he did. His heart was definitely singing. Not only was he married to the woman he loved but his long-lost sister was found.

He heard a light laugh. Allis. She came through the arch with her sister on one side and his on her other. Their hands were linked and all three were smiling.

The words *I love you, Allis* hovered on the tip of his

tongue. He bit them back. This was not the right time. He would wait until they were alone. Irritating though it was, Leon would save his declaration for when he had his wife's undivided attention. He loved her with all his heart, and he hoped and prayed that she loved him. For it was love, rather than their marriage, that had made Galard his home.

The four of them were soon talking as though they had known each other for years.

'It is such a pleasure to meet you, Sister,' Allis said to Blancha. 'I have prayed for a happy outcome, ever since Leon told me about you.'

They talked and talked until, eventually, a bell rang. Lady Bernadette rose. 'Sister Catharine, we ought to go. Mother Margerie will expect us in chapel.'

'So she will. Leon, bless you for coming. Seeing you has lifted a weight from my heart. I feel reborn.'

'Will you see us again?'

His sister's expression clouded. 'It may not be permitted. Strictly speaking, we're not meant to have visitors, though it does happen sometimes.'

Allis cleared her throat. She was patting her bulging purse. 'We could bring a monetary gift.'

Blancha gave a splutter of laughter. 'I've never known Mother Margerie turn down a gift.'

'Then *au revoir* for the time being, Sister Catharine,' Leon said. 'I look forward to seeing you again soon.'

Amid a flurry of hugs and kisses, they exchanged promises of further visits and left the convent.

# Chapter Seventeen

It was late afternoon when they reached Galard village. The merchants' stalls were open for business. Leon was counting down the moments until he could have Allis to himself, and he realised he would have to wait a little longer when her gaze strayed longingly towards the cloth stall. He recalled her stepmother saying she was on the lookout for some English worsted. Winter jackets must be made for the newly enlarged household, which meant, Leon realised, he and his men.

Seeing Allis, the cloth merchant's face lit up. 'Good afternoon, my lady.'

Allis reined in. 'Good afternoon, Jean. Your wife is well, I hope?'

'Very well, my lady, thank you for asking.'

Allis looked questioningly at Leon. 'Are you in a hurry to get back?'

Leon leaned on his pommel. 'I'm in no rush. Please, look your fill.'

'Thank you, I will.' Dismounting, Allis handed him Blackberry's reins.

Leon caught Vézian's eye. 'That will be all, Sergeant, you may take the men back to the castle. My squire is to muck out the stables.' At Peire's grimace, Leon looked coolly at him. 'There'll be no whingeing. Mark you, Lord Michel is extremely disappointed. Do a good job in the stables and I'll put a word in on your behalf.'

'Thank you, sir,' came the chastened reply.

Having dismissed their escort, Leon turned to Allis. She was fingering a bolt of green cloth.

'Leon, this is very fine. See how well the green matches the Galard colours.' She arched an eyebrow. 'And with your eyes, it will suit you too.'

'I knew it,' Leon said drily. 'You married me because I will look well in the Galard livery.'

'So I did, sir. Why else would I wed you?' She smiled warmly at him, so teasingly, it quite removed any sting from her words.

At which point Leon's tongue tied itself in knots to lock in his declaration. He was so slow in responding that Allis glanced across the square. She stiffened and let go of the green worsted. The teasing light was gone. She was white as a sheet.

Leon followed her gaze. Smoke was creeping out from under the door of Eglantine's cottage. There were no flames and the roof looked sound. How very strange. His mind began to race. The cottage had a working chimney, it must have been blocked. The only reason he could think of for doing such a thing was that whoever was in there was trying to hide. They clearly hadn't bargained for all that smoke.

Biting her lip, Allis turned back to the cloth merchant. 'Thank you, Jean, that is all for today. Be assured I will return later.'

The cloth merchant bowed. 'I look forward to it, my lady.'

Leaning out, Leon touched Allis's shoulder. 'Didn't Eglantine and her father take the infant to Carpentras?'

Mouth tight, Allis shook him off, picked up her skirts and marched towards the cottage.

'Allis, wait!' Leon swung off Titan. 'Jean…' he held the merchant's gaze '…would you take charge of our horses?'

'Yes, sir.'

The man might have said more, Leon didn't wait to hear, he was too busy racing after his wife. 'Allis!' What did she think she was doing? Protecting the reeve's cottage? Anyone could have broken in. The shutters were closed which was odd for the time of day, so if anyone was inside, they were definitely hiding. A gang of thieves? An outlaw? A murderer?

'Don't go in. *Allis!*'

He was wasting his breath. She took no notice, lifted the latch, and entered. Leon tore after her.

The main room was dark. Acrid air stung his eyes and caught at the back of his throat. The fire was sluggish. Badly built, it was burning so close to the front of the hearth that orange embers spilled across the floor. A lone pot hung over the flames. Leon had no doubt but that the chimney had been blocked in a crude attempt to conceal the fact that the cottage was being used as a hiding place. It was a dangerous and stupid mistake. The entire cottage could yet be reduced to ash.

He wedged the door open to expel the worst of the smoke and opened a shutter to admit more light. To one side of the hearth, he made out two figures. Allis was staring at a man Leon hadn't seen before. A knife flashed.

A heartbeat later, Leon was across the room. Reacting instinctively, he punched the fellow square in the jaw and watched him fall to his knees before toppling to the floor.

Allis let out a shaky laugh and something in her posture touched a nerve.

'You know him?'

She covered her face with her hands and nodded. 'To my shame, yes.' Her voice cracked.

Leon looked from his wife to the dark-haired man on the floor. Through the clearing smoke he could see that the fellow was well-built. His skin was swarthy, he must spend most of his time outdoors. His features were regular and clear cut. In all, he was remarkably good looking. It was easy to imagine women falling over their feet to gain his attention. Leon hadn't been at Galard long, but he recognised faces. This man was a stranger.

'I've not seen him before,' he said slowly.

Allis looked across, eyes clouded with worry. 'I don't suppose you have.'

The words of a guard at the castle gatehouse came back to him: *'That Simon is a handsome devil.'*

Leon's stomach knotted. 'He's called Simon.'

'Aye.'

'Eglantine's brother?'

A nod.

'And your lover.' A rush of understanding roared through Leon in a confused flood of feeling. Jealousy. No, not jealousy, for this man held no claim on Allis's heart. Anger, rather. Fury. Leon nudged the fellow with the toe of his boot. This was the careless ne'er-do-well who let pleasure rule him. He'd robbed Allis of her innocence with no thought for the consequences. He'd botched things so badly that it was amazing the wretch hadn't given her a lifelong aversion to men and marriage.

And there she stood, white about the mouth, eyes huge. She was staring at Leon as though her world had collapsed.

'My lover?' she whispered. 'I suppose you might call him that.' She hung her head. Her hands were bunched into fists. Leon couldn't bear to see her in such distress, she who had done nothing wrong, save fall for a handsome face. He strode across, took her hands, and encouraged her fingers to unclench. They were ice cold.

'Allis?'

She looked up, eyes drowning in misery.

'It's all right, my love.'

'Is it?'

'It is.' Leon slipped an arm about her shoulders and hugged her to him. 'Don't upset yourself over him. He's not worth it.'

She clutched his arm. 'Leon, I'm not upsetting myself over him.' Her eyes were glassy with tears. She blinked impatiently and her jaw dropped. 'You're not angry.'

'Oh, I'm angry,' Leon admitted, 'but not with you.'

Wonder dawned on her face. 'Truly? I… I was sure you would be outraged.'

'Of course not. You've explained how it was. He didn't treat you well. You didn't enjoy it. The man's nothing but a scoundrel.'

'It started with kisses. I liked it at first. He got carried away.' Her voice wobbled. 'And then it was too late.'

'He's an irresponsible fool. Allis, it was not your fault.'

She sagged against him. Hugged him back. 'Thank heaven you understand.'

'It was not your fault.'

Allis peered at the man on the floor. 'Leon, I was under the impression he'd left the district.'

'So was I,' Leon said. The way Allis had responded on their wedding night had told him more than words could ever do that she had no feelings for this Simon.

However, it was hard to imagine that any man, having known her, would give her up without a struggle.

'Allis, just now he was threatening you with a knife.'

She gestured at the pot over the fire. 'He was cooking, Leon, that's all. Cooking.'

'Is he violent? Do you think he's dangerous? Jealous, perhaps?'

'Simon? Jealous?'

'You were his lover, and you were meant to marry Claude.'

'It's possible Simon's pride was injured when I told him that what had happened between us would never happen again. He accepted it, though. He knew from the outset that our liaison had no future. Besides, he is the most outrageous flirt. I fell for his looks and didn't discover until far too late that he likes nothing better than to flit from one woman to the next.'

'Aye, I heard that elsewhere.'

'Oh?'

'It's amazing what you learn in the guardhouse.'

'The guardhouse?' Allis went red. 'Don't tell me that the men know that Simon and I...?' Her voice faded.

'Be easy. Your name was not coupled with his.'

'That's a mercy.' She sighed, rubbing her brow. 'Leon, something's been bothering me about Claude's injury. He was incredibly vague when I asked him how it happened. He insisted he didn't see who stabbed him, and then in the next breath he mentioned Simon.'

Leon stilled. '*Chérie*, this must be investigated.'

'Must it? Leon, I very much doubt that Simon is capable of violence like that.' Her shoulders drooped. 'On the other hand, I've thought for some while that the only woman Simon truly loves is his sister. If he felt vindictive towards anyone it is likely to have been Claude.'

Leon nodded. 'Because Sir Claude got Eglantine with child and Simon feared she was about to be cast aside.'

'Exactly.'

Simon stirred and groaned. His nose was bleeding. In case Allis was mistaken and the fellow became aggressive, Leon set her firmly behind him. He would never take chances with Allis's safety. 'Trust me, my love,' he muttered, for her ears only.

Hand to his nose, Simon scuttled crabwise away from Leon. 'You broke my nose,' he said thickly.

To Leon's ears he sounded surprised, which rankled. 'You were waving a knife about in front of my lady. You're lucky to come off so lightly.'

'I wouldn't hurt Allis!'

'So she informs me. However, from what I hear, you may not be so squeamish where Sir Claude is concerned.'

Simon took his hand from his nose, stared blankly at the blood on his palm and wiped it on his jacket. 'I've no idea what you're talking about.'

Leon leaned down, took him by the arm, and hauled him towards the door. 'You are coming with me.'

Allis followed. Leon was thankful to see she kept well out of the man's reach.

Simon blinked. 'Where are we going?'

'To hand you over to the castle guard. A few hours in a cell will doubtless clear your thoughts. Unless, of course, you are prepared to tell us whether you were responsible for the attack on Sir Claude.'

Simon's hand was back over his nose—he was clearly in pain. He coughed. Groaned. 'I might have hauled him off his horse.' His gaze met Leon's. 'I didn't mean to scratch him, but my knife got in the way.'

Allis gasped. 'You might have killed him!'

Simon glowered. 'Sir Claude is no better than a

beast, getting my sister with child and then refusing to marry her.'

Leon let out a harsh laugh. 'Your reputation is no better. How many women have you abandoned? How many children have you sired? Do you even care?'

Silence.

'You, my man, are coming with me. Lord Michel will be interested to hear what you know about the attack on his godson.' Ignoring his wife's gasp of dismay, Leon hauled Simon back to the horses.

His declaration of love would have to wait. He could only hope that after this debacle, Allis would accept it.

By the time they reached her father's office, Allis's nerves were in tatters. She trailed in behind Leon and Simon, heart beating like a drum. Thankfully Papa was alone. Did he know about her less than perfect past? Had he known all along? Allis wanted her father to have supported her marriage to Leon because he'd seen Leon's merit. It would be dreadful if her misguided, reckless affair with Simon was the real reason Papa had asked Leon to propose to her.

Her father leaned an arm along the armrest of his chair and studied Simon and his bloodied nose. 'You're the reeve's son, as I recall. You're Simon, a pedlar.'

'Yes, my lord.'

Leon leaned past Allis and closed the door. 'Excuse us for interrupting you, my lord,' he said, 'but my lady and I have recently discovered that this man is implicated in the incident in which Sir Claude was injured.'

'Simon?' Lord Michel's gaze narrowed. 'Explain yourself.'

Simon launched into a rambling account, mentioning Eglantine, Simon's fears for his sister's welfare, and his desire to secure a future for her and the baby. He fell to his knees and clasped his hands together.

'My lord, I'm truly sorry. I never meant to hurt Sir Claude. We struggled and my knife slipped. I wanted him to agree to do right by Eglantine.'

Lord Michel grunted. 'You admit your knife cut him?'

'Aye.' Simon was holding his hands so tightly, his knuckles gleamed white. 'I regret it more than I can say. I wanted to make him think of her future.'

'Nevertheless,' Lord Michel said, sternly. 'You pulled a blade on a knight, one who is my godson.'

'An eating knife, my lord. It was only an eating knife.'

'It was sharp enough to draw blood. My godson had to be stitched.'

Face tight, Simon gulped. 'I know it. I've been thinking of nothing else for what feels like an eternity. I'm sorry, my lord.'

'Hmm.' Lord Michel took a thoughtful breath. 'Your meddling is surprising, particularly given your colourful reputation with women.'

Alert for the slightest sign that her father knew about her disastrous liaison, Allis stopped breathing. Mercifully, not so much as an eyelid flickered in her direction. Her chest eased. Hope.

'That is in the past, my lord,' Simon said, hoarsely. His mouth trembled and he twisted to glance back at Allis. 'Truth to tell, my lady, I'm glad you and your husband found me. These last few days have been hell. I've been living in fear and I've had plenty of time to reflect. There is much I regret.' His face was white, his eyes strained. He looked terrified. The careless charmer who'd seduced her was no more. Nor, thankfully, was Simon giving any sign that he was about to betray her less than perfect history. He was plainly choosing his words with care.

Papa looked doubtfully at Simon. 'You insist you are a reformed man? That you've mended your ways?'

'Aye, that's it. My lord, you must believe me. I meant to give your godson a scare, nothing more.' Simon's head drooped. 'I've learned a hard lesson, my lord.'

'We shall see.' Papa said. 'Sir Leon?'

'My lord?'

'Get someone to take this fellow to the lock-up, will you? He can cool his heels there for a few days. I shall decide what to do with him later.'

'Yes, my lord.' Leon bowed and gestured at Simon. 'Up you get.'

Simon clambered to his feet and stood very straight, as though braced for a heavy blow. 'You won't hang me, my lord? I beg you—'

'Get along with you,' Lord Michel said gruffly, and waved him out.

When the door closed behind Leon and Simon, Allis stayed behind. Pulling a quill from the stand, she ran her fingers along the feathered edge. Her father sent her an absent smile, reached for a letter, and started to read.

Allis ached for Simon. He was frightened out of his wits. It was unbearable not knowing what judgement her father might come to. Surely he wouldn't have him executed? She bent the quill this way and that. If her father knew about her misstep with Simon, he might decide that Simon's impertinence—deflowering his lord's daughter—must be punished.

'Papa?'

'Mmm?'

'What will happen to Simon?'

Her father looked up. 'I am undecided. I shall interview him again and discover whether his contrition is heartfelt.'

'For what it's worth, Papa, I believe it is. Like most of us, he is a trifle selfish, but he is not vindictive by nature.'

Her father's eyebrows lifted. 'You know him?'

Somehow, Allis kept her countenance. She shrugged. 'He has the reputation of being a light-hearted man. A little careless, perhaps, although I think that what happened to his sister has taught him much. I cannot believe he meant to hurt Claude.'

Her father grunted. 'He seems a feckless fellow. On the other hand, it stands in his favour that he was quick to admit that it was he who hurt Claude. As I said, I shall come to judgement shortly. Until then, Simon stays where he is. Heavens, Allis, what on earth are you doing? You've wrecked that quill.'

'Sorry, Papa.'

The door opened. Leon was back. He took Allis's hand in a firm grip. 'My lord, you will excuse us. I need to speak to your daughter.'

Lord Michel waved them away with a smile and before she had as much as blinked, Allis found herself in their bedchamber.

Leon threw his cloak aside and removed his gambeson. Silently, he held his hands out to her. He had the strangest expression on his face. Unable to read it, Allis walked slowly towards him. He took her arms and looped them about his neck.

Nimble fingers unfastened her cloak. He put her cloak brooch on a coffer and the cloak slipped to the floor. The atmosphere thickened, it seemed full of promise and something else, something Allis was unable to define.

'Leon?'

'Hush.' He wound his arms about her waist and leaned in for a kiss.

His mouth was warm. Subtle and determined. Allis closed her eyes, breathed in his scent and her pulse began to thud. The kiss drew out, and her breathing hitched, just as Leon's was doing. She touched her tongue to his and wriggled pleasurably against him. A pressure against her thigh told her Leon was as eager for her as she was for him. Physically, at least.

She opened her eyes and drew back. 'Leon, thank you for being so understanding about my foolishness with Simon.'

He lifted an eyebrow. 'Allis, before we married, I committed the odd folly myself. Before we were married. Never again.' He kissed her cheek and moved on to nibble her ear.

'Never again? That sounds like a vow.'

He stilled. Green eyes, eyes that were dark with desire, met hers. 'Be assured, it is. You are the only woman for me.'

Allis couldn't look away. She couldn't breathe. Gripped by a sudden urgency, she curled her fingers into his jacket. 'Leon, there's something I need to tell you.'

A dark eyebrow lifted. 'Hmm?'

'I'm sorry if you don't want to hear it but I must tell you. I love you. It is not lust. I am in love with you.'

He froze. 'Allis?'

She pressed her head against his chest, swallowing hard. 'I would give anything to turn time back so that I might be the perfect wife you deserve and I'm sorry that I'm not. I dare say you don't want my love, and I promise never to mention it again, but I love you so much.'

Strong fingers caught her chin, angling her face to

his. 'Allis?' His gaze was deep. Intent. And his mouth—he was smiling. 'Allis?' he repeated, voice husky.

'Leon, I love you.' Her heart gave a little jolt. His eyes fairly blazed. She bit her lip. She wanted the words. She needed them. 'Leon?'

He cupped her cheeks with his palms. 'Allis, I love you. I never thought to say this to any woman, for as far as I was concerned love was a delusion. You have shown me it is far from that.' He kissed her nose. 'I love everything about you.'

Her eyes widened. 'Everything?'

'Well, not quite everything.' His eyes danced. Lifting her skirts, he looked pointedly at her riding boots. 'At this moment I am not particularly enamoured of those boots.'

'I like these boots. What's wrong with them?'

Setting his hands at her waist, he lifted her and placed her on the edge of the bed.

'They would wreck Lady Sybille's embroidery.' Going down on his knees, he unbuckled her boots and tugged them off.

Allis took firm hold of his shoulders and leaned down to kiss him on the mouth. When he opened to her, she touched her tongue to his.

He groaned and stood up. In a trice, their limbs were tangled on the bed.

Allis pretended to sigh. 'Now isn't that just like a man.'

'What?'

She laughed. 'You removed my riding boots—what about yours?'

# Epilogue

*The Great Hall—two evenings later*

Leon and Allis entered the hall later than expected to find everyone gathered for supper. As they approached the dais, Lord Michel beckoned them to their places.

'Allis, where on earth have you been?'

'Papa, I am sure I told you we were going to the village. We've been doing the rounds, thanking people for their wedding gifts.'

'Well, you took your time about it,' her father grumbled, as she and Leon seated themselves. 'I've been waiting for an age to tell you. We've heard from Carpentras.'

'Oh?'

'Lord Robert has written to let me know what happened when Eglantine appeared on their doorstep. It's quite extraordinary. Claude had no sooner set eyes on her than he began talking about marrying the girl. He insists he will accept the infant as his. Insists.' Lord Michel shook his head. 'One look at the babe was all it took. Claude is refusing to take no for an answer.'

Allis stared. 'How has Lord Robert reacted?'

'Not well. At present, he and Claude are locked in a

battle of wills. Claude refuses to take anyone but Eglantine to wife, and Robert will have none of it. Robert has, however, agreed that Eglantine and the babe can settle in Carpentras.'

'Claude has something to fight for,' Allis said, exchanging glances with Leon.

'Aye, this could be the making of him,' her father said. 'Robert also mentions that he's invited Isembert to live at Carpentras and that he has accepted. So, Galard has lost its reeve. The advantage of that is that one of the Galard estate cottages has become free.'

'There are many good men in the village, we can find another reeve,' Allis murmured.

Her father nodded. The conversation paused as bowls of mussels cooked in cream were set before them. Wine was poured and around them conversations revived.

Allis reached for her spoon—she loved cream sauce. 'Papa, say the word if you need help finding a tenant for that cottage.'

Lord Michel tore off a hunk of bread. 'I will. By the way, I've released Isembert's son.'

Allis's spoon stilled. 'I am glad. I don't believe he meant to hurt Claude.'

Lord Michel lifted his eyebrows. 'The man's a knave, but for what it's worth I agree with you. None the less, I told him he was no longer welcome here. He left this afternoon.'

'Where was he headed, my lord?' Leon asked.

'Blessed if I know. He's a pedlar. He might go to Arles. Or maybe Toulouse. He might even go to Paris.'

Leon, Allis was relieved to hear, gave a snort of laughter, and she was able to turn her attention to the mussels in cream, tossing the empty shells into a waiting bowl with a satisfying clink. 'Papa, you are quite certain that Bernadette will be safe in Saint Claire's?'

Hugo, who was seated a little way down the board, looked up. 'She's surely safe in the convent, Allis. Why do you ask?'

'I was thinking about Sir Philippe. Papa, has there been news of him?'

'None. He's retreated to his lair, but you need not worry on Bernadette's account. Sir Philippe would never attack a convent.'

Hugo leaned forward, eyes intent. He had always been fond of Bernadette. 'You sound very certain, my lord.'

'I am. Despite the man's flaws, he respects Church authority. The Rector has made it plain that he cannot look for an alliance with our family.'

*'Dieu merci.'* Hugo smiled at Allis. 'It's bad enough we've lost Bernadette to the Church, she is certainly too precious to lose to Sir Philippe.'

'I wish she would come home,' Sybille said wistfully. 'I do miss her.'

Allis put down her spoon. 'I've never been sure that devoting her entire life to God is right for her.' With a smile she took Leon's hand and leaned into his warmth. 'I love you so much,' she murmured. 'And with luck, we have children and grandchildren to look forward to. I don't want Bernadette to miss out on all that. If only she could meet someone and be as happy as we are.'

Hugo cleared his throat and reached for his wine cup. 'Well said, Allis. I'll certainly drink to that.'

\* \* \* \* \*

# Get 3 FREE REWARDS!

**We'll send you 2 FREE Books <u>plus</u> a FREE Mystery Gift.**

**FREE**
Value Over
**$20**

Both the **Harlequin®️ Historical** and **Harlequin®️ Romance** series feature
compelling novels filled with emotion and simmering romance.

---

**YES!** Please send me 2 FREE novels from the Harlequin Historical or Harlequin Romance series and my FREE Mystery Gift (gift is worth about $10 retail). After receiving them, if I don't wish to receive any more books, I can return the shipping statement marked "cancel." If I don't cancel, I will receive 6 brand-new Harlequin Historical books every month and be billed just $6.19 each in the U.S. or $6.74 each in Canada, a savings of at least 11% off the cover price, or 4 brand-new Harlequin Romance Larger-Print books every month and be billed just $6.09 each in the U.S. or $6.24 each in Canada, a savings of at least 13% off the cover price. It's quite a bargain! Shipping and handling is just 50¢ per book in the U.S. and $1.25 per book in Canada.* I understand that accepting the 2 free books and gift places me under no obligation to buy anything. I can always return a shipment and cancel at any time by calling the number below. The free books and gift are mine to keep no matter what I decide.

Choose one:  ☐ **Harlequin Historical**
(246/349 BPA GRNX)

☐ **Harlequin Romance Larger-Print**
(119/319 BPA GRNX)

☐ **Or Try Both!**
(246/349 & 119/319 BPA GRRD)

Name (please print)

Address                                                                 Apt. #

City                          State/Province                    Zip/Postal Code

**Email:** Please check this box ☐ if you would like to receive newsletters and promotional emails from Harlequin Enterprises ULC and its affiliates. You can unsubscribe anytime.

**Mail to the Harlequin Reader Service:**
**IN U.S.A.:** P.O. Box 1341, Buffalo, NY 14240-8531
**IN CANADA:** P.O. Box 603, Fort Erie, Ontario L2A 5X3

**Want to try 2 free books from another series?** Call 1-800-873-8635 or visit www.ReaderService.com.

*Terms and prices subject to change without notice. Prices do not include sales taxes, which will be charged (if applicable) based on your state or country of residence. Canadian residents will be charged applicable taxes. Offer not valid in Quebec. This offer is limited to one order per household. Books received may not be as shown. Not valid for current subscribers to the Harlequin Historical or Harlequin Romance series. All orders subject to approval. Credit or debit balances in a customer's account(s) may be offset by any other outstanding balance owed by or to the customer. Please allow 4 to 6 weeks for delivery. Offer available while quantities last.

**Your Privacy**—Your information is being collected by Harlequin Enterprises ULC, operating as Harlequin Reader Service. For a complete summary of the information we collect, how we use this information and to whom it is disclosed, please visit our privacy notice located at corporate.harlequin.com/privacy-notice. From time to time we may also exchange your personal information with reputable third parties. If you wish to opt out of this sharing of your personal information, please visit readerservice.com/consumerchoice or call 1-800-873-8635. **Notice to California Residents**—Under California law, you have specific rights to control and access your data. For more information on these rights and how to exercise them, visit corporate.harlequin.com/california-privacy.

HHHRLP23

# HARLEQUIN
## PLUS

Try the best multimedia subscription service for romance readers like you!

---

## Read, Watch and Play.

Experience the easiest way to get the romance content you crave.

Start your **FREE TRIAL** at
<u>www.harlequinplus.com/freetrial</u>.